Down & Dirty: Diesel

Dirty Angels MC®
Book 4

Jeanne St. James

Jeanne St. James

Editor: Proofreading by the Page
Photographer/Cover Artist: Golden Czermak at FuriousFotog
Cover Model: Nick Pulos

www.jeannestjames.com

Sign up for my newsletter for insider information, author news, and new releases:
www.jeannestjames.com/newslettersignup

Keep an eye on her website at http://www.jeannestjames.com/or sign up for her newsletter to learn about her upcoming releases: http://www.jeannestjames.com/newslettersignup

Author Links: Instagram * Facebook * Goodreads Author Page * Newsletter * Jeanne's Review & Book Crew * BookBub * TikTok * YouTube

Acknowledgments

I'd like to say thank you to everyone who belongs to my Facebook reader group! My "down & dirty crew" motivates me to keep writing with their positive words and support.

I hope you love Diesel as much as we all do.

You can join us here: Jeanne's Readers FB Group

Chapter One

DIESEL GROANED and rolled to the left, hitting a soft, naked body. The woman dropped to the floor with a squeal.

Shit.

He rolled to the right and hit another soft, naked body. That one fell to the floor with a yelp.

Fuck.

He kept rolling and knocked the third one out of his bed, too.

Jesus fuckin' Christ.

His bed at church was way too small for four people. What the fuck had he been thinking?

Fuck him, he hadn't.

A rustle of bodies in the dark, groans, grumblings and typical female bitching rose up.

"One of you bitches hit the light."

The room stilled and got quiet.

"Now!" he barked.

He heard scrambling, cursing and squeals from stubbed toes. Then the bare bulb in the broken light fixture over his bed blinded him.

A few seconds later, he sat up in the middle of his mattress while his gaze bounced from one of Dawg's new girls to the next. Three in total stood at the end of his bed blinking back at him like a bunch of brainless twats.

"Don't fuckin' just stand there, get dressed an' get gone."

"D..."

"No lip. Go."

The women quickly sorted through the piles of clothes and shoes on the floor, picking up pieces and handing them to their rightful owner. Occasionally they would sneak a peek at him and he'd growl back at them.

"Faster," he urged in a tone that encouraged no back talk.

Finally, when they were at least partially dressed, he pushed himself out of bed with a grunt, went to the door, opened it, and yelled, "Out!"

One by one they filed past him, still zipping, pulling and wiggling parts into place.

"Call me."

"It was fun."

"Anytime."

Fuck that. He slammed the door shut.

He fucked up royally by bringing them up to his room. He rarely did that. And he never fell asleep with anyone in his bed, either. *Ever*.

They got ideas if you did.

They were always looking for a way to dig their claws into you and drag your ass down. He'd never let that happen.

"Live free. Die free," was his motto right behind the club's "Down & Dirty 'til Dead."

He lumbered into his bathroom, scratching his balls. He took a piss, which luckily didn't burn, then checked for crabs.

He was the first one of the brothers to fuck those bitches, that's why he picked them. He wouldn't touch them again. Too risky.

He left the small bathroom and stepped over his own clothes, which were strewn all over the floor, to grab his cell phone from the nightstand. He pushed the power button to see the time.

4:33 AM.

Fuck, no wonder church sounded as quiet as a real church. The party was over. Everyone was passed out, asleep, had died or just simply left.

He picked up the box of condoms off the top of the scarred nightstand and peered inside.

Empty.

He glanced at the floor.

Damn.

He needed to get one of the sweet butts up there to pick up all the used condoms and discarded wrappers. She could do his laundry while she was at it. Because he'd let that go a little too long. He had more dirty clothes on the floor than he did clean shit in his dresser.

He was proud of himself, though. At almost thirty-three years old, he could still bang three women and last for hours. His endurance was legendary.

Yeah, in his own mind. He grunted.

Even so, he still had it. But he was getting too old for this shit.

These nameless, faceless fucks weren't satisfying him anymore. Yeah, they scratched an itch. But that was it. He saw what Z had with Sophie, Jag with Ivy, and now his brother, Hawk, with Kiki.

Hell, even what his father, Ace, had with his mother. Thirty-five years of marriage and they were still going strong. And they hadn't tried to kill each other yet, either.

What the fuck was he thinking? Was he getting soft like them?

Hell no.

Live free. Die free.

Fuck, it was supposed to be "Live free, ride free." *What-fucking-ever.*

He glanced at his phone again and realized he had a message.

Shit.

He hit the voicemail icon and put the phone to his ear. His blood ran cold when Jewel's voice came through the speaker.

"D... Fuck! Why aren't you answering? Damn it! This is the fifth time I'm calling. I need you to come get me. *Please.*"

Her voice didn't sound normal. That was not Jewel's typical smartass self. No, she sounded like she was in some sort of trouble.

Again.

And here she was calling the club's Sergeant at Arms, the enforcer, who was so busy fucking three cunts that he missed her calls.

Fuck!

Nothing had better have happened to her or he'd never forgive himself. He needed to find her and needed to do it now.

He hit the Send button on his phone and pressed it to his ear. She answered on the first ring.

"D." Her voice was breathless and low.

A prickle ran up his spine. "Where the fuck you at?"

"In the 'burgh. Come get me?" She was whispering.

"Why the fuck you whisperin'? What's goin' on?"

"I just need out of here."

"Where?"

"I'm at a... house."

His jaw got tight and a muscle ticked. "With who?"

"Nobody."

Fuckin' *nobody*. Bullshit. "This nobody drive your ass there?"

"Forget it, D... I'll call my brother."

"Address," he muttered.

"What?"

"Fuckin' address," he barked louder.

She gave it to him.

As he listened, he felt his blood start to boil. She was not in a good section of the city. And she was alone.

"Gonna beat your ass."

"I—"

He hit End. After finding his jeans, he yanked them up, threw on the nearest T-shirt, shrugged on his cut and tucked his phone into his back pocket. He sat on the edge of the bed after finding a half-decent clean pair of socks that didn't have any holes in them, tugged them on, then shoved his feet into his boots and zipped them up.

As he pushed to his feet and scrubbed a hand over the stubble on his chin, he realized he hadn't had a chance to wash the pussy off him.

Too fucking bad. If it bothered her, she could find another way home.

With a curse, he locked up his room and headed out.

JEWEL PACED the dark sidewalk back and forth, pausing to listen carefully every few minutes.

Nothing.

It would soon be dawn and she should've been out of here a long time ago. In truth, she shouldn't have come here at all.

But she had been bored. She didn't want to go to the party at church last night and Kelsea convinced her the party she was headed to would be fun.

Little did she know, her club sister had a motive for coming to this party in the city. She'd been hanging with some questionable people lately. And she'd hooked up with a guy that was a DAMC hang-around. Plus, she said with the two of them there, they could keep an ear open for any activity of the Shadow Warriors. Maybe hear where that asshole former prospect Squirrel and his buddy Black Jack were hiding out.

As Jewel had mingled with a much younger crowd than her, her first clue she shouldn't have agreed to come was that she suddenly found herself deserted there alone. And most of the party attendees ended up either drunk, high on drugs, or both.

Not her scene. She gave up that kind of partying years ago. Not that she was old. At twenty-eight she still liked to party. But being at a house in a questionable part of the city with no vehicle, and surrounded by a bunch of wasted twenty-one and -two-year-olds had her really rethinking her choices.

So, here she was outside a rowhome waiting for Diesel to come "save" her.

He would be pissed but that was nothing new for the club enforcer. Still, as the club's Sergeant at Arms, it was his duty to protect and take care of her.

Or that's what she wanted to believe. She wasn't so sure Diesel would agree. Maybe on the protect part. But that's where he'd insist it ended.

He was too busy being a walking, talking—no, that wasn't right —*grunting* testosterone-filled beast, to worry about taking care of anyone but himself. And by "taking care of" she meant sticking his dick in every conscious vagina he could find.

Every vagina but hers.

"Hey, baby."

Jewel jumped as a male voice she didn't recognize drifted her direction. She looked around but couldn't see anybody or even any movement. The hair on the back of her neck stood up.

D, hurry up.

"You out here by yourself? You need a friend?"

The voice came closer and Jewel's heart began to race. She squinted, trying to get a bead on who the voice belonged to.

"No. I'm good. My man's coming to pick me up."

"He stood you up, baby. I'm here for you, though."

She patted at her jeans' pockets hoping a knife or some sort of weapon would magically appear.

She was going to kill Kelsea.

"Just so you know, he's really jealous. He'll kick your ass for just talking to me."

A shadow moved between two of the cars that were parked along the curb.

"Is that right?"

"Yeah."

"Then we should go somewhere he can't find us."

Holy fucking shit!

Why didn't she ever take a self-defense course? The only thing she knew how to do was kick a guy in the gonads, scratch his eyes out... or call Diesel.

Fuck my life.

She looked down at her fashionable high-heeled boots. She couldn't run in those things. She could hardly even walk in them.

They were strictly for looking good and making her legs look hellishly long.

Which they did. But that wasn't going to help her out right now.

The shadow moved again and Jewel bit back a scream. She couldn't act afraid, she had to act fearless.

Right.

"Whoever you are, get gone!" she yelled, bracing her feet wide apart.

"Really, baby, you don't want me to do that. We can have some fun."

"Not looking for fun," she said firmly, hoping she sounded like the tough biker bitch she was.

Riiiiight.

"I am."

"My man's a mean biker, he'll kick your ass." Silence. Which made the skin on the back of her neck prickle. "He's huge, too. Killed a man."

Oh, Jesus. If someone told her that, *she'd* be the one rolling her eyes.

Jewel let out a yelp when the male voice came way too close to her ear and a hand wrapped around her bicep. "Well, we won't tell him."

"The fuck I won't!" she yelled desperately. The guy wore a baseball hat and it was too dark to see his features. She yanked at her arm, but he wouldn't let go.

No shit.

"Got a place we can go."

"I'm fine where I'm at," she assured him, trying to keep her voice steady since she was starting to unravel. This shit was getting serious. She yanked at her arm again. "Let me go!"

Suddenly, she was yanked so hard that she found herself off balance and tumbled backwards, landing on her ass. All the oxygen escaped her lungs in a *whoosh*.

"Get up, bitch." The guy pulled at her.

She pulled back. "Fuck you."

He pulled her harder. "Get the fuck up!"

"No!"

She needed to get a good kick in with her high-heeled boots right in his dick. Then he'd leave her alone. Once he was down, she'd sink one of those heels right into his eye socket.

That'd teach him to fuck with her.

She yelped again as he grabbed her hair and began to drag her over the ground.

Her arms started flying as she tried to whack any part of his body she could make contact with. Which wasn't much.

Jesus. She really needed to learn self-defense.

Then she heard the roar of the straight exhaust pipes and relief flowed through her. When the single headlight came at them at a high rate of speed, the relief quickly fled. She was going to get run over.

She squeezed her eyes shut as the sled came to a sliding stop inches from them, the man was off the motorcycle and the guy who was trying to drag her away was no longer moving.

Face meet fist.

He was now flat out on his back, groaning. Even in the dark, Jewel knew Diesel was furious. She could feel the waves of controlled rage rolling off him. Good thing it wasn't directed at her.

"What the fuck you doin'?" D bellowed, grabbing her by the arm and hauling her to her feet.

"Me?" she squeaked.

"Yeah, fuckin' you!" In the glow of the headlight, she didn't miss him checking her out head to toe. "What the fuck you wearin'? Jesus fuckin' Christ."

Jewel yanked her short skirt down, since in the tussle it had ridden up to her crotch. Good thing she had thrown on some panties before she left her apartment.

"You gotta be fuckin' kiddin' me. Your fuckin' ass in a bad section of town, wearing that fuckin' bullshit?"

Jesus. She had thought she'd looked nice. Hot, even.

Diesel stalked back over to the man on the ground, who was still groaning, holding onto his face, but trying to get to his knees.

D pointed his finger her direction but was talking to the guy. Well, not actually talking, more like bellowing in a scary fashion. "You see this bitch again, run the other direction, got me? Not walk. Run. Otherwise, huntin' your ass down. Got me?"

The man put up his hand in surrender, then pushed shakily to his feet.

"Now, get gone!" D yelled so loudly even Jewel winced.

The man quickly stumbled away and once he was out of sight, D's head swung in her direction.

Uh oh.

"Jesus fuckin' Christ. How many times do I gotta bail your ass out of a jam, woman? How many?" He stalked over to her, grabbed her upper arm firmly and steered her toward his bike.

She yanked at her arm. "I should've called Jag."

He didn't release her until they stood next to his Harley. "Yeah, right. Do that next time. Sick of this shit."

Grumble. Grumble. Grumble. Jewel frowned. The man was nothing but a Debbie Downer.

"How long you been out here?

She shrugged. "A while."

"Ever think of callin' a taxi?"

"My wallet was in..." *Shit.*

He eyeballed her. "In?"

"The car," she finished reluctantly.

"Whose car?"

Her mouth twisted.

With a curse, he mounted his bike. "Get on my sled. Discussin' this somewhere other than here."

"D, I don't think I can straddle the bike in my skirt."

"Take it off."

Her eyes bugged out. "What?"

"Take. It. Off."

"I'm only wearing a thong," she whispered.

He dropped his head and stared at his boot for a second, then two, then for more than thirty seconds.

Finally, with a tight jaw, he shrugged his cut off his shoulders, ripped his T-shirt over his head and without even looking at her, held it out. "Put it on. Take that shit off, then burn it. Don't want to see you in that again."

There was no way she was burning her skirt. It was cute and she looked good in it. She just wouldn't wear it to church. Or the garage. Or in front of Diesel.

With a sigh, she plucked the oversized tee from his fingers, yanked it over her head and then, after unzipping it, she shimmied out of her skirt. His T-shirt was so big she felt like she was wearing a muu-muu. It covered her practically to her knees.

She wrinkled her nose. And it smelled funky. She couldn't quite place it.

"You done?"

"Yeah," she answered.

"Then why we still sittin' here?"

After a slight hesitation, she climbed on behind him, grabbing onto his thick waist over his leather vest, which he had shrugged back on over his bare torso.

Well, his anger would have to keep him warm on the ride back, she thought. At least she had his shirt covering her formerly bare legs since the nights were starting to cool down as they approached the end of summer.

"Gotta hold tighter than that, woman. Otherwise, your ass is gonna be on the pavement."

With a sigh, Jewel wrapped her arms as much as she could around his waist and pressed her cheek to his back. She jerked her head back. She finally recognized the smell. "You and your shirt smell like pussy."

"Yep. Shit you get when you call me in the middle of the night."

"It's morning."

"Like I said, middle of the fuckin' night." He kicked his starter and the bike roared to life, his straight pipes rumbling through the city streets, echoing off the rowhomes.

Chapter Two

HE'D JUST FUCKED three bitches not more than an hour or so ago and now with Jewelee wrapped around his back, he had another fucking hard-on.

Jesus.

The fucking woman drove him crazy.

He'd been doing everything he could to keep his hands off her for the past few months. That day he carried her upstairs to his room at church when she'd totally sent him into a tailspin by waiting for him outside of the restroom, he'd been a cunt hair away from doing just that. He'd lost his mind when he came out of the bathroom after fucking another nameless, faceless cunt and saw Jewel sitting at the end of the bar, arms crossed and looking like a pissed off little hellcat. But once he carried her upstairs and had thrown her onto his bed, the fog in his brain had cleared. Or at least enough for him to realize he couldn't stick his dick in her after just fucking another woman. Hell, he couldn't stick his dick in Jewel at all.

Even though she had been sprawled on his bed where she landed, her tits heaving, her tempting, fuckable mouth parted, her blue eyes wide and her cheeks flushed, he couldn't touch a hair on her head.

Then it hit him, that if he did so, it would be the worst mistake of his life.

So instead, he had taken a deep breath to get his shit together, bitten off a curse, turned on his heel, and stormed out of his room, slamming the door behind him.

That was the closest he'd ever come to losing his shit around her. It could never happen again. But now with her clinging to his back, her tits pressed against him, and her pussy nestled tightly against his ass as they headed toward Shadow Valley, the thoughts running through his head were the same ones he'd been trying to fight.

He had to remain strong and not slip, or he'd be fucked.

Or she'd end up good and fucked. What a goddamn mess that would be.

He was still torqued about what she'd been wearing tonight, too. A *way-too-short* skirt, *fuck-me* high-heeled boots, a snug top that bared both shoulders and showed most of her cleavage. Large gold hoops hung from her ears and another smaller hoop circled the side of her nostril.

His jaw tightened and he ground his back molars. She'd been out trolling for strange. And if he hadn't shown up in time, she might have gotten some strange she hadn't bargained for.

His nostrils flared and he twisted the throttle harder, causing the bike to lurch forward with the sudden increase in speed. They were just minutes from his pop's pawn shop where Jewel now lived in the apartment above. She'd moved in a couple weeks ago after Jag and Ivy got a house and moved out.

He would have preferred that Jewel remained living with her mother, Ruby. Because now that she lived on her own, she could bring all kinds of strange home.

Jesus fuckin' Christ.

He took the corner into the alley fast enough that Jewel had to hold on even tighter, then he rolled his sled into the side lot of the pawn shop and parked his bike at the base of the metal stairway that led up to her place.

He kicked the stand down, shut the engine off and sat staring up the steps.

He was going to take her upstairs, get her inside safely, get his shirt back and then get gone.

That's what he was going to fucking do.

Doing anything else would mean complications and drama. And he liked simple. Clean. Neat. Nothing holding him back. Nothing holding him down.

"Get off," he ordered.

With an irritated sigh, Jewel dismounted from the bike, then stood there, his worn Ocean City Bike Week T-shirt just about swallowing her whole. It hit hard how much smaller she was than him. About half his size.

He followed her off the bike and stood next to her. She was on the smaller side of all the DAMC women, a whole foot shorter than his six-foot-four.

She might look delicate and petite in his oversized shirt, but he knew better. Her attitude and personality was pure DAMC, one hundred percent biker bitch. She wasn't afraid of shit. And she had a mouth on her that would curl a preacher's hair.

His gaze dropped to that mouth and he ground his teeth to remind himself he couldn't touch her.

"Let's go," he barked, grabbing her arm. Before he could get a good grip on it, she yanked free and huffed toward the metal steps. When she started hoofing it up the stairs in those high-heeled boots, her hips rocked and rolled, making it impossible to miss the jiggle of her ass under his tee.

Jesus fuckin' Christ. He rolled his eyes upward to the early dawn sky and sucked in lungs full of the cool morning air.

When he finally heard her hit the landing, he moved. Taking the steps two at a time, he kept repeating in his head: *she's not mine, she's not mine, she's not mine, she's not mine.*

He followed on her heels as she unlocked the door and entered the dark apartment.

A couple of steps in, she turned, planted her hands on her hips and said, "Thanks. You can go now."

He shook his head, shut the door firmly, twisted the dead bolt and pushed past her to the middle of the small living room. She hit the switch by the door and the room lit up.

When he glanced around, he noticed that Ivy had left her furniture for Jewel so the apartment was fully furnished. But even so, it had definitely changed. Jewel had put her own touches on the place. She loved Harleys and the MC life as much as any of the brothers and her decorative touch certainly showed that she was a complete biker babe meant to be on the back of some brother's bike.

Just not his.

"You can go now," she repeated, staying near the door.

He shook his head again. "Gotta talk."

She faked a yawn. "Too tired. We'll talk later."

"Didn't want to deal with the shit, shouldn't have called me."

She shrugged. "My mistake."

"Woman," he growled.

"Fine," she huffed and moved closer to the couch to toss her skirt she'd been carrying onto one of the cushions.

That thing needed to be burned. The skirt, not the couch.

"Fuckin' looked like one of Dawg's girls," he muttered.

"Just your type," she muttered back.

His jaw tightened and so did his chest. Dawg's strippers were only a means to an end. But he kept that to himself, since she was smart enough to figure that out on her own. Not that he gave a shit.

"Start talkin'."

"About what?" she asked, her face suddenly looking innocent.

Which was total fucking bullshit because she was anything but innocent. Her ass was always scheming, trying to find ways to get into trouble.

Drove him fucking nuts.

"Talk!" he barked so loudly he didn't miss her body jerk in response.

"D—"

"Went to score drugs?"

Her blue eyes bugged out. "No!"

"Went to score strange then?"

Her hesitation was telling. He struggled to keep a lid on his temper.

"No," she whispered.

He didn't believe it. "For fuck's sake, is this why you weren't at the party at church?"

"I get tired of that shit sometimes. I wanted to do something different."

"What, gettin' some strange?" he asked again.

"I said no, D. *Jesus*!"

"He ain't gonna help you." He took a step closer and she quickly scrambled around the couch, putting it in between them. "Who fuckin' drove you there?"

She bit her bottom lip and avoided his eyes.

"Jewelee, ain't screwin' around here," he warned. "Gonna find out. Might as well tell me."

She pressed her hands over her face, then sighed. "Kelsea," she said softly.

Jesus fuck. Kelsea. Another one who was always looking for trouble. And though his cousin wasn't much younger than Jewel, she still acted like a teenager and tended to hang around with a bunch of young partiers.

"An' she left you?"

"Yeah."

For fuck's sake. "Need to worry 'bout her?"

Jewel's eyes slid to the side. "No."

"She gettin' strange?

"No."

His mouth got tight. He was going to have a sit-down with his cousin. She needed to learn that she didn't leave a DAMC sister in a bad section of the city in the middle of the night. Specially to get laid. "She fuckin' someone on the regular?"

Jewel's gaze dropped to the floor. "Yeah."

"Who?"

"Can't—"

"Who?" he shouted and took another step forward.

Jewel's narrowed eyes landed on him and she didn't step back this time. Instead, she rounded the couch and got into his face with her hands on her hips.

"One of the hang-arounds. Gotta ask her. It's not for me to say, D. You wanna know who your cousin is fucking, you..." She jabbed him in the chest with her finger. "Ask..." Jabbed him again. "Her."

Diesel grabbed her hand, pulled her close and pinned her against his chest. He stared down into her face, her eyes flashing, her breathing rapid. He wrapped his hand around her chin, tilted her head up and held her gaze. "Know her reason now. What's yours?"

Her baby blues shifted.

"Eyes on me," he demanded.

And, fuck him, if she didn't comply. After holding her gaze for a few moments, he had to ignore the fire that burned in his gut. He also ignored his dick trying to punch a hole in his jeans.

She's not mine, she's not mine, she's not mine.

Ain't gonna make her mine, either. Too much other snatch out there without strings.

"Woman."

Jewel blinked slowly, her mouth opened, closed, then opened again. Her words came out in a whisper. "I was trying to keep an ear out for Squirrel Dick and that soon-to-be-dead fucker Black Jack."

His body lurched. She was doing *what*?

His fingers tightened on her chin and she winced. He didn't care. She needed to pay careful attention to his next words.

"Leave that shit to me. Got my crew on it. Got the Knights keepin' an eye out. Don't need you gettin' in the middle of shit."

"D—"

"No. Fuckin' listen, woman. Stay outta that shit. Got me?" When she flattened her lips, his blood pressure skyrocketed. She wasn't getting it. "You forget what they did to Jazz? To Kiki?"

"No."

"Want that shit to happen to you?" And, hell, it almost did tonight. Maybe not by a Warrior, but there were plenty of other predators out there. He'd never forget the sight of finding Kiki and Jazz in an abandoned house after being beaten to the point of being unrecognizable. Jazz being raped and having "SWMC" carved into her belly with a knife. Shit he'd never forget and still haunted him when he tried to sleep.

He also couldn't forget the sight of Bella after what happened to her. She'd been left just as broken and scarred as Kiki and Jazz but by someone who was supposed to have loved her.

He'd never forget any of that shit because it was burned permanently into his brain, as well as his soul.

If that shit happened to Jewel, too...

"No, D."

"Stay the fuck outta it. Ain't fuckin' with you, Jewel. Tan your fuckin' hide, you do this shit again."

"You can't tan my hide."

His heart pounded like a drum in his chest. "Try me," he ground out.

With a strangled voice, she whispered, "Your beast is showing."

His nostrils flared and he sucked in a breath. She had started calling him that just months ago. She was trying to get him to his breaking point. He wasn't going to let her push him to that. No, he wasn't.

"Stop with that shit or you'll get a taste of my 'beast.' Ain't sure you're gonna like it."

"Try me," Jewel echoed him.

Diesel's head jerked back and he tipped his chin down to her. Her face wasn't hard. Fuck no it wasn't. It was soft, her eyes inviting.

Jesus fuckin' Christ.

He needed to get the fuck out of there. He let her go and shoved her away. "Gimme my shirt."

Her eyes held his for a moment, then she grabbed the hem of his T-shirt and yanked it over her head, taking her own top with it.

"Jesus fuckin' Christ," he muttered out loud this time. He swallowed hard as she stood in the middle of her living room only wearing a red thong and her black leather knee-high boots.

Fuck me.

He had never seen the woman naked and in the past had imagined it many times, but what stood before him was so much better than his own visuals.

Way fucking better.

"Jesus, Jewelee," he said quietly. He was frozen in place because if he moved forward he was going to toss her over his shoulder, take her to her bedroom and then fuck her until neither of them could move.

But if he moved toward the front door...

Yeah, that's what he needed to do. He needed to grab his shirt from between her fingers and get the hell out of Dodge.

But, for fuck's sake, he couldn't stop staring at her. And she made no move to cover herself. His shirt hung from her fingers by her side. Her tits, not huge but perfect for her smaller frame, were firm and the nipples peaked into hard points.

Her lips were parted and her eyes hooded.

And his dick was screaming at him to take action.

Until now, he had no clue that she had a tattoo of a red rose with thorns over her right hip. And a belly button ring. Her stomach and hips had just enough flesh so she wasn't skinny; her thighs looked soft and inviting.

Too fucking inviting.

He wanted her to turn around. He needed to see her ass with her red thong up the crack.

Jesus. That'd be like unwrapping a birthday gift. It'd be the best fucking birthday ever.

But reality hit him that today wasn't his birthday and he needed to get the fuck out of there before he did something really fucking stupid.

Something that neither one of them would forget.

"Jewelee."

"Yeah?" A look of hope crossed her expression.

"Shirt on the couch. Go to your room an' lock the fuckin' door until you hear me leave. Then come out and lock the front door."

She frowned. "D—"

"Do it. Now."

She lifted her hand that was empty, pleading, "D... don't go." Her voice was low and husky and it shot all the way down into his already steel-hard dick.

He shook his head but his eyes never left her. He couldn't stop himself from letting his gaze roam her tight little body once more. He swallowed again. This time it was more difficult. "Gotta go."

"D."

"No, woman, ain't playin' this game of yours."

"Why?"

"'Cause you'll end up clingy an' a fuckin' nag."

She winced but quickly hid it. "Just a one-time thing. Promise."

Oh, fuck no, he wasn't falling for that trap.

He was going to say something and knew he'd regret it, but he had to snap himself out of whatever trance he was in and he had to hit her with some hard reality so she'd do the same. It was the only way he was going to get out of her apartment without driving himself deep inside her.

"Just had three of Dawg's strippers on my cock not more than an hour ago, woman. Want sloppy seconds?"

This time when she winced, it stuck. Her eyes hardened, her demeanor changed. And her mouth became an angry slash as she threw his shirt on the couch and turned.

Jesus. That ass with only that scrap of red cloth parting those round cheeks... *Fuck.*

She strode in those damn high-heeled boots down the hallway and not a second later he heard the slam of her bedroom door.

He closed his eyes, took a shuddered breath and cursed himself. He opened his mouth to call her name but when his eyes opened they landed on her *way-too-short* skirt abandoned on the couch.

He shrugged off his cut, grabbed his T-shirt, yanked it over his head, slid his cut back on and was out the fucking door before he made a very bad decision.

DIESEL GROANED and flipped onto his back. His eyes were squeezed shut, his palm was wrapped around his dick and he yanked at it as he struggled to get the picture of Jewel wearing only her thong and boots out of his head.

His hips rose and fell onto his mattress following the rhythm of his fist. The hand not full of cock was twisted in the sheets as he tugged harder, his balls tightening painfully.

He needed to wipe that vision of Jewel out of his head and he hoped a good jerk off would do it.

As much as he'd wanted to touch her, he couldn't. He couldn't. She wasn't his and she'd never be his.

She wasn't a quick fuck. She wasn't a woman he'd fuck against the wall in the bathroom.

She wasn't the kind of woman he'd just fuck to drain the load from his balls.

And that's all he was looking for because he didn't want anything more. He didn't want an ol' lady. He also didn't want to make the mistake of sticking his dick in snatch that would expect to become his ol' lady, either.

That shit wasn't for him.

Never was. Never would be.

So this was why he was jerking on his own pud right now. To try to get Jewel, her sweet body, and the speculation of what her tight, wet cunt would feel like wrapped around his dick, out of his mind.

But, fuck him, it wasn't working.

He groaned again, flipped over to his belly and punched his bed in frustration. Grabbing his pillow, he tucked it under his torso and imagined it was Jewel under him, with her legs wrapped around his waist while he was buried completely into her slick, wet heat. He tilted his hips back and forth, driving his cock up and down on his mattress.

This was what he was reduced to. Dry humping his fucking bed when he could've stayed and took what was offered. The real thing. He could've driven his cock deep into her sweet pussy and then her tight ass, blowing his load only when he'd had enough.

But no.

Gritting his teeth, he pumped his hips faster, the friction from the sheet making him suck in a breath. Squeezing the pillow under him harder, he shoved his face into a second pillow and with a final pump, he came with a grunt. His cum shot between his stomach and the sheet, making a complete mess.

Just like his fucking life.

Chapter Three

DIESEL GAVE a chin lift to the prospect that stood outside of Dirty Dick's tasked with keeping an eye on the line of Dark Knights bikes parked out front.

"Gonna get greeted," the young, light-skinned prospect warned.

"Right," D grunted and yanked open the door anyway.

Loud music Diesel didn't recognize assaulted his ears, tangy smoke that was more of the illegal than legal variety burned his nostrils, and the typical sounds of a rowdy biker bar on a Friday night hit him. As eyes turned his direction, his skin prickled.

He had to remind himself that the Knights weren't rivals but instead more like allies. The Dirty Angels had no beef with them and he wanted to keep it that way.

A dark-skinned man almost his size suddenly blocked his way. Almost his size, but not quite. D had a good inch and about twenty pounds on him. But even so, he looked like a bad motherfucker that D wouldn't want to be enemies with.

They clasped palms and bumped shoulders.

"Magnum," D greeted.

"D," was the grunt in response. He jerked his chin toward a corner in the bar. "Step into my office."

D grunted in return and followed the large man, who was the Knights' Sergeant at Arms, just like him.

They hit a table tucked in a corner, but one in a location where the whole bar could be watched. Magnum settled into a chair where his back was against the wall and his eyes scanned the bar before landing on D.

D pulled out a chair, swung it around and dropped his weight into it backwards, his arms resting along the chair back. He didn't want to be caught between the table and his seat if anything went down. Not that he expected it to, but one never knew. Better to be ready to move, than get stuck. And fucked.

Magnum eyeballed him for a moment then lifted his large hand over his shoulder. A pretty dark-skinned woman with hair cropped close to her head, dark eyes and heavy tits barely contained in a tight tank top, approached the table.

Diesel's eyes raked over her curves stuffed into tight short shorts and her long, endless legs with skin so smooth that they gleamed.

"Like what you see?"

D's gaze fell back on Magnum. "Yeah."

"Don't mind sharin' our women. 'Specially if you like the chocolate variety."

D glanced back at the woman who stood there patiently, wearing a welcoming smile. Normally with an offer like that, he'd say yes. Tonight he wasn't feeling it. "Just a beer."

Her eyes flicked to Magnum and so did his. The Knights' enforcer gave her a slight nod and D watched her move as she headed back to the bar. The way her hips rolled, he guessed she'd be a pro at riding his cock.

"She's good, brother."

"You had her," D stated.

"Yeah."

"Then I can't compete."

Magnum threw his bald head back and laughed. When he finally sobered, he cocked a brow D's way. "Don't know. You're a big fucker. Could be hung bigger than me."

"Could be," D replied. He leaned forward. "Not here to compare dick sizes."

The laugh lines around Magnum's dark eyes disappeared. "Yeah. Got that. Whataya here for?"

"Warriors."

"Right, brother. Been keepin' an eye out for those fuckers."

"Got that an' appreciate it."

"We find 'em, we'll deliver 'em to the Valley on a silver fuckin' platter."

"Got that, too."

The woman came back, slid a frosted mug of beer in front of D, giving him another inviting smile as she did so, slid a bottle of beer in front of Magnum, then when the Knight waved his hand, she quickly, but with noticeable reluctance, disappeared.

A woman who didn't give lip. D could appreciate that.

He turned his attention back to Magnum. "Got an event comin' up."

"'Nother fundraiser like *Dogs & Hogs*?"

The Knights were one of several clubs that had attended the fundraising event the DAMC held a couple months back. His brother, Hawk, and the club's attorney, Kiki—now Hawk's ol' lady—had planned the event that benefited veterans with PTSD so his brother could work off the community service part of his sentence. He'd been thrown in jail after they had *played with* a few of the Warriors in South Side at an Irish pub.

And by *played with* he meant beat the fuck out of. Diesel had been arrested, too, but luckily his charges had been dropped. Hawk hadn't been so lucky and did a ten-day stint in County. The only good thing that came out of it was him hooking up with his permanent piece, Kiki.

Of course, all the money they raised for the charity during the fundraiser was a bonus, too.

But the end of that event had turned into a complete clusterfuck when the Warriors tried to steal some of Kiki's hard-earned donations.

"No," D finally said. "Somethin' else."

Magnum raised a dark brow.

"A weddin'."

Magnum leaned back in his chair, crossing his arms over his broad chest. "Yours?"

"Fuck no."

A slow smile crossed Magnum's face. "Ain't a fool then."

"Nope. Our former prez is marryin' his ol' lady."

"Z, right?"

"Yeah."

"Saw his ol' lady at *Dogs & Hogs*. The sweet little baker. Can see why he'd wanna lock 'er down."

"Yeah."

"Still don't get why you're here."

"Need a favor."

Magnum waited.

"Gonna be an outdoor weddin'. At a lake. Too much shit has gone down with the Warriors lately, an' we're all gonna be occupied with the formality of Z handin' over his balls. Got my crew on tap to help keep a lookout, but need more eyes than that to keep shit safe."

The Knight nodded, then reached for his beer bottle. He put it to his lips and drained half of it. "Take it inside," Magnum suggested when he finally put the beer back on the table.

D shook his head. "Z's ol' lady's got a dream. An' it ain't gettin' married in a church. One with a steeple or the one attached to The Iron Horse."

Magnum smirked. "Bitch got his balls in a vise, for sure."

"Yeah."

"Got it. Askin' for our protection."

"We'll repay the marker when you need it."

Magnum nodded. "To be expected. But, brother, why you here instead of your prez? Your prez should be talkin' to ours."

D took a sip of his beer, then another one before setting it back down on the scarred wooden table. The truth was their president, Pierce, was a dick. And the brothers were going to plan an upheaval sooner than later, but Diesel couldn't admit what they were planning or even that there would be any shift in power. Any admittance of kinks in the chain of command would be a sign of weakness.

They also weren't sure of when it was going to happen. Right now Z was concentrating on getting hitched, not taking back the head of the table. Once all the wedding shit was settled, they could move on to the next order of business.

They also needed to find and bury six-feet-under their former prospect Squirrel and this Black Jack. And any other Warrior they could get their hands on.

"Pierce's occupied with some other shit right now. Got me handlin' this." Sort of a lie, sort of wasn't. The man sitting across from him wasn't going to know that either way.

"The redhead gonna be there?"

D cocked a brow in surprise. What the fuck was that about? "Ivy? Yeah."

"That brother get her ass under control? If not, a few of my brothers want a shot at 'er."

Blood rushed into D's ears. He needed to keep his shit together and do his best to not make enemies today. "Talkin' 'bout my cousin, brother."

"Yeah, and?" Then Magnum smiled and D realized the man was busting his balls. Testing him.

"Right," D grunted in relief.

Out of nowhere, a blonde white woman approached Magnum, wrapped her hand around the back of his neck, leaned over and kissed the top of his head.

"Talkin' business here, woman," Magnum grumbled but snaked his arm around her hips and pulled her tight against him. The man's eyes landed on D. "Got an ol' lady?"

"No."

He tilted his head to his. "Good. Don't. Pain in the fuckin' ass. All of 'em."

The woman laughed, and said, "You got it good, ol' man."

"Yeah, 'cause you got a temper an' you like those angry fucks like that redheaded bitch."

How Magnum knew that about his cousin, D didn't know and didn't want to know.

"Those are the best fucks," the blonde said, her green eyes flashing a challenge.

D couldn't agree with them because he never had one. All his fucks were easy, quick and disposable. To him, those were the best kind.

He didn't need any drama in his life or in his bed.

"We done here?" Magnum asked.

"Yeah, if you're in agreement."

"Gotcha covered, brother. Give me the details when you got 'em, an' we'll get your back."

Diesel nodded. "Good."

Magnum unfolded his big body out of his chair. "Stay, finish your beer. See somethin' you like, let me know. Like I said, willin' to share." He steered his woman around with a hand spread along her lower back. Before he walked away, he tossed over his shoulder, "But we'll expect the same courtesy."

D didn't like the sound of that at all. There was no way they were sharing their women with another club. Dark Knights or not.

Hell, it was bad enough that Axel, not only Z's brother, a cop, and the VP of the Blue Avengers MC, was chasing Bella.

That wasn't going to happen, either. Not as long as Diesel was breathing.

The brothers were spread out over the clubhouse courtyard. The night air was starting to cool down a bit since it was getting toward the end of summer. Jag, the Road Captain, had organized a run earlier in the day. Mama Bear and some of the sweet butts, as well as the prospects, had prepared the rest of the shit for tonight's party. But the evening seemed a bit more on the mellow side and D wasn't going to bitch.

Nash's band, Dirty Deeds, seemed to be keeping their music on the more mellow side, also. Though, Dawg was out in the trampled grass by the light of the bonfire still finding the slow rock songs fast enough to bump and grind on some of his girls.

Some of the hang-arounds, guys that liked to hang with the brothers but who had no desire to prospect, were enjoying the attention of the strippers, too. They and the prospects were allowed to touch them. They couldn't touch the sweet butts since those women were only available to the patched members and they definitely couldn't touch any of the ol' ladies. Not if they wanted to find themselves breathing the next day.

The band's version of ZZ Top's *Rough Boy* filled the courtyard.

Dex, the club's secretary, was hanging onto one of the sweet butts named Tequila, a hand on one of her huge fake tits, and the other on her ass which hung out of her obscenely short cut-offs, as he ground against her while they swayed in a slow circle. Crash had his arms wrapped around one of Dawg's new girls, one of the three strippers that D had kicked out of his room a week ago. The man had a wide grin on his face as he ground against her ass. And D was pretty sure he was sporting a boner.

Crash could have her. Dawg's girls were a once and done for D. Once they started getting passed around, he wouldn't touch them, with not only his own dick, but anyone else's.

Dawg's stable was large enough that he could have a full complement of dancers working the poles on a Saturday night at Heaven's Angels Gentlemen's Club and still bring the freshest, newest ones here to church parties as "entertainment."

He noticed that Dawg hadn't brought Goldie around lately. He wondered if he kicked the aging, well-ridden stripper to the curb finally. In the last year, the woman had become desperate to get her claws into one of the brothers, hoping to become a permanent piece. No brother in their right mind was putting her permanently on the back of his bike or in his bed.

Zak leaned into him, a bit blitzed. "Get any of the new girls?" He had a beer hanging between two fingers. It had to be at least his tenth by now.

Though, Z could normally put them away, he never drank to the point of losing his shit. So D could only chalk it up to pre-wedding jitters. Especially since the DAMC women were all inside church planning the big day. And scheming, of course, because bitches were always scheming.

Diesel followed Z's gaze toward the strippers dancing by the band's stage, which had become a permanent fixture in the yard. Some of the prospects had finally built something worth keeping up all year round.

"Yeah." He twisted his head back toward his best friend and club brother. "Miss it?"

Z took another pull from his beer then shook his head. "Fuck no. Don't need nobody else other than Sophie."

"Bitch got your balls in a sling," D grumbled.

Z whacked him on the back and laughed. "Don't hear me bitchin', do ya?"

No, he didn't. D raised his own beer to his lips and let the cool brew slide down his throat. He scanned the courtyard again, looking for someone he could drain his nuts into. Wasn't looking good. Nobody was catching his eye tonight.

For the past few nights, it had been just him and his palm. And they needed to break up.

Maybe he should've taken Magnum up on his offer last night.

He blew out a breath. *Right.*

Closing his eyes, he couldn't get rid of the image of a naked Jewel that was burned into the back of his eyelids.

He pushed to his feet. He needed to find some fresh snatch right now and fuck that memory right out of his head.

"Where ya goin'?" Z asked, a slight slur in his question.

"Gonna hit the head," he grunted.

Zak laughed, knowing exactly what that meant.

Diesel scanned the courtyard once more and his gaze landed on a female that he'd never seen before hanging by the fence near the beer kegs. He strode across the yard on a mission and within seconds, found himself staring down at the woman, taking a closer look.

She'd do.

"Hey," she said, wearing a small smile. "I'm—"

"Don't give a shit who you are. Who you with?"

"My girlfriend brought me—"

That was all he needed to hear.

She squeaked as D grabbed her wrist and tugged her along behind him toward the side door of the clubhouse.

"I, uh—" she started.

D stopped suddenly. He cupped his dick through his jeans. "Want it or not?"

"Uh…" her gaze dropped to his crotch. Then her eyes widened. "I… Sure," she finally whispered.

With a nod, he continued his trek to the door with her in tow.

She was the complete opposite of Jewel, which was a relief. She was blonde, leggy, a bit on the thick side, and had huge tits. And at that moment, he could give a flying fuck if they were real or fake. He wasn't planning to get to know her well enough to find out.

He yanked open the door and encouraged her to step inside when his hand shoved her ass. She stumbled to a stop just inside the door and he ran into her with a grunt. "To the left," he directed.

Then he realized why she had stopped. She was staring at a group of women surrounding the bar, who were all staring back at them.

Jesus fuckin' Christ.

"Hey," she called out a weak greeting.

D groaned as some of the DAMC women answered her, wearing smirks.

Someone yelled, "Breaking the seal, D?"

Jesus.

"Think the room's already occupied," someone else called out, sounding a bit amused. It sounded a lot like Diamond, Jewel's sister.

Right.

Ignoring them, he circled his fingers around the nameless woman's bicep and steered her toward the restroom.

"Is your room this way?" she asked, surprised.

"Yep," he grunted.

He grabbed the doorknob and before he could open it, she asked, "Why does it say 'chicks'?"

He yanked open the door and stopped dead.

Jewel had her back to them and it looked like she was fastening her jeans. "Sorry," she called out without turning around. "Didn't lock the door. Come in, just gotta wash—" She finally twisted her head around and froze.

Her eyes widened. D's narrowed.

And the blonde squirmed. "This is a bathroom," she whispered.

Genius. But he didn't need her for her brains, just...

"What the fuck?" Jewel shouted as she spun to confront him.

Jesus fuckin' Christ, here comes the fuckin' drama.

"What's her name, D?"

D ground his teeth.

The blonde began, "It's—"

He scowled down at her and she shut up.

"I should go," she whispered. "I'm not really into hooking up in bathrooms."

"No?" Jewel asked. "Diesel's a pro at it. Aren't you, D?"

D ground his teeth harder. So hard, he wouldn't be surprised if he cracked a few.

"I should go," the blonde repeated again and pulled her arm from his grasp.

"That would be smart," Jewel advised, her eyes never leaving Diesel's. "Unless you like the imprint of wall tiles on your ass."

The blonde disappeared. He didn't have to see her leave, he felt it.

She was gone and now it was just him and Jewel.

Her eyes snapped at him and so did her words. "Sorry I messed up your fucking *date*. I'm sure it was going to be meaningful and extremely romantic. She could've been *the one*."

"Shut up, Jewel."

"I offered myself up to you like a goddamn fool and you turned it down. You'd rather have any strange you can get against a bathroom wall instead." She shook her head, her face flushed with anger. "Nothin' but a goddamn *beast*," she hissed.

Diesel twisted and slammed the door behind him. He punched the lock on the knob before twisting back to face Jewel.

"Fuckin' call me that again," he challenged her.

Her eyes flashed and her nostrils flared. "Fucking beast!" she shouted, her face twisting.

D lost his mind. Totally fucking lost his mind. Right there. Right then.

He jerked forward, grabbed her arm and shook her. "Wanna be like the rest of 'em?" he growled in her face.

Jewel opened her mouth and nothing came out, her face suddenly pale.

"Wanna be like the rest of 'em?" he repeated, much louder and so much more pissed this time. He spun her around to face the wall—the one he knew so well—and shoved her forward. She stumbled and caught herself on the wall with her palms.

He swore she whimpered but he didn't give a shit. He was past giving a shit. Or even a flying fuck.

He was going to do what he'd been trying to avoid. But the damn woman needed a lesson. She needed to realize she wasn't going to get what she was looking for with him.

"Pants off," he barked. "Up against the wall."

"D—"

"No, woman, this is what you wanted."

"No."

"Sure fuckin' is. Kept pushin' it, pushin' me. Want it, gonna get it. Get your pants off. Now."

Her chest rose and fell rapidly, her eyes looked wild, her face went from pale to flush in a heartbeat.

"D—"

"Shut up, woman, an' take your pants off. Can't fuck you against the fuckin' wall when you're wearin' those fuckin' jeans."

With trembling fingers, she reached for the top button of her jeans.

D's head spun. She was going to do it. She was going to *let* him do it.

Jesus fuckin' Christ.

No.

No.

No.

He was not going to fuck her in this bathroom, against that wall, like any other piece of ass.

He wasn't going to do it.

He needed to teach her a lesson, but not here. Not in this bathroom.

His mouth went dry and a sharp pain shot through his temple, and before he knew what he was doing, he had her thrown over his shoulder, was barreling out the door and across the common area of the clubhouse.

From a distance, he heard gasps, and both his and Jewel's names being called. Worried voices. He ignored it all.

His heavy boots pounded up the steps to the second floor and then down the hall to his room.

As he dug into his jeans for his keys, he realized Jewel wasn't struggling at all. She wasn't fighting, she wasn't bitching. She was too quiet.

His heart thudded in his chest as he unlocked his door, kicked it open, took a step inside, kicked it shut, then slid the bolt lock home.

Within two strides, he had her tossed onto the bed where she bounced, all of her dark hair flying about wildly. Her eyes were focused on him, as he remained standing at the end of the bed.

Jesus. He needed to save himself and leave like the last time he carried her upstairs. He needed to do that before there was no going back.

Before he got past that point of no return.

Without a word, she got to her knees and pulled her DAMC tank top over her head, then she reached behind her to unclip the black lacy bra she wore.

When her tits were free, she unbuttoned and unzipped her jeans. She tugged off her sandals and tossed them onto the floor, then laying back on his bed—*his* bed—she shimmied out of her jeans and panties.

And all that time, he remained frozen in place, watching her tear each piece of clothing off until she was fully naked in *his* bed.

"Woman, you don't know what you're doin'," he finally muttered through clenched teeth.

"The fuck I don't," she lay on his bed, propped up by his pillows and cupped her tits, thumbing her own nipples, "*beast.*"

D's nostril's flared and he ripped off his cut, tossing it to the side. His eyes never left her as her fingers slid down her belly to her cunt and she slipped two fingers along the slit of her pussy.

Jesus fuckin' Christ.

His chest felt as if it had caved in, but he yanked his shirt over his head. Bending over, he unzipped his boots and toed them off. He ripped off his jeans and socks at the same time, then straightened, his cock in his hand.

He closed his eyes for a second as he stroked it, but for that whole second he was thinking what a huge mistake this was.

There was no going back from this.

She's not mine, she's not mine, she's not mine.

The reminder didn't help as he put a knee onto the bed making it sink under his weight.

He was going to do this.

They were going to do this.

There was no going back.

"Show me," he grunted.

The fingers she had in her cunt scissored to show him how slick and pink her center was.

"Show me," he grunted again.

Her fingers disappeared inside herself and she moved them rapidly, her other hand joining in, her thumb circling her clit. She was shaved bare and he hated that on women since it made them look like a little girl. And she was far from a little girl. He needed to tell her about that.

His thoughts quickly fled as her hips rose off the mattress as she fucked herself with her own fingers, her face flush and her lips parted as she whimpered. Her head rolled back and she cried out as her hands began to move at a frenzied pace.

His chest heaved as he struggled to breathe while watching her. He never saw anything so beautiful before.

Never.

Jesus.

And he hadn't even touched her, yet. He realized he was squeezing his dick so hard that it was turning purple and the veins were bulging. He released the pressure and slid his palm up and down his length as Jewel's hips shot off the bed again.

She groaned, moaned and when little mews escaped her, he could hardly hold himself back any longer.

But he wanted to watch her come first.

And when she did, he just about lost his shit.

She even called his fucking name when she came.

Before she was even done with her orgasm, he was up and over her, driving his cock deep.

Then he stilled once he was fully seated inside her.

His mind swirled, his body tensed, and he couldn't believe how warm, wet and tight she felt.

"Woman," he grunted, shoving his face into her thick hair and inhaling her scent.

There was no going back from this.

He was careful to keep the majority of his weight off of her as he began to move, slowly at first, marveling at how she squeezed him tight. Her legs circled his waist and she tilted her hips, giving him a better angle to hit that right spot. The one that made her wetter with each thrust.

"Diesel."

He lifted his head and stared into her blue eyes. Slightly unfocused, their intensity could still be felt all the way deep into his soul.

She's not mine, she's not mine, she's not...

Mine. She's mine. She's fuckin' mine.

She's mine. Makin' her mine an' only mine.

He grunted as she whimpered with each pump of his hips. He ground deep and she took every inch of him without complaint. Her nails raked his ass, her teeth scraped the strained cords of his neck, his back flexed as he curled over her as he thrusted over and over.

Everything fell away until there was nothing but her underneath him, encouraging him to make her come. And he did just that. More than once. Every ripple, every squeeze along his dick, made him want to give her more, make her come once more. Just once more.

He wanted to feel her come again. And again. He wanted this to be endless.

Their bodies were slick with both their sweat and her juices as she kissed along his shoulders before sinking her teeth in hard.

He groaned into her mouth when he took it, claiming that part of her, too.

Every inch, every curve, every digit, every strand of hair was now his.

He lost his sense of time because he couldn't get enough.

"I was right... you are a beast," she breathed. "You gotta come, D. I can't take much more."

He wasn't done. He'd never be done.

Pushing his weight into his hands, he dropped his head until he was face to face with her, their eyes locked. "Gonna come inside you."

"Yes," she hissed.

"Want that?"

"Yes."

"Makin' you mine."

"Yes," she answered on a ragged breath.

He tensed, his balls pulled up and with a loud grunt, he spilled everything he had inside her.

Chapter Four

DIESEL GROANED and rolled to the right. Planting his feet on the floor, he pushed to a stand, yawned and scratched his balls.

Something was... off. He glanced down. Damn. He needed a shower. He had pussy juice caked...

His head twisted to look at his bed. His *empty* bed.

Jesus fuckin' Christ.

She had bailed after he fell asleep.

The fuckin' bitch bailed on me.

He rounded the bed, snagged his phone from the nightstand, and then stopped, staring at an open box of condoms. Four hours of fucking and they hadn't even used one.

Jesus.

He looked down at his dick.

Jesus.

He hit the power button on his phone, scrolled through his contacts and hit Send.

The phone rang.

And rang.

Finally, Jewel's sleepy voice answered. "What?"

What?

"You fuckin' left."

"Yeah."

Yeah?

He sucked air through his nostrils, held it for a moment, then blew it out of his mouth loudly. He was trying to keep the lid on his temper, but his blood was boiling so badly the lid was quaking dangerously.

"You didn't want a clinger and a nag," she reminded him and then hung up.

Hung up.

His head jerked, he pulled the phone away from his ear and stared at it.

Good thing that lid was imaginary or he'd take it and whip it across the room.

He tapped in a text. With his fat fingers it took him three tries to get it right.

Then he threw the phone on the bed and stalked into the bathroom to wash her off his dick.

JEWEL STUDIED the text D sent.

Dont u fuckn move! Nota fuckn inch!

She smiled as she placed her phone back on her nightstand. Still wearing that smile, she got out of bed to unlock her front door since Ace probably wouldn't be happy if Diesel busted it down. It already had to be replaced when Ivy lived there.

Then she went back into her bedroom, dug out her sexiest negligee and slipped it over her head.

After adjusting her breasts into the lacy cups and setting the thong more comfortably in her ass crack, she climbed back into her bed, pulled the covers over her and fell back asleep.

Still wearing that smile.

HEAT SEARED JEWEL'S BACK. Having Diesel spoon her was like being curled against a furnace. He was way too fucking hot.

In more ways than one.

And who would have thought D even knew how to spoon?

Crazy.

Her eyes landed on the digital clock on her nightstand. It was two in the afternoon. She doubted she'd be able to walk after their marathon fuckfest.

The man had stamina, that was for sure.

Though, between sessions he would be just about knocked out cold. The man could sleep like the dead.

When she had fallen back to sleep early this morning after he called and texted, she'd been sleeping like the dead, too.

She hadn't heard him knock, or pound his meaty fists, if he even did, which he might not have since she'd left the door open for him. And she awoke to find him standing next to her bed, staring at her, his expression dark and stormy.

Clearly, he hadn't been thrilled that she'd fled from his room super early this morning. Though, not thrilled was a bit of an understatement.

Actually, he'd been furious. But it definitely made for good sex.

The man was a beast in bed, just as he was in life.

But now, his right arm was curled under her with his hand cupping her right breast, his fingers twitching every so often in sleep. His left arm snaked over her waist, and his hand, with the fingers spread wide, pressed along her lower belly.

Her pussy clenched at the thought of how close his middle finger was to her clit. Even though she was sore and tired from the most back to back sexcapades she'd ever had in her life, she couldn't resist the need for him to touch her again... *there.*

His face was nuzzled into the hair gathered at the back of her neck and she could feel his warm breath steadily beating against her skin. His cock, now soft, nestled in the crack of her ass.

Like the rest of the DAMC women, she had seen his ass on more than one occasion as he screwed some random female against the wall in the women's room at church. But she had never seen the actual tool that he used.

She had to say it was impressive. Like the rest of him.

Her fingertips traced some of the many tattoos that covered his arms. Unlike most of the brothers who had inked sleeves, his didn't stop at the wrists. His continued over the backs of his hands. The fingers of his right hand had the letters D-I-R-T-Y tattooed onto them. The fingers of his left hand had the letters A-N-G-E-L.

He was DAMC through and through. No doubt about it.

But then, so was she.

She never denied it, not like some of her club sisters. She knew the drill of being an ol' lady and all that it entailed.

But she also was in no way submissive. So, she wouldn't openly admit she wanted to be an ol' lady.

And not just anyone's ol' lady.

D shifted in his sleep and his left hand moved lower, now cupping the mound of her pussy.

Her fingers slid along his and encouraged him, even in his sleep, to press harder.

In the last twelve plus hours, she had a record number of orgasms, but one more couldn't hurt.

Because she was sure once he woke up, he'd split.

He had stated he didn't want a clinger or a nag and even though she wouldn't be either of those things, she wasn't going to beg him to stay.

She wasn't going to ask shit of him.

She decided she was going to play it cool from now on. Act like she didn't give a shit whether he wanted her or not.

That's what she was going to do. But right now...

His middle finger curled and slipped between her folds, teasing along her clit and lower. His breathing remained steady, his hand on her breast, for the most part, relaxed.

Every part of her body began to tingle. Everywhere. Her nipples hardened and her pussy clenched even harder.

Jesus, it was like she couldn't get enough of him. Which worried her a little. That might make it a little difficult to act like she didn't care.

As his long finger slipped inside her, she stopped worrying. A long, low groan escaped her as she tilted her hips to give him better access.

She began to move her hips in a matching rhythm to his hand, and when his thumb pressed her clit as his middle finger fucked her, she closed her eyes, pressed her head back into his collarbone and came once more.

It was that easy. That quick.

And oh so satisfying.

Once her breathing slowed, she turned her head slightly, listening to his.

He was *still* asleep.

Amazing.

With a sigh and his finger still buried inside her, she closed her eyes and let sleep claim her once more.

DIESEL GROANED AND ROLLED, his eyes opening when the smell of sex, and a lot of it, hit his nostrils.

He blinked.

He was not at church. This was not his bed.

He flipped onto his back and blinked up at the ceiling.

His reflection blinked back at him.

Jesus fuckin' Christ. Who the hell had a mirror on the ceiling anymore?

He turned his head and surveyed the room. He was alone.

Second time in over twenty-four hours in which he'd woken up after Jewel deserted him while he slept.

He wasn't liking that.

Not. At. All.

He rolled again, planted his feet on the floor and stood with a groan. He twisted at the waist and groaned again as his spine cracked.

He glanced down. Yeah, his dick was still attached. He was

surprised that, with all the sex he'd had in the past day and night, it hadn't fallen off.

He grinned. The fucking woman was greedy when it came to his dick. And his tongue. And a few of his digits.

Without bothering to pull on his jeans, he barefooted it out into the hall, hit the head, then made his way into the living room that opened to the small kitchen. He followed his nose to the coffeemaker, saw a pot of hot fresh-brewed coffee, and a mug sitting next to it with a note.

He lifted the Harley Davidson notepad to read it.

Coffee. Towel - back of bathroom door. Went to work. Thanks.

Thanks?

He tossed the pad back where he found it, poured himself a mug of steaming black coffee, then leaned his naked ass against the counter as he took a sip.

Thanks.

Son of a bitch.

Jewel glanced up and groaned when she saw who was approaching the door to the office at Shadow Valley Body Works. She clicked the button on the mouse to save the invoice she was working on and leaned back. Just waiting.

This should be good.

Once Diesel had shown up yesterday at her apartment, she had shut off her phone. And when she turned it back on this morning, the missed calls, voicemail messages and texts were too numerous to read or listen to. Since she already knew the content of them all, she deleted them without doing just that.

And now she was going to pay for it as she watched her sister, Diamond, yank open the door and step inside.

The only good thing about her showing up was she carried a large pink box with the name Sophie's Sweet Treats on the side.

Her sister just got an automatic ten points for that.

If it was full of some of Bella's killer stuffed cupcakes she'd get another fifteen. She was feeling generous this morning.

Diamond smiled at her and lifted the box up. "I come bearing bribes."

Jewel arched an eyebrow and sighed. "See that."

Di slid the box onto the corner of the desk and propped her ass on the edge. Jewel blinked up at her and she blinked back.

Her sister was waiting for Jewel to dish the gossip.

"Well?" Di finally asked, slightly annoyed.

"Well?"

"Jewelee."

"Di."

"Seriously," Di said, now miffed.

"Seriously," Jewel confirmed as her gaze was drawn back out of the large office window.

Oh no. No. No. No.

Bella was carrying another pink box from the bakery, heading toward the office, and right on her heels was Ivy.

Shit.

Diamond's head turned to glance the direction Jewel's was. "I didn't tell them I was coming here."

Jewel shot her sister a frown. "You didn't have to, apparently. It probably wasn't hard to figure out."

Ivy held the door open for Bella and they both rushed inside. They stopped short, spotted Diamond and then laughed.

Ivy grinned. "Like minds and all that shit."

"Jesus," Jewel muttered. "Did you invite Kiki, Sophie and Kelsea, too?"

"Sophie's holding down the fort at the bakery but I have to report any juicy details to her ASAP," Bella said, sliding the second box of cupcakes next to the first one.

"Break those bitches out," Jewel muttered. She might as well overdose on sugar if she had to get through what she was sure would be a thorough grilling.

As soon as they popped the box lids open, Jewel leaned forward to stare at the wondrous confections that came from Sophie's bakery.

Her baked goods were addicting. And hip widening.

"Got anything with a shitload of chocolate?" Jewel asked Bella.

"Death by chocolate. Chocolate cake, dark chocolate ganache, and stuffed with chocolate mousse. And don't forget the dark chocolate curl shavings on the top. Expertly put there by me," Bella announced.

She lifted the heavenly sight out of the box and handed it to Jewel, who promptly peeled off the paper baking cup and muttered, "Death by anything would be welcomed about now," before shoving it into her mouth.

The rest of the women grabbed a cupcake and shoved them into their pie aka cupcake holes. Which meant Jewel had a minute or two before the torture commenced.

Good thing none of the guys were around or they'd all be sporting wood hearing the loud moaning of the women. Anyone listening on the other side of the shop door would think they were having an orgy.

And they were. Just in their mouths.

Jewel took a sip of her coffee to wash down the overly sweet chocolate frosting.

She sighed and looked up to see three sets of eyes staring at her, waiting.

"What?" she asked them.

"*What*?" Diamond shrieked. "What do you mean *what*? Spill, sister! I didn't bring cupcakes because I love your ass."

Ivy and Bella nodded in agreement.

Great.

"I don't know what you want me to say," she began and quickly took another sip of coffee.

Damn. Coffee and cupcakes first thing in the morning. That hit the spot.

Kind of like D's finger on her clit.

She closed her eyes and cursed silently.

"Having flashbacks?" Bella asked, amusement in her voice.

Jewel's eyes popped open. "Maybe."

"Shit! We were all dying when he came charging out of the bathroom with you over his shoulder."

"Thanks for stopping him."

Ivy made a noise. "You *wanted* us to stop him? You didn't seem to be fighting it."

Crap. That was true.

"Then he went running up those steps like an Olympic athlete and like you weighed *nothing*."

Jewel rolled her eyes at her sister's words.

"And we waited and waited…" Ivy started.

"For you two to come back down," Bella finished.

"And you didn't," Di added in a whisper.

"Yeah," Jewel said, avoiding their eyes.

"*Yeah,* she says," Di scoffed. "*Yeah*!"

"Then you ignored all of our texts and calls yesterday."

"Saw his sled parked by the steps *all day*," Ivy said.

Of course she would, she probably worked Sunday at Shadow Valley Pawn. As well as did Ace and Dex.

Shit.

That meant by now, *everyone* knew she and Diesel had hooked up.

"It was going to happen eventually," Ivy stated, brushing her red hair away from her face.

"It was?"

"Yeah, that day I brought Bangin' Burgers over here and he charged into the office, I could cut the tension with a knife."

"You could?"

Ivy frowned at Jewel. "Jewelee, seriously, we all knew it was going to happen."

"Now that you two are together—" her sister began.

Jewel's eyebrows shot up. "Together? We're not together."

"What?" Diamond.

"Bullshit." Bella.

"Right." Ivy.

Fuckity fuck.

Jewel leaned over, grabbed another cupcake out of the box and swiped her finger through the icing before shoving the big sweet glob into her mouth. Today was going to be a two-cupcake day.

Yes, it was.

"It's nothing. You know D likes his conquests."

"Right," Bella muttered.

"He normally doesn't take his conquests up to his room," Ivy added, helpfully.

"Nor does he stay all day and all night in a woman's apartment." Bella was also being *way* too helpful.

"You don't know that," Jewel insisted.

Bella cocked a dark brow her direction.

"Okay. Maybe so."

"I think D finally met his match," Ivy crowed gleefully.

"Just because he didn't... We didn't..." She squeezed her eyes shut for a second, then muttered, "Shit." She opened her eyes. "It was nothing."

"Mmm hmm," came from one of them.

Jewel frowned.

"Jewelee," her sister said softly. "You've wanted him forever."

"I never said that," Jewel insisted, though her sister was right. She wanted Diesel ever since she hit puberty and realized boys weren't yucky. And at five years older than her, D had never looked her way. He'd been too busy chasing women who were older and more experienced, while adding notches to his belt.

"You didn't have to. It was hard to miss."

"Now you have the hook in him, you just need to reel him in." Ivy pretended she was holding a fishing rod and reeling in a fish. Di snorted.

Her arms dropped quickly when the shop door swung open. Crash strode in, followed closely by Rig.

Their attention immediately fell to the pink pastry boxes.

"Fuckin' holdin' out again!" Crash yelled. He went over and snagged two cupcakes, peeled the paper off the bottom of one and shoved half of it into his mouth.

Rig's gaze landed on Ivy. "Your man know you're in here hoardin' cupcakes?"

Ivy tossed her red hair and swatted a hand his direction. "I'll tell him when I'm good and ready."

Rig's eyebrows hit his forehead. He snagged one of the cupcakes, ripped the paper off, tossing it onto the desk, and bit into it.

Icing stuck to his raggedy, long beard and moustache that Jewel always wanted to shave off. The guy would be somewhat good-looking if he cut that messy crap off his face.

"That's disgusting," Bella said, her dark brown eyes squinting.

"What?" Rig asked, looking her direction.

"That shit in your beard," Bella answered, pointing to his overgrown facial hair.

"Flavor savor," Rig said with a laugh, then he stroked the moustache that curled over his upper lip with his tongue.

"Gross," Jewel muttered.

"Bitches love it," he said, still laughing.

"Whatever," Bella said and then shoved him toward the shop door. "These *bitches* are busy with important business. So, get gone."

He grabbed a second cupcake and left.

Crash was already halfway through his second one. "Tellin' your ol' man you're in here," he told Ivy with a mouthful of cake and icing.

Ivy shrugged. "Go ahead. I don't give a shit."

"In here cacklin' like a bunch of fuckin' hens."

"Do I need to repeat myself, Crash?" Ivy asked.

"Nope."

"Good. Get gone."

"This is my shop," he complained. "You can't kick me out of my own office."

"Jewel's office," Ivy corrected him.

"She only works here."

"*Only*?" Ivy screeched.

Crash frowned. "Whatever," he grumbled and left, slamming the door behind him.

Jewel rolled in her lips to avoid laughing. She loved working at the body shop, but sometimes dealing with the guys on both the body shop side and the towing side, which was Rig's baby, could be like running a daycare.

"We were saying?" Diamond asked, her blue eyes landing back on Jewel.

"We weren't saying anything," Jewel said. "It's nothing; move on."

"But you guys..."

"Di, who are you bringing to the wedding?" Jewel asked to change the subject.

Her sister shut up about Diesel. "Not sure."

"Slade?" she prodded.

"Not sure."

Jewel knew Diamond would love to go to the wedding with Slade. The guy was freaking *hot* and was about to be the newest patched member. He seemed to have his shit together and was *hot*, which was a plus. And he was *hot*, so there was that.

Ivy cut into her thoughts. "Think Z's parents are going to show up for the wedding?"

They looked to Bella. "What about Axel?"

Bella's eyes bugged out. "Why are you asking me?"

They all just gave her a knowing look.

"It'll be a damn shame if they don't show up," Jewel said. "Did Z even ask them?"

That question hung out there for a minute since none of them knew the answer.

"Having Axel take you to the wedding would be a good excuse for him to show up there, Bella," Jewel suggested.

"Right. I'm not asking him, though. And I get what you're saying, however, even though he's Z's brother, he's still 5-0. Even if I did show up at the wedding with him, Hawk and Diesel would blow a gasket. Not to mention the rest of them."

"These men need to get over themselves. We can fuck who we want, when we want."

Bella raised a brow. "Oh yeah? You think D's gonna let you do that now?"

Jewel's mouth parted, she snapped it shut, and it parted again as a breath escaped. She shut it a second time, then muttered, "Shit."

Bella nodded. "Right. And anyway, I'm not fucking Axel."

"And I keep telling you, you should be," Di said. "Even though he's my cousin, I still can recognize the fact that he's as yummy as one of your cupcakes *and* he's a good catch, 5-0 or not."

"I'll keep that in mind," Bella muttered.

Di snorted. "And he wants down your pants in the worst way."

"Okay. Enough," Bella snapped. "Anyway, it's not like we need dates for the wedding. It's informal."

"No, but..." Di drifted off as the roar of straight pipes filled the office from the parking lot. All eyes slid to the window.

Diesel pulled his sled up in front of the office. He sat on his bike staring at them through the window the same way they were staring at him. But now Ivy and Diamond were plastered to the window with large smiles on their faces.

Shit. Jewel's heart flipped in her chest and the hair on the back of her neck bristled.

"D's here," Diamond called out.

"No shit," Jewel grumbled, unable to see him any longer with their noses practically pressed to the glass.

"For getting laid so recently, he sure doesn't look happy," Di grumbled. She twisted her head in Jewel's direction. "Do you suck in bed or something?"

"Di!" Bella snapped, grabbing her arm and pulling her away from the window. "He always looks like that. Has nothing to do with Jewel."

Jewel wasn't so sure of that, but she wasn't going to argue.

"No," Di continued, "he looks like Mr. Grumpypants more than normal this morning."

"What do you expect him to be like? Whistling and skipping?" Bella hissed. Then she suddenly said in a very normal voice, "Hey, D."

"Hey, D!" Ivy said, a big smile on her face.

"Hey, D!" Diamond said, winking at him.

He scowled at Diamond and pushed past her.

"Woman," D grunted as his gaze landed on Jewel.

"'Kay, we gotta go," Bella yelled out and shoved the other two through the front door.

Jewel's eyes slid from the door back to D, who she swore took up most of the space in the small office. And most of the oxygen, too.

She tilted her head back to stare up at him. "Want a cupcake?"

"Yeah," he said, not breaking their gaze.

A shiver ran up Jewel's spine. His brown eyes were dark and unreadable.

"Thanks," he grumbled.

"For what?" she asked, surprised. Since when did this man have manners and say please or thank you?

"Coffee. Towel."

Ah, shit. He was just repeating what she wrote in the note. "That's it? Just thanks for the coffee and towel?"

"Yeah."

"Okaaay," she drew out. "You stopped here for that?"

"No."

"Then what?" she prodded.

He finally stepped back, looked at the cupcakes, grabbed one of the boxes, then turned and walked into the shop with them, shutting the door behind him.

Jewel stared at the door and shook her head. She had no idea what that was about.

But she did note, as he was leaving, that his ass looked awesome in his black jeans today. She wondered how many scratches she'd left behind on those muscular cheeks.

Her pussy clenched as she thought about their all-day sex session yesterday. She should've woken him up and got one more shot at him this morning.

Maybe she could convince him to stop over tonight.

So much for playing it cool.

Chapter Five

DIESEL LEANED back in his desk chair, his booted feet kicked up on his messy desk. With his cell pressed to his ear, he listened to one of his guys as he reported in.

Two of his "Shadows" that worked for him at In the Shadows Security were on a long-term gig in the city being bodyguards for a well-known NFL player. One who liked to get himself in a bit of trouble. Drinking, constant partying, questionable women, DUIs, the list went on and on.

His guys had their work cut out for them, but they were a couple of his best. And they could keep their cool even in the midst of chaos. But still, he made them check in regularly.

As much as they were paid, they didn't complain about it.

All of his Shadows were former military and usually of the elite variety. Former SEALS, Green Berets, Night Stalkers, Delta Force, Force Recon, and any other special forces men he could recruit.

His "security" company had expanded in the past few years. He and his guys had a good reputation and word had spread. When he first opened the business, he and some of his club brothers did most of the grunt work, which were mostly shit jobs, like being bouncers at bars, nightclubs, and private parties. Now, with the crew he had, the demands on both investigative services and bodyguard work were increasing, as were his fees. He also offered some "elite" services that teetered on legality. But some of the stuff the club used to handle themselves was now dealt with by his crew, which kept the club on the right side of the law. For the most part.

He leaned toward the investigative side of things after Zak was set-up by those fucking bastards, the Warriors, and the cops royally fucked up the investigation. Whether on purpose or not, he didn't know. He hadn't found out that gem of truth yet. Though, that was not a closed case in his mind. The evidence had been fucked and it even screwed up Z's appeal.

Z did his ten-year stint, did it like a fucking pro, and when he got out, moved on to bigger and better things. Like Sophie. He didn't remain bitter and ignored any talk about making an effort to clear his name. He just wanted to be done with the whole thing and put it behind him. Especially now that he was getting permanently attached to his woman and D wouldn't be surprised if she soon got knocked up. Z was one of the brothers who wanted a family.

In one way, D understood letting the whole thing go, in another, he wasn't sure if he could do the same as Z.

No matter what, his woman stuck by his side, whether Z was labeled as a convicted felon or not.

The brother had a perfect ol' lady. Couldn't get any better than Sophie. Smart, successful, loyal, hot as fuck. And was a boss when it came to baking shit.

He'd downed three of those cupcakes this morning in about five minutes flat.

They were as sweet as fuck.

Like Jewel's pussy.

Fuck.

The voice in his ear went quiet. Then he heard, "Boss?"

D adjusted his dick, which was starting to chub up.

"Yeah," he grunted.

"You get me?"

"Yeah. Got you."

"Hangin' up now," came the amused voice on the other end.

"Yeah."

The phone went dead. D pulled it away from his ear and tossed it onto the desk.

Fucking Jewel.

He closed his eyes and remembered her yesterday. Legs spread, cunt soaked, moaning and whimpering, squirming beneath him, raking her nails down his back and over his ass. Her legs wrapped around him, nudging him hard with her heels like he was a fucking horse and he needed to "giddy-up."

He giddy-upped. That he fucking did.

His phone beeped at him. He snagged it and read the text.

Coming over?

He stared at the screen.

Fucking woman. Wanted more of his dick. Wanted him to get addicted to that pussy of hers so she could put a leash on him, nag him, try to control him, fill that empty spot on the back of his sled.

Ain't gonna happen. No fucking way.

His fat fingers tapped out four letters. *Busy.* He hit Send.

He waited, expecting drama, but got no answer. After a few minutes, he tossed his phone down, sighed, dropped his feet to the floor, and got to work.

Two hours later he slammed the back door of his building, locked it, then stepped out into the dark parking lot. He hated fucking paperwork, but it was a necessary evil. Especially if he wanted to get paid by his clients. He really needed to hire someone to keep his books, file shit, and whatever. But he hadn't found anyone he could trust yet. Someone able to keep the shit that went on, and the famous people they covered, on the down low.

He thought about asking Diamond because she had a shit job but the bitch couldn't keep her trap shut and she had an attitude as well as a smart mouth. He might end up firing her ass five minutes after she started.

He glanced at his phone. It was only ten. He could either go back to his shithole of a room at church, or stop in and visit with Hawk at The Iron Horse. He scrubbed a hand over his short hair. He really needed to get his own place. Hawk had a decent house in the 'burbs and, now that Kiki had moved in permanently, he was getting more and more domesticated.

D snorted.

Brothers were going down like flies. Jag even bought himself and Ivy a house. He wouldn't be surprised if those two had rugrats running around under foot soon.

Jesus.

Movement by his sled caught his eye and he froze. He wouldn't be surprised to come outside one night and find Warriors fucking with his Harley. Maybe even trashing it like they did Jag's. He needed to get some motion lights set up out back. He put that on his mental to-do list as he moved forward and saw someone sitting...

On his fucking bike!

Jesus fuckin' Christ.

Jewel sat on the seat, wearing only lacy panties and a bra, and freaking crazy high heels which she had propped on the back foot pegs. And by doing that, her knees were cocked and spread wide, her fingers were moving in between them.

"What the fuck?" he shouted.

She gave him a smile.

"What the fuck?" he repeated, because his brain and his temper were both boiling.

"I've been waiting," she said, her voice husky. "I didn't expect you to be busy for so long."

His eyes raked her. "How long you been out here dressed like that? Some of my crew could've come back at any time."

"Then I would've given them a message to send you out."

His head jerked back as he stared at her. She would've *what*?

He didn't step any closer to the bike or her, because if he did, he might blow a gasket, pull her off it, throw her over his lap and spank her fucking ass to teach her a lesson. And he'd do it until that smirk of hers was wiped clean away.

"Woman," he growled.

"I figured after a *busy* night, you could use a little relief."

She was being a smart ass.

Her fingers trailed back and forth over the center of her panties. She was probably slick and ready for him. One of her hands cupped her bra.

But when she buried her other hand *into* her panties, he'd had enough.

"Woman," he growled again, but the word got stuck in his throat. He swallowed hard to clear it.

"Yeah, D?"

Jesus fuckin' Christ.

His hard-on was now raging, his blood pounding in his ears, his heart thumping against his chest.

"Like fuckin' in public?" he asked, sounding a bit strangled.

She lifted a shoulder. "Yeah, sure."

Jesus fuckin' Christ! Just like that. *Yeah, sure!* Acting like fucking in public was an everyday thing for her.

His blood pounded harder. "Done it before?" he asked a little too loudly.

"Sure," she murmured. "You're so far away." Her voice caught as the hand down her panties moved faster.

He was about to self-combust. With a few long strides, he was at the bike, pulling her off it with a surprised squeak. He took her place on the seat, unbuttoned his jeans, ripped down the zipper, pushed the denim down far enough until his cock was free. Then he looked at her standing there in only those panties, bra and heels.

Fuck me.

"Get on," he barked.

With a smile, she placed a hand on his shoulder and didn't she just fucking pull her panties to the side and climb onto his dick.

Fuck yeah, she did.

As all the oxygen left his lungs at the unbelievable feeling of her pussy wrapped warm and wet around him, he dug one hand into her hair at the back of her head, and snaked an arm around her waist, shoving his face into her neck. His chest tightened as he inhaled her scent. And when she began to move up and down his cock, he closed his eyes and held her even closer.

Fuck him. He was so fucking fucked.

"D," she groaned in his ear as her cunt squeezed him tight.

She was so wet that she was dripping down his balls, which were jammed painfully against his zipper. But he didn't give a shit. A little discomfort was worth this woman riding him, making him want to blow his load deep inside her.

She's mine.

He took her mouth, shoving his tongue against hers and she fought him for control, their tongues twisting, pushing, circling. She groaned into his mouth. And when she tried to pull away, he wouldn't let her.

Not yet. Her mouth was his. Her pussy was his.

Everything about her was his.

He dropped the hand from the small of her back into her panties, and slid his middle finger down her crease until he found her tight, puckered hole. Curving his finger, he pushed inside her. One knuckle, two, then all the way to the third.

Now her ass was his, too.

She squirmed against him, rode him harder, faster, then bit his bottom lip. He reluctantly released her mouth and she cried out his name.

"That's it, woman, ride me." He grunted as she gasped, jamming him deeper inside her until he hit the end of her.

With a twist of her hips she ground herself against his lap, driving him to the edge.

"Tit out," he mumbled.

Her hand slipped into one of the bra cups, pulled her tit from the cup and he latched onto the nipple, sucking, biting, pulling it with his teeth.

That made her get even wilder.

Throwing her head back, she landed forcefully over and over on his cock. Until he felt it. The unmistakable orgasm that hit her, making her jerk in his arms as he felt the gush of warmth over his dick and down his balls.

He heard "D" breathed into his ear.

He didn't know if he could even answer. He was barely holding on by a thread. One that was badly frayed and about to snap.

"Ah, fuck, I'm going to come again," she moaned. And then did just that.

After that one, he was done.

Done.

With a grunt, he buried both his finger and his cock deep and let go. He released her nipple and shoved his forehead into her neck and long hair as his cock pulsed and his balls emptied deep inside her.

That tightness that had been felt in his chest was suddenly gone.

Nowhere to be found.

He flared his nostrils trying to slow his breathing. Her hands gripped both sides of his head and she tilted it up, then placed her lips on his, kissing him deeply.

Jesus, this woman.

He was so fucking fucked.

He grabbed a handful of her long, dark hair and pulled her head back to stare into her blue eyes.

"Don't get it, do you, woman?"

"What?"

"Ain't gonna be tied down."

She circled her hips and he grunted. "Didn't like it?"

"Didn't say that."

She nodded, a sly smile crossing her lips. Then with both hands planted on his shoulder, she pushed herself off his lap and off his bike, adjusting her panties back into place.

"Where's your clothes?"

She lifted her chin to somewhere behind him. "In my Jeep."

"Get 'em an' get gone."

She saluted him in a sassy manner, and without an argument, walked away in those crazy-ass heels of hers into the dark. A moment later he heard her car door slam shut and the engine start.

He remained where she left him, on his bike, his dick still hanging out, staring at one of his boots, while he heard her drive away.

He was so fucking fucked.

He tucked his cock back in his jeans, then threw back his head and bellowed a curse to the sky.

HE WAS SO FUCKING FUCKED.

As he watched her rise and fall on his dick, he dug his fingers into her hips, desperate to keep her at a slow pace. He didn't want to finish in this position. Not like this.

Last night on his bike, she was on top. Then after he found himself at her apartment not even a half hour later, he had her once doggy style, once bent over the bed, and, hell, once against the fucking wall.

He couldn't get enough of her. And luckily, his dick had kept up with his needs.

Now this morning, he wanted to finish when he was on top since she needed a reminder that she wasn't going to be the one to bring him to heel.

No, she wasn't.

She threw her head back, gasped, grabbed her own tits and pinched both of her nipples as she clamped down on him hard.

Fuck.

This woman had an insatiable appetite when it came to sex. And he wondered if she was normally like this. And, if so, who the hell she'd been getting her fix from in the past few years.

Certainly not him.

His nostrils flared at the thought, and the muscles in his jaw got tight as he tried to push away the thought of all the men that had come before him.

He wasn't going to fucking ask. He wasn't going to even bring it up. He was going to push that from his mind.

Suddenly, she was curled over him, her lips barely above his. "I'm gonna come, D."

And when she did, their eyes held, even when her face changed while the orgasm rushed through her, making her body twitch on top of him, her muscles tightening like a stretched rubber band then becoming so loose, it seemed every bone disappeared in her body.

She collapsed onto his chest, her breathing ragged, her fingers digging into his pecs, her long, dark hair spread across her back and shoulders.

He grabbed a handful of that wavy silk and rubbed the strands between his fingers.

Jewel lifted her head and her blue eyes flashed at him when she asked, "Taking a break?"

Hell no he wasn't.

With a grunt, he flipped her onto her back and she squealed then laughed as he kneed her thighs apart forcefully. The giggle died when he thrust into her hard, grabbed her wrists and held them pinned to the bed over her head with one hand. His other hand found her tit and he rolled the hard tip between his finger and thumb.

Her tits might not be big and heavy like he normally liked, but, fuck him, if they didn't do it for him and they fit her tight body perfectly. Again, he normally liked a lot of flesh on his women, and Jewel was more on the smaller side. Even so, she could handle his bulk on top of her just fine.

That was emphasized when he drove his dick home one more time and she took every inch of him, digging her heels into the backs of his thighs. With another grunt, his body curled over hers and he grounded himself deep inside her. Air hissed out of her as he did that over and over. Finally, he released her wrists and her nails immediately raked down his back, making him hiss, too.

"Fuck me like you mean it," she demanded.

Jesus fuckin' Christ. This woman.

"Mean it," he said.

"Show me."

"Showin' you, woman. Don't wanna hurt you."

"You're not going to hurt me. You haven't hurt me yet." She grabbed his face between her two hands and forced his gaze to hers. "Make me come."

"Made you fuckin' come."

"Again."

Jesus. "Demandin'."

"Fuck me harder."

He sucked in a breath.

"Fuck me like a beast," she whispered.

His head jerked back. "Jesus fuckin' Christ! You always like this?"

She blinked slowly then said softly, "Just with you."

His temper quickly fled when both her eyes and mouth softened as she studied his face.

I'm so fuckin' fucked! the voice in his head screamed.

He needed to bust a nut and get the hell out of her bed, out of her apartment.

He didn't scare easily. But this shit...

His heart was thumping so hard in his chest, he swore it was going to explode.

"D, you're not moving."

"Right," he grunted. Then, with willpower he didn't know he had, he disengaged from her, rolled onto his back, then kept rolling until he was sitting on the edge of the bed, his back to her.

His heart was beating so fast that he pressed his palm to his chest. Maybe he was having a heart attack.

The mattress moved and dipped as she came behind him on her knees, wrapped her arms around his neck and pressed herself to his back.

"D," she whispered, her mouth against his ear.

"Gimme a minute, woman," he managed to get out.

"You didn't get to come yet," she said softly.

"Gimme a minute, woman," he repeated more firmly. He dropped his head and raked his fingers through his short hair. He sucked in a long breath and let it go. He squeezed his eyes shut. "Shouldn't be doin' this, Jewelee."

"Doing what?"

"*This*," he barked.

"Having sex?"

Yeah, but not just the sex. All of it. Whatever she was doing to get into his head. To fuck him up. To make him question what he wanted in fucking life. For his future.

All of it.

Her fingers traced along the lines of his chest, over his collarbone, along his shoulders. Her tits were plastered to his back, her bare pussy at the top of his ass. Her tongue traced his ear, then it dropped to run a line down the side of his neck.

"Gotta stop doin' this, Jewel."

"Nobody cares that we're fucking."

But I fuckin' do, he shouted in his head.

"We're good together. It's good, D. You've made me come more than anyone else."

Jesus. Just what he needed to hear.

She continued, "We'll keep it simple."

Right. Like she was going to keep it simple. He knew better than that. Bitches were always scheming, trying to get into positions of control. Trying to lead their men around by their dick. He witnessed it one too many times.

That wasn't going to be him. He wasn't going to fall for that shit. No matter how good the pussy.

No matter that it was Jewel.

No matter that Jewel wasn't just any pussy to him.

Fuck!

She slid her hands down both of his arms and interlaced her fingers with his. And, fuck him, he didn't stop her from doing it.

"C'mon," she murmured. "You still have a hard-on that won't quit. Let's do something about that."

He stared at their linked hands which laid on his thighs. Her hands were so small compared to his. So delicate compared to his meaty paws.

"Can't expect shit from me, Jewel. Nothin' more than I'm givin' you right now."

After a hesitation he didn't miss, she said, "Got it, D. I won't expect *nothin'* more than you're giving me right now." She pressed her mouth to the back of his neck and sank her teeth in slowly.

His dick kicked at the rush that went through him. He couldn't get enough of her biting and scratching him.

Hell, he couldn't get enough of that wet cunt of hers, either.

If she was willing to keep it simple, then why shouldn't he take what he wanted from her and the same for her from him?

Keeping it simple. That's what she said.

She shifted and sank her teeth into the area where his neck met his shoulder. He felt that directly in his dick, too.

"Woman," he growled.

"Beast," she murmured against his skin.

He twisted, snagged her by the waist, threw her back on the bed and covered her quickly with his body. His eyes closed as he slid inside her, connecting them once more.

He took a couple deep breaths, brushed her hair out of her face before taking her mouth. He didn't let it go until they both came. This time together.

D's HEAD twisted on the pillow toward his ringing cell phone, which was on the nightstand next to Jewel's bed. He picked it up to not only check to see who was calling, but the time.

Jesus, Jewel was going to be late to the shop this morning. But they'd have to get over it. If anyone had a problem with it, they could come address it with him directly.

He tapped the phone's screen to answer the call.

"Son..." Ace started.

"Yeah."

"Anything I should know?"

Jesus fuck. "Nope."

"Second mornin' your bike's been in the lot."

Maybe it wasn't so convenient that Jewel's apartment was directly over his father's pawn shop. "Yeah."

Ace snorted. "Okay, glad we had this talk."

The phone went dead. He pulled it from his ear and stared at it for a second before sliding it back onto the nightstand.

"Something wrong?" Jewel asked, her voice husky from sleep.

"No."

"Who was it?"

"Pop."

"This early?"

"Ain't early, woman. Your ass is gonna be late to work," he grumbled.

She lifted her head from where it was buried in his neck. "What did Ace want?" she asked, her eyes rounded in surprise.

He stared at her for what felt like a full minute. Her arm was draped over his chest, and one of her legs wrapped around his. And that addictive pussy of hers was pressed to his hip. "Wanted to know what's goin' on with us."

"And you said?"

"Said we're keepin' it simple an' just fuckin' but you're tryin' to get your claws in me so you can be my ol' lady."

Jewel made a noise and rolled her eyes. "Really. What else did you say?"

"Are you fuckin' serious?"

Jewel laughed. She planted a hand on his chest and pushed herself up. "I have to get cleaned up and get to the shop before Crash and Rig have a coronary. Things go to shit when I'm not there."

"Yeah." He needed someone like Jewel to run his office. She had a knack for keeping the shop organized and running it like a well-oiled machine.

Instead of rolling out of the empty side of the bed, she climbed over him. He snagged her wrists and pulled her down on top of him. "Ain't goin' nowhere, woman. Takin' care of me first, then Crash an' Rig."

"Again?" she whispered, but he didn't miss the heat flaring in her eyes.

"Fuck yeah, woman. An' when I say takin' care of those two boneheads, don't mean in the same way you're gonna take care of me."

"Right," she whispered and with a smile, she slid down his body to settle between his legs. When she took him into her mouth, he closed his eyes and dug his fingers into all that thick hair of hers.

As her mouth and hand worked him, he couldn't help but think of how getting head in the morning from a beautiful woman like Jewel was anything but simple.

He was so fucking fucked.

Chapter Six

DIESEL GUESSED if you had to put a padlock on your ball and chain so it'd never come off, there was no better place to do it than by a large lake that had a few black swans swimming around it. And luckily, for late summer, the weather had held.

D swore his sac was shriveling up as he listened to Z and Sophie's short vows.

In a nutshell, Z announced that he was her ol' man and she announced that she was his ol' lady. Plus, they stuffed a few more bullshit words in there to make it sound pleasurable that Z was handing over his balls on a platter.

No rings were exchanged, since Crow would tattoo them onto their fingers at a later date. But when Buggy, one of the hang-arounds who happened to be an ordained something-or-other, told Z he could kiss his "biker bitch," Z jumped on that opportunity and gave his woman the full tongue for at least a minute to a chorus of hoots, hollers, claps, whistles, and boot stomps.

Just watching that kiss made his eyes slide to the right until they landed on Jewel. Since the ceremony was very short—they all wanted to get right into the after party—they hadn't even bothered with folding chairs out on the lawn. Instead they all stood gathered around the couple by the lake shore. Jewel stood to one side surrounded by some of the other DAMC women, like Bella, Diamond and her mother, Ruby.

His gaze raked over her and what she was wearing. She had stuffed herself into some tight red halter top dress, one that had a deep V where her tits were. The back was completely open all the way down to the top of her ass. And it was *short*, only coming halfway down her damn thighs. He knew damn well exactly what was at the juncture of those thighs. The high heels she wore were impractical for the grass that they were standing on, but they made her legs appear much longer than they were. Like they actually might reach all the way around his waist when he was fucking her.

As much as he'd fucked her in the last few weeks, he knew they couldn't quite reach, whether she was on her back, against the wall or in his lap with her arms wrapped around his neck and her face shoved against his throat.

He tried not to think about how much harder it'd been lately to climb out of her bed at night and head back to his shitty room at church. After those first couple of times, he'd made it a point not to stay overnight. He didn't want to get used to her being curled around him all night.

They were keeping it simple.

Surprisingly, she hadn't bitched once when he'd roll out of bed, pull on his clothes and roll out of her apartment in the middle of the night. Not once.

Which made him wonder if she was truly keeping it simple or she was up to something.

He couldn't think about that right now. The ceremony was over, Z officially had a leash on his dick, and all the brothers moved toward their bikes.

The club brothers lined their sleds in a row on one side and the Dark Knights on the other facing each other, which left a path down the center for Z to escort his now wife to the large reception/party tent.

"Start 'em up," Pierce yelled.

The roar of dozens of bikes filled the air. Everyone twisted their throttles as Z and Sophie stood at the far end, holding hands. Both wearing huge smiles, Z did a chin lift to his brothers as he took Sophie's arm and walked her down the "aisle" to the tent about a hundred yards away. Once they disappeared into it, Pierce waved his hand and they shut their engines down.

Diesel dismounted his bike and headed over to Magnum, the Knights' enforcer. They clasped arms and bumped shoulders.

"Brother," Magnum greeted.

D lifted his chin. "You an' your brothers are invited to party long as you got enough keepin' an eye out. Want no shit with the Warriors goin' down today."

The large man nodded. "Got you. We're on it."

"Got my crew out there, too. Ain't gonna see 'em but they're there."

"Heard about your crew."

Diesel grunted.

Magnum grinned. "Got you, brother."

"When this marker needs paid, lemme know."

Magnum's smile widened. "Got that, too." He turned and headed to a group of Knights awaiting orders.

D watched them for a moment, then twisted his head toward the tent, where a line of brothers and their women were filing inside. He waited until the end of the line disappeared, then a few moments later he heard the drummer in Nash's band tapping his drumsticks. The first strains of Steelheart's *I'll Never Let You Go* hit Diesel in the chest.

He sucked in a breath and made his feet move forward, even though he wanted to get on his fucking sled and leave. He couldn't and wouldn't do that to Z or even Sophie. They were family and the club was pretty much the only family that either of them had. He needed to suck it up and be there for them.

Pushing through the tent entrance, he saw everyone circling the temporary wood floor that had been laid down for the day. At his height, he had no problem seeing over the crowd. Z had Sophie wrapped tightly in his arms, her face pressed to his shoulder, one hand spread over the bare skin of her back and the other squeezing her ass. Even though she wore an informal white dress that was sexy as all fuck, Z wore black jeans, a white button-down shirt, his boots, and of course, his cut. All the brothers wore their cuts today in solidarity.

Z wore a big smile as he moved in a circle with his ol' lady in his arms. D's chest pulled tight as he silently hoped that the brother continued to be that happy next week, next month, next year, through their first kid, and through their last kid. Hell, he wished happiness on Z forever. The man deserved it after being shafted at such a young age.

No one moved until Dirty Deeds ended the song and moved on to Scorpion's *Still Loving You.*

Z smacked Sophie on the ass and then guided her to the front of the tent. The prospects scurried around handing out beers and booze to everyone. Once the couple got to the front, and everyone held a cup or bottle in hand, Ace stepped into the middle of the dance floor and lifted his beer. The band got quiet.

"Zak," he boomed. "Been like a fuckin' son to me an' Janice. Love ya, boy. Can't be happier on who tied you down. Got a good catch there. An', damn, the woman knows how to bake. We all love ya, Sophie. Happy you joined the fold an' became family. Can't do any better than that man by your side. Loyal as hell."

Diesel's nostrils flared as he watched his father get choked up.

Ace cleared his throat and continued, "Don't gotta say much more, other than you deserve this, Z."

Nodding heads and murmurs went through the tent.

"So, we're gathered here today to celebrate this union! Drink up an' let's get fuckin' down an' dirty!"

"'Til dead!" came the thundering response from the crowd.

The decibel level under the tent hit a record high as everyone cheered, raised their alcohol, then knocked back a healthy swallow or two.

Diesel raised his beer bottle, tipped it toward Z, who caught his gaze and gave him a slight chin lift. D returned it, then put his beer to his lips and let the cool liquid slide down his throat. He'd rather have whiskey instead but he wanted to keep his wits about him today. He needed to keep a sober eye out to make sure the day went without any issues.

Then his father was next to him, whacking him on the back. "Don't take it personal what I said to Z."

He dropped his gaze, but not by much, to his father. "What?"

"The part 'bout her not being able to do any better. You an' Hawk are my blood. Never forget that."

"Didn't give it a thought, Pop. Know what you meant."

Ace nodded and tipped his cup to his lips. After taking a long drink, he swiped the back of his hand over his mouth. "Good." He looked around. "'Specting another one of these soon."

D cocked an eyebrow toward his father.

"Not for you. Hawk."

D's gaze drifted through the crowd and he found his brother sitting at a nearby table with Kiki. "Think so?"

"Yeah. Don't expect it to be long before she's knocked up."

Diesel grunted. Their father was probably right.

"He's fucked," D finally said.

Ace frowned. "Nothin' fucked about findin' a good woman."

"Right."

"Got your mom, then got you two. Was like a pig in shit. Still am."

"Pop."

"Yeah?"

"Shut up."

Ace laughed and whacked him again. He lifted his chin to where Hawk and Kiki sat. "Gonna grab a seat. Comin'?"

D's gaze drifted back to his brother, where he was leaning over, his mouth pressed against Kiki's ear and she was smiling about whatever he was saying, her bottom lip caught in her teeth.

Jesus.

"Where's Ma?" D asked.

"Hangin' with some of the women. She'll show up when she's good an' ready."

Right.

He reluctantly followed his father over to Hawk's table, did a chin lift to his brother—once the man stopped whispering dirty shit into his ol' lady's ear—grabbed a chair and sank his weight into it with a groan. When the folding chair also groaned, he hoped his ass didn't end up on the ground.

After the current song ended, Nash's band remained quiet. D looked in that direction to make sure there was no shit going on he needed to get involved in. Nash was pointing at the front of the tent, so D's gaze swung that way.

Both Zak and Sophie were standing. Something was up. D's heart thumped as he scanned the tent, but he couldn't see anything amiss.

Z gave a nod to Nash, who leaned into the microphone stand and announced, "Listen up. Z's got somethin' important to say."

The tent became quiet and all eyes turned to their former president.

"Know it's a bit early yet, but wanted to share this with my family..." He took a deep breath, then shouted, "My ol' lady is knocked the fuck up!"

There was a brief moment of shocked silence then the shouting from the crowd became overwhelming.

"Now," he tried to yell over the noise. "Drink up, eat up, an' let's fuckin' party!"

Not even a second later Ace muttered, "Thank fuck." His eyes bounced from D to Hawk. "Don't know how bad your mother wants babies in this family. Look at 'er."

D's gaze landed on where his mother was squeezing Sophie so tightly that Z's woman was wincing.

"Got no idea how much she bitches 'bout it. Tried to shield you boys from her constant naggin'. She's been wantin' to be a grandmomma for a long time. Blood or not." He pinned his gaze to Hawk, who's eyes widened when he said, "Don't mean you're off the hook." He turned to D. "Or you, either."

D scowled and swatted a hand in his father's direction. "Ain't no fruit in these loins."

Hawk's lips rolled in and his eyes crinkled as he stared down at the table. Kiki didn't hide her laughter.

She quickly sobered when she said, "It's a shame that neither Sophie or Zak have family who are supporting them."

"They got each other," Hawk grumbled.

"And us." Ace added. "Plenty of family."

Kiki nodded. "Still… I'm glad my family isn't like that. My parents may be a little… *off*, but at least they accept all of my decisions."

Hawk curled his arm around her shoulders. "Yeah, your mom loves me."

"What's not to love, honey?" She cupped his cheek and pressed a kiss to his lips. "She really loves the fact that you've loosened me up. That, and she hated Landon."

"Ain't the only one," Hawk muttered, his eyes lifted to the dance floor. "Nash gonna play sappy songs all night? 'Cause if so, we may have a problem."

D followed his gaze. Kelsea was out on the dance floor bumping and grinding to Ozzy's *Just Want You* with one of the Dark Knights. His jaw tightened and his wasn't the only one. Pierce was on the edge of the dance floor, hands on hips, eyes watching Kelsea intensely.

D sighed. The Knight had his hands roaming up and down Kelsea's waist and hips. And as he watched, the man pulled her tighter against him.

Of course, Kelsea was eating that shit up. But for some reason, it was bothering the fuck out of Pierce. Guess D needed to figure out why. If Pierce was touching Kelsea when he shouldn't be, there was going to be a bigger problem that needed to be addressed than just removing Pierce from the head of the table. There should be no reason Pierce would be possessive of Kelsea except for one… the general rule that nobody should be touching DAMC property.

As Sergeant at Arms, D would let it slide today. The Knights were doing them a big favor and if they wanted to mingle with their women, he didn't have a problem with it. Now, if they wanted to take it any further, he just may. But he'd deal with that when and if he had to.

Right now, Kelsea was enjoying herself and there was no reason to cause any waves during a day that should be special for Z and Sophie.

"Supposed to be protectin' us. Not stealin' our women," Dex said from behind him.

D twisted his neck to look at the man. "Ain't stealin' 'em. If the women wanna dance, you gonna dance with 'em?"

"Fuck no," Dex answered.

"Then let 'em dance with whoever they can rope into that shit. Knights take it any farther, I'll step in."

"Right," Dex grumbled, then moved on.

D looked up to see a vision in white heading his way. Sophie approached, climbed into his lap and wrapped her arms around his neck, then pressed her lips to his cheek.

Jesus. He hoped the chair held.

"How are you doing, Grunty McGrunt?"

D ignored the snicker he heard from the other side of the table. Instead he grunted his answer.

She shook her head. "That good, huh?"

"Gotta be good when I got a beautiful woman in my lap. Ignore my *keys*."

Sophie's lips curled in but D didn't miss the corners of her eyes crinkling. After a second she said, "Have to confess... This isn't your baby. Sorry."

D grunted. "Good. Ain't changin' no shitty diapers, anyhow."

"Said you weren't off the hook," Ace reminded him. "An' I changed your shitty diapers."

D ignored his father.

"So..." Sophie started. "I have to thank you for arranging the extra protection for today, even if it doubled the catering bill."

"Club can afford it. Small price for protection."

"Are you sure it was needed?" Sophie asked quietly.

D just looked at her. She simply nodded, understanding he wasn't going to talk club business with her. Especially business that could put a damper on her day.

Z approached the table. "Tryin' to steal my woman?" Holding his hand out, Sophie took it. Z pulled her out of D's lap and into his arms. He placed a hand over Sophie's belly, even though she was in no way showing yet. "Gonna be addin' a hellion to the club."

"Future prez," Hawk said.

"Not if it's a girl," Sophie said with a soft smile.

"Woman, ain't no girl comin' out of this," Z said, grabbing his crotch.

"Oh good lord," Kiki mumbled.

Z laughed and looked toward Hawk. "You're next, Chicken Hawk."

"Right," Hawk answered, shaking his head.

"Yep," Ace added. "You're next," he said to Hawk then jabbed his thumb in Diesel's direction. "Then him."

"Jesus fuckin' Christ, Pop," D growled.

Ace put up his hands. "Just sayin'. Jewel—"

"For fuck's sake!" Diesel barked, cutting his father off.

"Whatever," Ace mumbled, but to D's relief he dropped it.

Zak shook his head, looking way too amused. "Gotta get my woman some food an' get this kid fed." And with that, Z dragged Sophie back up to the front of the tent.

After a few moments, D turned to his brother's ol' lady. "Hear from Jazz?"

He regretted asking that when a sad look came over Kiki's face. She shook her head. "I keep leaving messages. Either her parents are erasing them or she just doesn't want to talk."

D was staring at Kiki when suddenly everything around him faded away and he found himself back at that abandoned house. The shithole the Warriors had taken Kiki and Jazz to. He could feel himself lifting his knee and kicking down the door only to find the horror inside.

The women bloody and beaten, sprawled on the dirty floor, unrecognizable and naked.

He understood why his brother had fallen to his knees next to his woman and lost his shit. And he hadn't even come across her like D had. Her clothes had been cut away with a knife, her wrists bound, and she bled profusely from head wounds. Her bare legs were spread wide apart. He had at least used his cut to cover her as best as he could, then pushed her legs together before Hawk got there.

Jazz, he'd only covered with his T-shirt, since he didn't want to hurt her any more than she already was.

Jesus fuckin' Christ.

"D."

His brother's voice drew him from the memory, his nightmare, and his eyes lifted to where Jewel stood on the other side of the tent.

Jesus.

Yeah, he understood exactly why his brother had fallen to his knees at the broken and battered sight of his woman.

He understood it and might have done the same thing.

When her blue eyes met his across the dance floor, the tightness in his chest became almost unbearable.

"D," he heard again. He ripped his gaze from Jewel and turned his eyes to his brother. "Seven o'clock."

Diesel turned back to look over his shoulder in that direction. He noticed Zak's sister, Jayde, standing close to Abe, the latest prospect to become a fully-patched member. Even from where D sat, he could see she was flirting.

Fuck.

He glanced up to where Z sat with Sophie. The man had eyes on his sister, too. He leaned over to his wife and said something before beginning to move.

D pushed to his feet.

"Guess you're gonna handle it," Hawk said.

D grunted and took off at an angle, meeting Z on the dance floor.

"Brother, know you ain't out here to dance with me," Zak said, without taking his gaze from his baby sister.

"Nope. Your weddin', brother. I got it."

Z shook his head. "Don't mind her bein' with a brother, 'specially one like Abe. Good. Solid. Cool head. But know where it'll land her. Don't think she could handle bein' froze out of the family."

"Got you, brother. Will have a word with 'em."

Z raked a hand through his dark hair. "Wasn't expectin' her to show. Probably on the D.L."

"Yeah," D answered.

With another look in the direction of his sister, Zak blew out a breath, whacked D on the shoulder, then went back to Sophie.

Diesel headed the opposite direction. And he knew exactly when Abe realized he was headed their way. The man's body straightened and the lazy smile on his face disappeared. Abe's lips moved as he said something quietly to Jayde, but D had no idea what it was. Though he could guess, because by the time D hit them, Jayde had turned, her hand on her hip, already dripping attitude.

"Diesel," she greeted, looking a bit miffed.

"Shouldn't be here."

"It's my brother's wedding."

"Yeah. Your family know you're here?"

"D, I'm a freaking adult. I don't need anyone's permission."

D shook his head slowly. "Don't give a shit, not gonna cause drama for Z on his big day."

"I'm here to support him," she stated.

"Right. But your family don't want you 'round the club."

Jayde's eyes slid to Abe. Something D did not miss.

"Not their decision," she finally murmured.

"You livin' at home?"

Jayde frowned.

"Daddy buy you that fuckin' Camaro?"

Jayde's eyes narrowed.

"'Til you're out from under their thumb, you gotta do what they say. Z don't need to get grief from Mitch or Axel. Club don't need 'em breathin' our direction, either."

"D..."

"Fuckin' Jayde. Want you here. Family. Even though some of your blood denies it. Z wants you here, too. But it's gonna cause shit. Don't want shit today."

"Nobody's going to tell them. I'll just stay a little bit. I just want to dance and congratulate my brother and Sophie."

D cocked a brow. “Who you dancin’ with? Abe here?”

“His name isn’t Abe,” Jayde huffed.

“The fuck it isn’t.”

“It’s Lincoln,” she snapped.

D’s eyes fell on Abe, who stood still, keeping his face blank. “You talkin’ to her on the sly?”

“No.”

“Better not be. Voted your ass in, can vote your ass out. No touchin’ this one. Got me?”

Abe’s face hardened, but he said, “Got you.”

“Diesel! That’s not right.”

“Woman,” D grumbled. “Don’t be back talkin’ me or I’ll take you outta here myself. Go say your shit to Z an’ Soph, then get gone.”

Jayde opened her mouth to have the last word, but Abe’s hand went to her arm and she shut her mouth, looked at him, then nodded.

What the fuck was that about?

“Go,” D grunted.

With her mouth an angry slash, Jayde marched toward the front of the tent. Once she got there, D turned back to Abe.

“Fuckin’ her?”

He shook his head. “No.”

“Not gonna, either. The day she’s out from under that pig father of hers thumb, then you can approach Z. Not a fuckin’ minute before. Got me?”

“Got you.”

“An’ Z might not mind you up in his sister’s shit, but she’s gonna deal with the crap Z has to deal with when it comes to Mitch an’ Axel. Wanna be the cause of her family turnin’ their back on her?”

“No.”

“Then keep your dick outta her. No matter what Z eventually says.”

Abe glanced to where Jayde stood speaking with her brother and new sister-in-law.

Diesel studied the younger brother. Z was right. The guy was solid. Had a good head on his shoulders. Kept cool when needed. That’s why

Hawk liked him working at The Iron Horse. The guy could fight though, hold his own when he had to. He'd been a good prospect and now that he was patched in, he'd make an even better brother. The club needed more men like him. And he could understand his attraction to Jayde. She was pretty, had a body on her, and dripped attitude, which most brothers liked because it was a challenge. But Jayde was young and considered the "baby" in the DAMC family and, as so, was treated as such. Mitch didn't want his daughter hanging with the club, didn't want her around the brothers for good reason. D couldn't miss that Abe wanted to stick his dick in her. So it was probably best Jayde steered clear.

As long as being around the club and brotherhood was a risk to Jayde when it came to losing her parents and oldest brother, then D, Grizz, and some of the other brothers would step in to make sure she saw reason.

"Name's Lincoln?" D asked. Normally he didn't give a shit what a prospect's real name was. But the man was no longer a recruit. He was now a brother.

"Yeah."

"Shit name."

Abe stared him. "Go by Linc."

"Ain't a prospect anymore. Wanna be called Linc, just say so. Abe's a shit name, too."

"Yeah."

"See you're gone an' she's gone, gonna come lookin' for you. Got me, *Linc*?" D warned.

"Got you."

"Plenty of other pussy."

A look crossed Linc's face and Diesel waited for the challenge. But after a moment, when it didn't come, D just nodded and headed back to the table.

Smart man.

Jewel watched the whole interaction between Diesel and Abe with curiosity. And she wasn't the only one.

Bella nudged her in the ribs. "None of us have caught D in the bathroom in weeks. Wonder why?"

"I've been keeping him busy," Jewel answered Bella without tearing her eyes away from the man who'd spent a lot of time recently in her bed.

"Apparently. I've said this before and I'll say it again, I've never known him to go back for seconds, and definitely not thirds and fourths."

Jewel shrugged.

"*Are* you trying to reel him in, Jewelee? Because you know, he's not one to get caught. You might be disappointed if you're looking to end up on the back of his bike."

"Just trying to see what's there, if anything," Jewel murmured.

"Just don't expect too much from him," Bella warned. "Love my cousin. Want the best for him, which may very well be you, but... I know how he is, too. We all do."

Jewel finally looked at her. "Didn't think Hawk would get caught either, and look at him. Not only did he get caught, but class caught him."

Their attention was drawn to Hawk who had his arm wrapped around Kiki's waist. Her head leaned on his shoulder and his expression was soft as he stared down into her face as he talked. Her eyes were tipped up to him and there was nothing but pure love in the look they gave each other.

How the mighty have fallen.

So, seeing that gave Jewel some hope since Hawk and Diesel were a lot alike. Stubborn, domineering, alpha bikers.

Besides the first two nights at her apartment, he hadn't stayed the night again. She didn't know if it was Ace's phone call, or what, that made him stop staying over. But whatever it was, it needed to change. She knew her apartment was a thousand times better than that disgusting hole he lived in at church. She didn't know how he could stand it.

She saw D approach his brother and father. The man was as tall as Hawk but broader. Scarier-looking. Always had a serious look on his face, where at least Hawk had a sense of humor and had no trouble laughing at a joke or at someone doing something stupid.

One day Diesel was going to look at her like Hawk did Kiki. He'd smile at her and her heart would melt into a puddle at his feet.

She snorted. She was fooling herself. The man was hard. Impenetrable. Unbreakable.

Jewel had witnessed moments of softness with Hawk when it came to Kiki. But the only time Jewel saw D react with any emotion was at the hospital when Bella collapsed in what seemed to be a mental breakdown after Jazz and Kiki were kidnapped and assaulted.

That was the only time she could remember in all the years she'd known him, and she has known him her whole life. One thing about their generation of DAMC, was that they all grew up together.

Well, except for her cousins, Jayde and Axel, who were kept from the club because of Uncle Mitch. Zak was the only one who fought to be a part of the club and to follow in their grandfather Bear's footsteps.

He broke free from his immediate family only to find his relationship with them irrevocably broken. So because of this, Jewel was surprised to see Jayde here. She was risking the wrath of Mitch and Axel. Though Jayde was the youngest out of all of the DAMC "sisters" and "brothers," she was clearly no longer a child. Hell, she was now a college graduate.

As Dirty Deeds played their rendition of Judas Priest's *Angel* in the background, Kiki separated herself from her ol' man and joined the women where they gathered.

With Kiki's dark brown hair pulled up in a twist, it was hard to miss Hawk's name tattooed in delicate black script at the nape of her neck. She knew Hawk had asked Kiki to do it and Kiki obliged once she moved permanently into his house.

Kiki had also given up her job at her legal firm as well as her condo for her man. Yes, she had opened her own practice in Shadow Valley, but as independent, financially and otherwise, as Kiki was, it still surprised Jewel that the woman submitted to almost anything Hawk asked.

But then, if Hawk was nearly as good as D was in bed, she could see why the woman was easily influenced.

And D was a *beast* in bed.

He did not act tender, loving or caring in any way. Protective, yes. Bossy, yes. Which was part of who he was, and also what his role was within the brotherhood.

Bella was right, though. Diesel never went back for seconds. And definitely not for thirds. She wondered what D wanted from her. Or if he even knew what he wanted. Because it wasn't just sex. It couldn't be. He could get that anywhere and always had.

As Jewel studied Diesel, she was determined to crack that hard outer shell. She just didn't know how.

She gave Bella a look, then skirted the dance floor to where D now stood by himself, a beer bottle hanging from two fingers. The whole way over to him, his intense eyes never left her.

By the time she reached him, her pussy was throbbing, her nipples ached, and she was ready to climb onto his face.

Wouldn't that be entertaining at this celebration? Normally it wouldn't be anything new at a club party for a sweet butt or one of Dawg's girls, but none of the DAMC women had sex out in the open for everyone to watch.

It would be a first.

Jewel felt the heat land in her belly. Jesus. She couldn't get enough of this man. Why did she get stuck on one that would be such a challenge? And a headache.

"Just gonna stand there?" D asked gruffly.

She lifted her gaze to his. "Nope."

"What do you want, woman?"

"You know what I want," she whispered.

D raised his bottle to his lips and tipped it. Jewel watched his throat move as he swallowed. When he lowered the bottle his dark brown eyes hit hers. "Ain't gettin' it now, gotta keep a watch on shit."

"Right. Not now. Later," she agreed softly.

His eyes raked down her dress. "Got panties on?"

"No."

"Bra?"

"No."

"Fuck," he growled. "You wet?"

She smiled. "Yeah."

"Gonna fuckin' eat you later," he muttered.

"Yeah," she agreed, her thighs quivering at the thought.

"Then I'm gonna spank your ass for not wearin' panties 'round all these brothers."

Jewel's smile disappeared as she swallowed hard. Fuck, she wanted that. Her legs wobbled, making her reach out to catch her balance by planting her hand on his arm.

His eyes dropped to where she held him.

"Then I'm gonna—" He stopped abruptly.

She swallowed again, her eyes hooded, her pussy clenching hard, her thighs getting slick with her arousal.

"What?" she whispered. If he kept talking dirty to her she might just come where she stood.

D held her gaze as he shook his head. "Gonna be a surprise."

Shit.

Shit. Shit. Shit.

"Leave your door unlocked an' that dress on."

"Yeah," Jewel murmured as if she was in a trance. Every part of her body ached for his touch, for his tongue, for his cock.

She needed to snap herself out of this. There were hours to go before this reception was over. That wait was going to be torture if she couldn't get everything Diesel was going to do to her out of her mind.

She shook her head to clear it. She glanced over her shoulder when Dirty Deed's started a new song and she heard the women hooting and hollering on the dance floor. "Going to go dance."

"See you out there dancin' with a Knight, that spankin' ain't gonna be fun. Promise you that."

She nodded, unable to answer.

"See any of 'em touchin' you, woman, gonna be an issue."

She blinked at the look on his face.

Jesus. He was dead serious.

As she turned away from him, her daze cleared and she bit back her smile as she headed the direction she had come from.

Looks like she had more than just tonight to look forward to.

It seemed she had wormed her way under his skin enough that he may be laying his claim.

Chapter Seven

DIESEL CURSED and shoved at the paperwork on his desk. He couldn't fucking concentrate. Not one bit.

His mind kept going back to two nights ago at Jewel's apartment. The night of Z and Sophie's wedding.

When he'd finally left the reception, almost everyone else had cleared out. He was one of the last to go and it had been late.

He had no idea when Jewel had left. While he tried to keep an eye on her most of the evening, she'd disappear once in a while, pop up and then disappear again.

Drove him fucking nuts.

Every time he couldn't catch a glimpse of her, he wondered what trouble she was up to, what man was talking to her, or who was trying to get a piece of that tail.

By the end of the night he'd driven himself mad.

So, when he finally got to her apartment, he had let himself inside and stalked right to her room.

And it surprised the fuck out of him when the woman had listened. She waited for him on her bed still wearing that red dress. And her high heels. After that night, that dress needed to be burned along with that short skirt of hers.

Hell, he needed to go through her damn closet and make a bonfire.

"About fucking time," she grumbled.

"How many times did you come already?" he asked, because the flush on her face certainly wasn't from her being bored.

"None."

"Bullshit," he grunted as he slid his cut from his shoulders and threw it aside. "Lyin' gets you some extra swats."

"Good," she whispered.

His head jerked as he stared down at her. Her blue eyes challenged him.

"Can't wait, can you?"

"No," she answered on a breath.

His dick kicked in his jeans. All night he couldn't stop thinking about smacking her ass until it was red and her cunt was soaked.

He bent over, unzipped his boots, toed both them and his socks off, ripped off his T-shirt, unbuttoned his jeans but, at the last minute, decided to leave them on.

It was only fair since he was leaving her dress on for what he had planned.

He sat on the edge of her bed, grabbed her ankle and dragged her to him, then barked, "Over my lap."

And didn't she fucking drape herself right over his fucking lap?

The fuck she did, too.

Her dress had ridden up her thighs and he could just see the bottom curve of her ass cheeks.

"You seem happy to see me."

"No shit," he grumbled as he traced a finger along the edge of that dress over the warm flesh of her ass that barely peeked out. "Gonna spank that ass."

"Yeah," she whispered.

He could not only feel but see the shiver that went through her. "Want it?"

"Yeah," she breathed.

Fuck him.

"Gonna wear dresses without panties again?"

"Yeah."

Jesus fuckin' Christ.

Tucking a finger under the hem, he slowly pulled the bottom of the dress up over her ass until those perfect globes were right there at his fingertips.

His palm itched to make contact, his dick painfully hard and leaking in his jeans.

He slipped a finger down her crease and then through the slick wet of her cunt. "Want my dick?"

"D," she whispered. He'd take that as a yes.

He circled and pressed her clit until she wiggled on his lap. Which did not make him lose his mind at all. No, it fucking didn't.

His cock was jammed uncomfortably in his jeans and he needed to get this show on the road.

Like quickly.

He grabbed her hair in one hand and tugged her head back until her neck arched. "Gonna spank your ass," he announced again.

"What the fuck, D! Just do it!" she shouted, a flush crawling up her stretched throat to her cheeks.

He ignored her impatience, stopped playing with her pussy and then brushed his palm over her cheeks. They were so fucking perfect.

He raised his hand and her whole body jerked in anticipation. He lifted his hand higher and she did it again.

He looked at her face, pulled up by his hand gripping her hair, and she had her eyes squeezed shut.

"Jewelee," he said softly. Her eyes opened at her name and, when she wasn't expecting it, his hand dropped, smacking her hard on her right cheek. She jerked in his lap as she yelped and he just about lost his load in his jeans.

His balls were painfully tight as he smacked her again, the other cheek this time.

She moaned and ground herself harder into his lap.

Fuck. Him.

Her fingers had a death grip on his thigh and when he spanked her a third time, her eyes rolled back. He jerked her hair harder.

It took everything he had to ask, "Likin' that?"

"Fuck, D." Her words came out husky and that turned him on even more.

"Yeah you do." His gaze roamed over her bare back in the dress, where the fabric gathered at her hips, then the red marks on her ass cheeks.

Jesus, he wanted to sink his teeth into her round, soft flesh.

"Gonna wear panties next time," he stated.

"No," she groaned, shoving her hand underneath herself to find her own clit.

Whap.

"Gonna listen."

"No," came her ragged whisper. Her fingers moved furiously.

Whap.

"D..."

"Woman," he warned.

"Gonna come," she said on a groan.

Jesus, this woman.

"Again," she urged.

Fuck him. His dick jerked with each strike and it throbbed violently, needing relief.

Whap.

He struggled to suck in a breath.

"Again," she demanded.

Whap.

He slowly let his breath back out.

"Fuck," she cried out. "Again!"

Whap.

"Coming," she wailed.

When her back arched even more, he grabbed her chin with his hand to twist her face toward him, bending over to take her mouth as she came. He swallowed her cries as her body jerked in his lap. After a moment, her body went lax and her hand stilled. He released her hair and she went boneless, her eyes shut, her lips parted as she panted.

Nobody was ever going to see her this satisfied again. Nobody but him.

No one else was going to taste her, touch her, fuck her, kiss her or...

Fuck him.

He was so fucking fucked.

"What're you doin' to me, Jewelee?" he muttered under his breath before he could stop himself.

She turned her head to look up at him with her gorgeous blue eyes. "Nothing you don't want done," she answered.

Fuck him, she was right.

After fucking her three times that night, he now sat there in his office unable to keep his mind on what he needed to because he couldn't wipe out that memory. The whole thing played in his mind on a continuous loop.

Business was not on his fucking mind.

Jewelee was.

When he finally got around to forcing himself from her bed that night, she had been wrapped up in a sheet, everything about her relaxed and satisfied, her eyes soft and sleepy while she watched him dress.

Not once did she ask him to stay.

Not a peep.

And if she had asked, or even begged, he wouldn't have anyway.

Because he was so fucking fucked.

When he walked out of her bedroom and then her apartment, his feet felt as though he was stuck in quicksand. His boots were heavier than normal and it was hard to move himself forward.

He wanted to turn around, rip off his clothes and slide back into bed with her, wrapping her up in his arms and holding tight.

He had to argue with himself to keep moving, to step outside, to take a deep breath to suck in the cool night air, to put his ass on his sled and go back to church.

That was where he belonged, not in Jewel's bed.

Because it was dangerous. And he was so fucking close to being caught, done, trapped forever. He teetered on that edge and if he fell he would be finished.

It wasn't just these feelings he was afraid of. It was the power that Jewel would have over him. And the power his current and future enemies would have over him when it came to Jewel. She could be used very easily as a pawn if they knew what she meant to him.

And that shit couldn't happen.

He couldn't let it.

"Boss," came a deep voice from the open doorway of his office. He dropped his hands from his face and looked up at Mercy.

"Yeah," D answered with a chin lift, an unspoken invitation into his office.

Mercy was one scary motherfucker. Almost as big as D, he had a noticeable scar that ran diagonally across his face that made him look it, too. He was not only one of his best Shadows but one who'd been with him the longest. The former Delta Force operator had skills like no one else.

Some D didn't even know about. And he probably didn't want to, either.

"Got intel on those motherfuckers."

D straightened in his chair. "Thought you were guardin' that NFL douchebag?"

"Was. Night off. Walker took my spot."

D nodded. "Night off but you went huntin' Warriors?"

"Yeah." He stepped closer to D's desk, his fists pinned to his thighs. "Can't get that shit I saw out of my head."

D said nothing because he understood it. Mercy was with him when he found Kiki and Jazz in that shithole of a house. The sight affected his men as much as it had affected Diesel. And his crew had seen some bad shit during their stints as special forces.

"Shoulda got 'em that night," Mercy said. Though his voice was soft, his expression was not and his eyes were diamond hard.

"Yeah." But they didn't. "Whataya got?"

"Out of PA, that's for sure. Heard chatter that they were in West

Virginia, then Kentucky. Heard they may be headin' back this direction. Last known location was twenty klicks south of the Mason-Dixon."

"Gonna hit us again," D stated, then scrubbed his palm over his head. He sucked in a breath.

"Could be."

"Least they didn't hit Z's weddin'."

"Too risky. You did right by gettin' the Knights involved an' makin' it known ahead of time."

"Yeah," D grunted.

"Gonna come in quiet. When you least expect it."

D didn't answer. Mercy was right. Those fuckers knew both the Angels and the Knights were waiting for them to show up. So if they tried to hit DAMC again, they'd have to do it stealth-like. Though, he wasn't sure if those dumb fuckers were capable of that.

Even so, D wasn't sure how to protect everyone and all the businesses, too. They were too widespread throughout town. And not only were the brothers independent, so were the women. Which made them easy targets.

Even the brothers who had ol' ladies couldn't watch them twenty-four seven.

If it was up to him, he'd have everyone moving into church or, at least, out to Ace's farm. Keep everyone close. Keep an eye out. Unfortunately, no one would go for that nor would it be practical. Also, the fact was the beef between the two clubs had been going on so long, it may never end. Even if he could get everyone at one location he couldn't keep them there forever.

The only way to keep everyone safe would be to take every last Warrior out.

Every last fucking one.

He wasn't even sure that was possible. Being nomads, D never could get a good read on how many there were. They were always adding prospects and patching in new members. Like that pencil dick Squirrel.

D had kicked his ass, then kicked him out of the club for disrespecting Ivy. Then the useless piece of shit went on to join up with their enemy. And even worse, was involved in the violent assault on the women.

Even as classy as Kiki was, he was sure she wanted a piece of Squirrel herself. Hawk was in line, too, and D had promised his brother that he'd keep both the prospect and that Black Jack asshole breathing once they located them so Hawk could get his pound of flesh from their asses.

Truth was, Diesel wasn't sure if he'd let his brother do that. He didn't want Hawk ending up back in jail, torn away from the club, torn away from his woman. D had better ways to handle revenge. And his crew was chomping at the bit to help with that.

His cell phone vibrated on his desk and the screen lit up. Both sets of eyes dropped to the picture that popped up on the screen. And, fuck him, if it wasn't Jewel sending him a picture of herself in a very compromising position.

"Fuck," he muttered, snagging the phone quickly and hitting the power button so the screen went dark.

"Damn," Mercy responded. His eyes tipped back up to his, the corners of his lips curling just slightly. "She yours?"

D scrubbed an agitated hand over the whiskers along his jaw. He forgot to shave this morning since he apparently had other things on his mind. And the woman who just showed her fucking goods to one of his crew was one of them.

She must need another lesson.

Which he'd be happy to give to her.

When D didn't answer him, a surprised look crossed Mercy's scarred face. "Hold up. Was that Jag's sister?"

"Yeah. An' you didn't just see shit," D finally stated, his eyes narrowed on his man.

Mercy nodded, now amused. "Got you, boss. Didn't just see shit."

"Right," D grunted.

"Should get outta here if you got that hot number waitin' on you."

D's nostrils flared and his back straightened. "Watch yourself. Got me?"

Mercy's lips now curved into a full smile. "Got you. I'm out. Gonna go hit some local bars an' listen for news."

"Ain't on the clock, brother," D reminded him.

"Like I said, can't get that shit outta my mind. Willin' to help on my own time. Plus, could use a drink."

D lifted his chin in thanks and Mercy gave him one of his own before spinning on his heel and striding out the door.

"An' I need to find somethin' like that for myself," he tossed over his shoulder.

D could hear him chuckling while traveling down the hall.

Shit.

As soon as he knew Mercy was out of range, D hit the power button on his phone and studied the picture. Jewel was on her bed, legs spread, fingers on her clit, hand cupping her tit, eyes hooded, mouth parted. And the fucking picture was a reflection of all that in the mirror above her bed so, of course, she was easily identifiable.

Jesus fuckin' Christ.

If she was going to send shots like that she needed to learn to exclude her face just in case they were sent to the wrong person by mistake. Like her brother, Jag, or his father. Or, hell, any of the club brothers.

His phone vibrated again with another incoming text. It was one word: *Waiting*.

Waiting.

She was going to be waiting for a while. He was not going to come running whenever she beckoned.

Or sent dirty pictures.

No, he fucking wasn't.

He pushed up from his chair, went over to his office door, slammed it shut and locked it.

His phone vibrated again as he went back to his desk.

She had sent another picture and it was even better than the first.

Jesus. He now had a raging hard-on.

He settled his ass back in his chair with a groan, unfastened his jeans, propped the phone up so he could see the screen, and fisted his cock.

As much as he wanted to head over to her apartment and sink into her tight, wet heat, he was not going to let himself fall into the bottomless pit he wouldn't be able to escape from.

His fist would have to do.

Chapter Eight

Jewel's stomach churned as she drove past the sign that welcomed them to West Virginia. She foolishly let Kelsea talk her into going to this party to meet up with her man of the month, another guy she met at a party. Not the club hang-around she was doing last month.

At least this time, Jewel insisted on driving. There was no way she was going to be left behind again and this time in another state. Especially one where she knew no one. And if for some reason she was, she certainly couldn't call Diesel to save her ass this time.

If any of the brothers knew where the two of them were headed, any and all of them would blow a freaking gasket.

But, hell, after trying to tempt D over to her apartment the other night and not even getting a single response to her pictures—and she'd sent a half dozen of them—she decided maybe she needed a change of scenery.

She really needed to just give up on the man. He was being a stubborn shit. She kept offering herself up and, though, he'd take advantage of what she was offering, that was it. A booty call.

Sex and nothing more.

Even though she loved and craved the sex, she wanted more than that from Diesel.

So much more.

And every time he rolled out of bed in the middle of the night to leave her apartment to go back to his room at church, it was a blow to her self-esteem.

What was wrong with her that he didn't want to stay?

His brother, Hawk, and Kiki were happy.

Her brother, Jag, and Ivy were happy.

And Zak and Sophie were over the moon, especially between the wedding and her pregnancy.

Why didn't D want any of that?

Maybe he did, but just not with her. And that was a fact she had to face.

"He's probably just playing hard to get," Kelsea said from the passenger seat as if she could read Jewel's mind.

"Right, because being a tease is exactly what Diesel's striving for," she muttered in return.

"Why don't *you* try playing hard to get? Make him chase you. You're being too easy."

Jewel shot a look over at Kelsea. "You're calling *me* easy? You're chasing dick in a whole different state."

Kelsea laughed. "Yeah, but it's a big dick."

"If anyone knew where we were headed..." Jewel began.

"Don't say shit and they won't."

"Probably planted chips in our necks when we were born so they can track us by GPS."

"Did they even have GPS when we were born?"

Jewel frowned at the windshield and tightened her grip on the steering wheel. "You got the directions for this place?"

"Yeah, in the map on my phone. Keep going. I'll tell you when to turn."

The problem was they were headed into the country, not into any town. This worried Jewel even more. "You sure about this guy?"

"Yeah. Met him at the party in the 'burgh."

"I know, but you were there with that hang-around, what's-his-name."

"Yeah, but this one is better."

"Jesus," Jewel said under her breath.

"I heard that."

"And?"

Kelsea snorted. "Look, I'm glad you're coming with. Di won't go. Of course, Bella won't, I wouldn't even bother asking her. So you're it."

"You could always ask Jayde," Jewel suggested.

"Right. And risk the wrath of Axel and Mitch. Uh-huh."

That was true. Most of the DAMC women stayed clear of Jayde. No one wanted to create waves. For the club or for Jayde herself.

"Turn here," Kelsea urged.

"I know I should've asked this earlier but... is this an MC party?" It took her club sister too long to answer and Jewel's stomach dropped. "It is, isn't it?"

"Yeah," Kelsea said softly.

"Jesus, Kels. What club?"

"Deadly Demons," tumbled from Kelsea's mouth in a rush.

Jewel's head spun in her direction. "You shitting me?"

"Turn here. This is it."

"I should be turning around and taking us home, for fuck's sake."

"But we're here. It'll be fine. I promise."

Right.

As the headlights of Jewel's car hit the house and then the lines of bikes, Jewel's stomach twisted even harder. This was so not a good idea.

The Deadly Demons were known one-percenters. And they lived the typical outlaw biker lifestyle. Why Kelsea wanted to hook up with one of them, Jewel would never know.

It was stupid.

And she was about to say something to that effect to Kelsea as she put the car in reverse to back out of the driveway, but the woman shoved open the passenger door and jumped out before Jewel had the chance.

"Hey!" Jewel yelled and watched Kelsea run through the beam of light from the car's headlights and toward the house.

Fuck.

She shoved the shifter into neutral, set the emergency brake and stared at the house which was all lit up. An orange glow could be seen from the backyard of the house which meant a bonfire was roaring. She wasn't sure if the loud music she heard was from a live band or a blaring stereo.

Shit. Shit. Shit.

She shut the car off, pulled the keys from the ignition and reluctantly got out. There was no way she was leaving Kelsea here on her own. Not like D's cousin did to her at the party in Pittsburgh.

She really needed to check out the biker she was doing, too. Maybe if she could make Kelsea see some sense, they could get out of there sooner than later.

A group of bikers, all wearing DDMC colors, hung out on the front porch of the two-story home. This wasn't your typical grandmother's farmhouse. No, it fucking wasn't. There was shit everywhere in the yard, on the porch, including bike parts, kicked kegs, old couches, beer cans and bottles, a turned-over refrigerator, and even just piles of garbage.

Whoever lived there was a pig. This could even be their church. She had no idea.

But what she did know was as she approached the group, she shivered and the hair on the back of her neck stood up.

She never should've dressed the way she had. She was glad she at least pulled on jeans and knee-high boots instead of heels since she figured the party would be outside and she wanted to stay somewhat warm. However, she had worn a cute, snug sweater that emphasized her cleavage. Now she wished she had worn a turtleneck and a parka.

This was the last party she was going to with Kelsea. That was for sure.

Some "Hey, baby's," crude comments, and low whistles came from the group.

Her nostrils twitched at the smell of joints being passed around. And the closer she got to the porch, the more strongly the smell of piss hit her. Nice.

"That your sister that just went inside?"

"Yeah," Jewel answered.

"C'mere, baby, come say hi to your new daddy," one of them said. He was short and had a huge beer belly on him that pushed out from his cut and made him look as if he was nine months pregnant. His beard was long and scruffy and his face as ugly as sin. And when he smiled... Jewel figured he may have never visited a dentist. In his whole life.

He was so not her new "daddy."

"Got an ol' man already. But thanks anyway."

"Yeah? Who?"

"If you didn't know already, my sister and I are property of Dirty Angels."

"Bullshit. Whatcha doin' down here then?"

"My sister's got a friend in your club, that's all. She's going to say hi and then we're outta here."

"Can't be rushin' off. Gotta stay an' party with us."

She was going to kill her "sister."

"Who's your ol' man? That ol' fuck Grizz?"

She left the male laughter behind as she pushed past them and into the house. Jesus, she'd take Grizz any day over anyone in that motley crew.

Though, just the thought of being with Grizz, who was like a grandfather to her, turned her stomach and bile crept up her throat. She pushed that creepy thought out of her head quickly as she walked down a narrow hall toward the back of the house.

"Kelsea!" she called out as she went. "Kels!"

She walked past a doorway that looked like it led to an old-fashioned parlor. A biker leaned back against a wall with peeling wallpaper and at his feet was a woman with long, stringy hair on her knees, sucking him off. Jewel's gaze lifted and hit the biker's. He gave her a smile and held out a hand, an unspoken invitation to join them.

Right. That was one big, fat nope.

She kept moving, passing a couple skanky women who looked like they were as high as kites.

"Who are you?" one of them asked as she eyed Jewel up and down, a catty look on her drawn face.

Jewel ignored them and kept moving. Finally, the hallway spilled into a kitchen at the back of the house.

It was a kitchen that she would never want to eat or cook in. It was filthy, piled with dirty dishes and rotten food. And it stank.

Gross.

Why the fuck did Kelsea want to be with one of these guys?

Three Deadly Demons stood around a beer keg that was buried in ice in a big blue plastic half-barrel. They looked up when she stepped into the room.

She decided to pull on her bad biker bitch persona. She drew herself up to her full height and slapped a bitchy look on her face. "Lookin' for my sister. You assholes seen 'er?"

One of them gave her a crooked smile. "Damn, you're a fuckin' good-lookin' piece of ass."

Jewel deepened her voice and growled, "Ain't tellin' me nothin' I don't know. But ain't the fuckin' question I asked."

"Tough fuckin' bitch, huh?"

"Gotta be when I'm surrounded by a buncha assholes like you."

"Hey, now!" one of them yelled.

"Bitch like you prolly likes it rough, dontcha?"

"Love it rough an' my ol' man knows how to give it to me like that, too."

"Your ol' man here?" another one of them asked.

"Nope. An' you don't want 'im to be. Just warnin' ya."

One of them laughed and put up his hands in surrender. "Scared now. Don't be siccin' your ol' man on us."

"Tell me where my sister went an' I won't."

"Don't see ya wearin' your ol' man's cut. Means you ain't claimed."

Shit.

Jewel swallowed hard. She was going to have to drop names. Or one in particular. And that very well may get back to that person.

Which was not good.

For her.

Or for Kelsea.

"I'm claimed." She moved to head out of the back door of the kitchen to join the party out back to see if she could find Kelsea, but one of them snagged her arm as she passed.

She was swung around and the biker raked her body with his gaze.

"Little on the skinny side, but you'd probably ride my dick just fine. Prolly a wild thing, too."

Shit.

Jewel sucked in a breath, trying to make it seem less shaky. "Know what happens when you touch DAMC property?"

"No, tell us," one said, sounding amused at her tough biker bitch act.

"Get fucked up, that's what."

One of them laughed.

Shit.

"Fuckin' DAMC turned soft. Ain't no challenge there," another one said.

"DAMC's not soft," she claimed.

"Goin' all legit an' shit."

"Didn't make 'em soft," Jewel insisted.

The one who had her arm pulled her closer. So close that she could feel his heat against her.

Shit.

She was never going to forgive Kelsea for this crap.

"Who's your ol' man?" the one holding her asked, his face way too close to hers.

Shit.

Shit.

Shit.

She was going to regret this, but she had no choice. "Diesel," she finally let slip from her lips.

The biker released her immediately and not expecting it, she stumbled back a couple steps until she could catch her balance.

"Right," the guy said, sounding like he didn't quite believe her but didn't want to risk it if it was true.

"You're Diesel's ol' lady?"

"Yeah," she growled. "Don't believe me? Ask 'im."

Shit. Shit. Shit.

"Now I'm gonna go out an' look for my sister," she said and headed out of the back door, her heart beating a mile a minute.

She stepped outside, and as her eyes adjusted to the dark, smoke from the bonfire, cigarettes and pot hit her. The only light came from the roaring fire made up of what looked like tires, pallets and some other questionable things.

But the bodies surrounding the fire and scattered throughout the yard were just dark figures. She couldn't tell who was who. Or where Kelsea was. And she certainly wasn't going to call out her name, which would draw unwanted attention.

Luckily, she didn't have to search. Kelsea approached her. Of course with a biker hanging on her, an arm possessively hooked around her neck.

"Hey, was wondering where you were at," Kelsea started.

Jewel glared at her. "Yeah? Would've been nice to wait for me."

Kelsea shrugged, the biker's arm rising and falling with her shoulders. "This is Slash."

What the fuck? *Slash*?

"Really?" Jewel cursed her voice coming out like a squeak.

"You DAMC bitches are fuckin' hot," Slash said, checking her out.

Jewel did the same to him. She had to admit Slash wasn't half bad himself. She could see why Kelsea was attracted to him.

Only problem was that he was in a *fucking outlaw biker club* where anything could happen.

She was so not speaking to Kelsea ever again after they got out of there in one piece. She was totally disowning her ass.

Kelsea leaned toward her and said in a loud whisper, "He's hung like a stallion."

Slash grinned and said, "Yeah, I am."

"Nice," Jewel responded, arching an eyebrow Kelsea's way, wondering when Kelsea was ever around a stallion to know how they were hung. "But I don't care."

Jewel's ass started to vibrate. She pulled her phone from the back pocket of her jeans. Staring her in the face was a text from D.

Shit!

U 2 aint the brightest bulbs in the bitch box, r u?

Jewel's jaw dropped, then snapped shut.

"Don't be jealous. You bitches can share," Slash continued, like he was stud muffin of the year.

Jewel's eyes hit Kelsea's. She tipped her chin toward her phone and mouthed, "D."

Kelsea's eyes rounded and her face paled.

Jewel's phone vibrated again. *Ur ass is mine. Get the fuck outta there now.*

"Oh, shit," Jewel said softly.

"What?" Kelsea asked, panic crossing her face.

"What's the matter, babe?" Slash asked.

Kelsea plastered on a fake smile and looked up at her new man. "Nothing." She looked back at Jewel. "You need to go, then go. Slash can get me home."

B waitin for u at ur place.

"Fuck," Jewel groaned softly after reading the latest text.

Got 1 hour. Thats w droppin K off 2.

"Ain't takin' you all the way back up to Pennsylvania, babe," Slash complained.

"Slash," Kelsea whined.

"Uh, Kels," Jewel began then another text made her cell vibrate.

Dont want me comin 2 get u 2.

No, she didn't.

"What?" Kelsea asked.

"Might want to rethink all of this..." Jewel jumped when her phone rang.

She turned the phone toward Kelsea, who whispered, "Shit," when she saw who was calling.

Jewel sucked in a breath then hit the Answer button. She could hear him bellowing before the phone actually hit her ear.

"Woman!"

"Yeah?"

"Where you at?"

"On our way back," Jewel lied, her eyes meeting Kelsea's.

"Better be. Got eyes there. Gonna check if you're lyin'."

Shit.

"We're heading out now."

"Kelsea, too."

"Yeah, she's coming, too."

"What? No!" Kelsea shouted.

Jewel held out her cell phone to her. "You want to tell him that?"

Kelsea's expression went blank. "No."

"Didn't think so," Jewel said, putting the phone back to her ear. Then decided it was less deafening to hold it about an inch away. She had no problem hearing D "speaking" from there.

"Heard all that. Get gone now."

"Right," Jewel whispered.

"Times tickin', woman."

"Right," Jewel repeated. Then the phone went dark.

Shit.

"Gotta go, Kels," Jewel said, though she was a bit relieved they were getting out of there. Not so relieved that D would be waiting for her. Especially when he was pissed.

"Fine," Kelsea finally huffed. Then Jewel had to stand there waiting while they swapped spit and tongues for almost five whole fucking minutes. Jewel tried to ignore the roaming hands.

"Need to fuck you, babe," Slash told Kelsea when he finally let her mouth go.

"I know," Kelsea whined softly.

"Oh, God, really?" Jewel asked, staring up at the dark sky and hoping for divine intervention.

"Next time," Slash promised.

Oh, there was *not* going to be a next time. Not if Jewel had anything to do with it. Or Diesel. Or anyone else who caught wind of this. Which, she had a feeling, would eventually be all the brothers.

Shit.

JEWEL HAD DRAGGED Kelsea out of there, past more grabby-hands Demons, shoved her in the car, then once she was in the driver's seat, locked the doors. Not that locked car doors would stop anyone who wanted to get at them.

Then she drove as fast as possible, trying to not get stopped by West Virginia cops for speeding and also not hit a herd of deer. Especially since it was getting close to rutting season and the bucks were running around like brainless twits because they were desperate to fuck whatever doe was in heat.

Kind of like bikers.

She had delivered Kelsea home safely with barely a word between them and all the way back to her apartment her heart had tried to beat a hole in her chest.

And now…

Now, she sat in the dark in her car, both hands gripping the steering wheel so hard her knuckles were white as she stared at Diesel through her windshield and he stared back at her.

Totally pissed.

No, like a volcano ready to blow.

He leaned back against the railing at the bottom of the metal steps to her apartment, arms crossed over his chest, his ankles crossed.

To anyone else, he might look relaxed, casual.

Jewel knew better.

She could see his tight jaw, tight muscles, and this tightly strung temper from where she sat. She had parked on the other side of the lot because she was afraid if she pulled up next to his bike, he would drag her out of the car right away and the club's enforcer would be meting out his form of punishment immediately.

Instead, she watched him watching her.

She blew out a shaky breath when she realized she couldn't sit in the car forever. Though, she'd like to.

Maybe she could go spend the night at her mom's.

Yes, that sounded like a smart plan.

"Longer you sit there, the worse it's gonna be," Diesel shouted across the lot.

Jesus, she felt like a child about to be disciplined. She knew she had to face him sooner or later, she just couldn't help but want to put it off.

Maybe she could sweet talk his temper down. Or offer him head.

Fuck! She needed a freaking plan.

She couldn't come up with a single one. Besides not dying tonight.

She snorted. That was ridiculous. She was an adult. He was an adult.

They were going to handle this like two adults.

She pulled the key from the ignition and shoved open her door. Tentatively putting one booted foot out on the macadam and then the other, she waited for the earth to swallow her whole. Actually hoped for it.

When it didn't, she stood, shut her door and slowly turned her head to glance in his direction.

He hadn't moved a muscle. Though she was sure one ticked in his jaw, she couldn't see it from where she stood.

She had to woman up and get this over with. Putting one foot in front of the other, she crossed the lot like she was about to walk the plank of a pirate ship.

She swallowed her thumping heart back into her chest.

"D…" she began as she came close enough that she didn't have to yell.

"Woman, don't even," he warned.

"D…" she began again, trying to formulate in her brain something, *anything*, to say to reduce his blood pressure.

He pushed off the railing and blocked both the front of the steps and her escape.

Though he was now standing instead of leaning, he kept his arms across his broad chest, probably to refrain from grabbing her. Or… whatever.

"You're my ol' lady, huh?" he growled, going toe to toe with her. "That's what you told those fuckers?"

"D…" she started saying to his chest.

"They're too stupid to know my ol' lady would never be at one of their parties. *Ever*," he yelled in her face. "'Specially if I wasn't there with her."

She winced and whispered, "Wasn't my idea."

"Don't give a shit whose idea it was. Tired of gettin' your ass outtuva jam."

"You didn't."

"Yeah, I did. Gotta call from a Demon to confirm you bein' my ol' lady was true. So, yeah, saved your fuckin' ass. Again."

"You mean you said I was?"

"What the fuck did I just say?"

Oh.

"Got you outta there safely. Otherwise, who knows—" he stopped abruptly.

What would've happened, she finished for him silently.

Yeah, he got them out of a jam.

She felt the fight or flight leave her. He was right. She was wrong. And Kelsea was an idiot. Not that she was any better for going along with the younger woman and not asking enough questions beforehand.

"Bad enough we're dealin' with Warriors an' their bullshit, then you an' my genius cousin decide to head outta state to party with an outlaw club. A fuckin' outlaw club!" He emphasized the last part with a shout and a shake of his head. He finished by muttering, "Fuckin' crazy bitches."

"D..." she started again, but she honestly didn't know what to say, to make it better, to excuse their stupidity. Besides, "Sorry."

"Sorry? When you gonna learn, woman?" he grabbed her upper arm and gave her a shake. "When?"

"D..." she whispered, her eyes starting to burn, her throat closing up. She finally realized that the man was showing some emotion. Toward her. He *cared*. And it wasn't because he was the club's Sergeant at Arms. It was more.

He had feared for her safety. For Kelsea's safety. She recognized it now.

"Never gonna learn, Jewelee. Keep puttin' yourself in harm's way an' you've been lucky."

"I know how to take care of myself," she whispered lamely.

"The fuck you do!" he bellowed inches from her face, making Jewel wince. "They decide to gang rape you, what you gonna do?"

Jesus. Jewel bit her bottom lip. She hated that he was right. She, or even Kelsea, would've been outnumbered and unable to stop them. Then add a mob mentality on top of that.

They would've been fucked.

"Ain't nothin' markin' you as mine. What the fuck were you gonna do if they decided to take turns with you?"

"D..."

He raised a hand to stop her. "No. No fuckin' pleadin'. Ain't gonna drop it. Want an answer. Can take care of yourself? What were you gonna do, woman? Cry, plead an' beg 'em not to?" He snorted. "Lotta good that woulda done. Jesus fuckin' Christ," he shouted to the sky. Then he closed his eyes and Jewel watched something cross his face. A memory. Something. His demeanor completely changed. "Jesus fuckin' Christ," he repeated more quietly. He dropped his head, pinned his hands on his hips and stared at his boots for a moment. Two. Three. Then he shook it and gave Jewel a look.

And that look scared her more than his angry beast. This was something totally different.

Lightning shot through her, from her head to her toes. Every part of her tingled, every nerve stood on its end.

"D," she whispered and put a hand under his leather cut onto his chest. His heart thumped strong and rapidly under her palm.

"Jesus, woman," he said much more quietly. "Killin' me."

She leaned into him and whispered, "No, not killing you. Making you feel."

He shook his head. "Don't want that shit."

"Sometimes it's not a choice. Can't help what you feel."

He blinked slowly at her.

"I'm yours, D, if you want me," she offered softly.

His head jerked back and he stared down into her face. "Woman."

"Beast," she whispered, her voice husky.

His nostrils flared and something in his eyes changed. He covered her hand that laid over his heart with his own. He left it there for a moment, then pulled her hand off of him and stepped back.

"Go upstairs, Jewelee. Get inside. Lock your door. Had enough shit for tonight."

"D..."

"Fuckin' do it," he said, his voice now hard, his expression even harder.

Jewel's stomach twisted and the tears stung her eyes again.

Before she started crying, revealing how much it hurt that he didn't want her—or, at least, didn't want to admit to wanting her—she pushed past him and ran up the steps.

She fumbled with her keys, but finally was able to unlock her door. She rushed inside, then slammed the door shut. Leaning back against it, she bit her bottom lip to stifle the whimper that wanted to escape.

Then she ran to her room, threw herself on her bed and no longer fought any of it.

Chapter Nine

"DIESEL."

D scowled into his glass of whiskey. He was not in the mood to listen to this woman's bullshit.

No, not a woman. She didn't deserve to be called that because she sure didn't act like one. She had a lot of growing up to do yet, even though she was already in her mid-twenties.

"Diesel," she called.

"Fuck me," he muttered.

Hawk's eyes were on the woman as she approached, and he muttered, "Ain't got a choice, brother. Gotta deal with 'er."

"Right," D said into his glass of amber liquid before tilting it to his lips and draining it dry.

Kelsea slid her ass onto the stool next to him. "You ignoring me?"

D twisted his neck to look at her. "Hard to do when you're screamin' my name across church."

"I was trying to get your attention."

"Well, you got it."

"I know your pissed at Jewel—"

"Don't know shit," he growled.

"But don't take it out on her. It's all my fault."

"She drove," he stated. He did a chin lift toward his brother, who filled his glass again. Hawk then leaned against the counter behind the bar and crossed his arms over his chest, settling in to hear the conversation.

D took another swallow, letting the warmth of the whiskey slide down his throat into his gut.

"Yes, but I didn't tell her everything."

"She ask?"

Silence.

Right.

"What are you doin' fuckin' with a Demon?" Hawk butted in.

"He's cool," their cousin answered.

"What the fuck," D muttered.

"He's cool?" Hawk repeated. "Are you fuckin' serious?"

"Look..." Kelsea began.

"No, you look," D shouted, pointing a finger into her face. "Don't be doin' stupid shit an' don't be draggin' Jewel into your stupid shit, either."

Kelsea chewed on her bottom lip.

"Out of state. Outlaw club. Drunk an' high fuckers. Two bitches not claimed. Your asses were hangin' out there for anyone to take advantage," Hawk barked. "No reason to be hookin' up with a Demon."

"Hawk," Kelsea started, her eyes narrow.

"No lip," Diesel grumbled.

"Don't need your approval," their cousin muttered.

D sucked in a breath, ready to rip her a new one when Hawk's hand landed on his arm. "Brother. Step back." Though Hawk's voice sounded like he was under control, D knew his brother was as torqued as he was.

D released his held breath and swallowed the scorching words he was going to head Kelsea's way. He lifted his glass and finished it off instead.

He needed more than what he drank so far to take the edge off him.

"Know you growin' up without a father, Kels," Hawk started, a little more calmly, "was tough. An' with Doc doin' life, didn't even have a grandfather to point you in the right direction. That's why Ace an' me an' D step in. Not just because D's the enforcer. Not because we're blood. All of us are lookin' out for you. Whether you want it or not."

Diesel expected her to argue, to stir up shit. But she didn't. Instead, she nodded at Hawk, who was also just as surprised as D was.

"Got it," she said softly. "I have to go. But D..."

She turned toward him and he steeled himself to hear whatever stupid shit she was about to say next.

"Gotta give Jewelee a chance."

Jesus. His fingers gripped the empty glass still in his hand. He didn't say anything as his cousin pushed off the stool and headed toward the back door. When she was gone, D returned his gaze to his brother.

"She's fuckin' right, brother. Gotta quit fightin' it. Rippin' you apart."

"Bullshit," D grunted.

"Can see it. Rippin' Jewelee apart, too."

D sucked a hard breath through his nostrils and shoved his glass toward Hawk. "Gimme another."

Hawk smiled, shook his head and poured him another whiskey.

And not a minute later one more.

DIESEL GROANED and rolled to the left, hitting a soft, naked body, which dropped to the floor with a squeal.

He groaned again when he opened his eyes and the bare bulb hanging from the drop ceiling not only blinded him but shot a shard of pain through his head.

"Jesus fuckin' Christ," he grumbled.

He blinked and looked over the edge of the bed to see one of the sweet butts on the floor.

Tequila.

Jesus fuckin' Christ.

He couldn't remember shit from last night except that as long as Hawk was filling his glass, he was downing them.

After that... nothing.

And, fuck him, now Tequila was pushing her naked ass up from his floor, or trying to since she was tangled up in some of his dirty clothes.

"How the fuck you get in here?"

Tequila shook off the shirt snarled around her wrist and hauled herself up to a stand.

Her fake tits didn't even jiggle when she did so. That shit might turn other men on but it didn't do squat for him.

He glanced down at his limp dick. "We fuck?"

With a huff, Tequila said, "No. Not for a lack of tryin', either. Helped you up here an' then you passed the fuck out."

Oh, thank fuck. He was afraid he'd have to take a torch to his dick if he accidentally stuck it in her. "Why you still here an' why you naked?"

Why the fuck was *he* naked? He didn't remember taking off his clothes, either.

"Figured when you woke up we could fuck."

D sat up in bed and cocked an eyebrow in her direction. "Ain't happenin'. Get the fuck out."

"D," she whined, eyeballing his lap.

"Out!" he shouted. "Now!"

"What the fuck," she grumbled, picking through the piles of clothes on the floor to find her own. She took her time pulling them on.

"Hurry the fuck up," he growled. "Come back later, clean up this room an' do my laundry. Got me?"

Her dark eyes widened, then narrowed quickly. "Ain't your slave."

"Fuck you ain't. Wanna hang 'round this club, fuck brothers, then you earn your keep."

"Ain't enough brothers—"

"Out!"

"Christ, you're an asshole."

D ignored her and swiped his cell from the nightstand, powering it up to check for messages and texts. He glanced up when she hadn't moved. "Got thirty seconds 'til I shove you out into the hall, with your clothes or not. Not like you wear much, shouldn't be much to find."

"Whatever, asshole," she grumbled, snagging her boots from the corner of the room and tucking them under her arm. "Glad I didn't fuck you."

D grunted.

With a last look toward him, she huffed and then pulled his door open.

Jewel stood in the hall, her fist raised as if she was ready to knock. Her eyes widened as she faced Tequila, who cursed and shoved past her, knocking her backwards and out of the way.

Jewel lowered her hand and planted both of them on her hips, glancing from the hallway to D.

"Tequila!" Diesel bellowed, then said to Jewel, "Get 'er the fuck back here."

"Yo, skank, you're being paged," Jewel shouted down the hallway.

"What?" Tequila griped, peering her head around the door not a second later.

"Touch her again, you're out. Come in my room again other than to clean, you're out. Got me?"

"Whatever," Tequila mumbled, then her head disappeared, only leaving her hand behind in the doorway as she flipped him the bird, then even that disappeared.

Jewel stayed in place watching what he could only assume was the sweet butt heading down the hall.

"Fuck you, too, Jewel," he heard Tequila call out.

Jewel's lips twitched and she waved an exaggerated goodbye in the other woman's direction before stepping into his room and slamming the door shut. Then she replanted her hands on her hips as she stared at him sitting naked in the middle of his bed.

He couldn't miss her eyes raking over his body. His dick didn't miss it either and decided it was time to wake up.

Tequila couldn't turn him on when she was totally naked. Jewel could do it fully dressed.

He was so fucking fucked.

"Was she good?"

He scratched the stubble on his chin and tried to figure out her mood. Since it was Jewel, he gave up on trying. He was just going to give it to her straight and she could think whatever the fuck she wanted to think. "Didn't touch her."

Jewel paused, then asked, "She touch you?"

He didn't answer.

She arched a dark eyebrow. "Don't know?" she asked, stepping closer to the bed.

"What're you here for, woman?"

Her eyes dropped to his lap and his now hard dick. "Not that."

He waited impatiently.

"I should have texted first, but I didn't think you'd have Tequila in your bed."

"Didn't touch her," he grumbled again.

"Yeah. I heard you the first time," Jewel muttered.

"Then fuckin' spill it, woman. Why the fuck you here?"

"Because..." She stepped to the side of the bed.

Now she was within arm's reach. He could snake out a hand, snag her and have her beneath him in a few seconds flat. But he didn't. He fisted his fingers in his lap instead.

"Because," she began again. She took a visible breath. "I've decided this shit between us has to stop."

D beat down the surprise that wanted to cross his face. "You decided."

"Yeah."

"Told you we shouldn't be doin' it in the first place," he reminded her.

"I know."

He snorted. "Now *you* decided we ain't doin' it anymore."

"Yeah."

"Fuckin' lost your mind, woman," he grumbled.

"No... No, I didn't. You want to be free, you're free."

He frowned. "When wasn't I free?" he asked, confused.

"You sure acted that way every time you were in my bed. You couldn't wait to roll out. Didn't want to be with me for longer than you had to to get off."

Right.

She was right on that one. He couldn't wait to roll out. But not for the reason she was thinking.

It wasn't her. It was him.

And, yeah, maybe freedom had something to do with it.

Jewel continued, "Sex was good. No, to be honest, it was great. But I can get that elsewhere."

His head jerked back. What the fuck did she just say?

"I didn't want only sex with you, D. I thought I was clear about that from the beginning. I know you can get it anywhere. And so can I. However, apparently we don't want the same thing."

So can she?

"Where you gettin' it?"

"What?"

His blood rushed through his veins like a freight train. "Where you gettin' it other than me?"

"I—"

He snaked his hand out, snagged her wrist, and twisted them both until she landed onto her back on the mattress. He stared down into her face, his nose a cunt hair from hers.

"Where... you... gettin'... it?" he asked slowly.

When she tried to turn her head, he grabbed her chin firmly, holding her gaze.

"Woman," he warned when she didn't answer.

He watched her throat move as she swallowed. "Nowhere right now."

Good answer.

"But, D, I'm done with this."

"Done when I say you're done."

"No," she said, her voice thick. "I'm not going to keep throwing myself at you to only be rejected."

"Ain't rejectin' you when my dick's inside you."

"Yeah, but..."

"Want too much from me, Jewelee. Can't give it to you. Told you that. Nothin' changed."

"And that's why I'm done with this."

"No."

"Yes, D. Yes! I can't keep doing this to myself." She closed her eyes. "I can't," she whispered.

"Doin' what? Just what're you doin'?"

When she opened her mouth, the last thing he expected came out.

"Loving you when you don't love me back."

His chest tightened as all the breath rushed out of him and he stared down at the woman beneath him. Her head on his pillow, her hair wildly spread out around her. The spark in her blue eyes gone. Her lips turned down.

Disappointment. She was swallowed up in disappointment.

He did that to her.

He did it.

"Jesus, Jewelee," he grumbled softly.

"Nothing changed. Nothing's going to change. So like I said, I can't keep doing this to myself."

The hurt in her eyes twisted his gut. "Supposed to be keepin' it simple," he reminded her as well as himself.

"I know," she said softly. "I can't do it, D. You said I was killing you." She tried to shake her head, but he wouldn't release her chin. "But, truth is, you're killing me. I have to move on."

Hawk was right. This was ripping her apart. He should have seen it. He was a stupid fuck.

This wasn't simple at all.

For him or for her.

And this was why he was so fucked. He knew deep down he would never be able to let her go. And that's why he also kept coming back to her, to her bed.

He thought if he could just be with her just for a brief time here and there, he could easily pull himself back out of that hole he was sliding into.

But he couldn't. He had fucking fallen in deep.

And he didn't even know when it happened.

No, he knew. He just wanted to deny it.

It was the first time he took her. Made her his even though that wasn't his intent. And since then, there hadn't been anybody else but her.

Jesus fuckin' Christ.

"So, please, let me get up and get out of here," she whispered, her eyes shinier than normal.

He had never seen Jewel cry. Not once. Not even while growing up. Not even when she wrecked her bicycle trying to jump a ramp the boys had set up for their dirt bikes. She screwed it up, got all banged up, skinned her knees and needed stitches on her leg. She didn't cry that day. Hell, no. She got mad at herself for doing something stupid. And even back then, he'd recognized the frustration on her face for being unable to prove she could do what the boys could.

But now...

Holy fucking shit.

Now, he was the reason the woman was going to cry.

"Jewelee," he murmured, sweeping a strand of her dark hair away from her face.

"D, don't," she begged, wiggling underneath him. "I need to go." A tear leaked out of the corner of her eye and slid into her hair.

Jesus. She really *was* killing him.

"Want you, woman."

"I know," she answered, blinking quickly. Her voice caught when she added, "But not enough."

"Care about you," he admitted gruffly.

"Again, not enough."

His heart skipped a beat when he stated, "You love me."

"Yeah," she said on a ragged breath, another tear leaked out of her eye, rolling down her face to disappear.

He thumbed the third one away.

"Don't know why."

"I don't, either," she answered.

She was trying to be a smart ass, but what she said was probably true. He didn't know why or how she could love someone like him. A beast like she called him.

He could be a beast. His stomach burned at the thought that he'd always be one.

He could not be what she wanted.

"Always gonna be me, woman. A beast like you say. Never gonna be soft, tender."

"I've seen it."

"No."

"Yes, with Bella."

"She's my cousin. Different."

"You protect her."

Of course he did and always would. "Been through too much shit."

"Yes, and you're there when she needs you."

"She don't like it when she's weak."

"Yeah, but you still step in when she is. You help make her strong again." Jewel slipped a hand between them and pressed a finger into his chest. "It's inside you, D. I've seen it. You just don't want to share it with me."

She was wrong. So fucking wrong.

"And I get it. I'm not *the one*."

Jesus.

"When you find *the one*, you'll share it with her."

Jesus fuckin' Christ.

"Just don't short change yourself. When you find her, show her. Make sure she sees it, sees all of you."

For fuck's sake, it wasn't a finger she had pressed to his chest, it was a knife and now she was twisting it.

"Jewelee."

Jewel wiped a hand over her eyes. "What?"

This woman. "Need to shut up."

She nodded slightly. "I need to go."

He should let her go like she wanted. Roll off her, give her her freedom. Go let her find a man that will fulfill all her needs.

Because it wasn't him.

Jesus fuckin' Christ.

He wanted it to be him. He wanted to give her everything she needed. If he didn't, someone else would. And there was no way he could sit back and watch that.

No fucking way.

"D, I have to go to work."

He couldn't stop staring at her. Her blue eyes still shiny with tears, her mouth parted slightly, the gold ring in her nose. Her long, thick lashes.

Without saying a word, he snagged his phone from the nightstand, pushed a few buttons and hit Send.

"What are you doing?" she asked.

"Brother, Jewel ain't comin' in today." His eyes hit hers, which had widened. He listened to Crash bitch on the other end of the phone. "Don't give a fuckin' shit. Got a problem with it, come find me." Crash shut up. "Right," D grunted then hit End.

He tossed his phone, then rolled up and off her. "Go home, Jewelee."

"What?"

He offered her his hand. "Go home. Gotta shower. Be there in thirty. Ain't fuckin' you in this bed."

"What?"

"Didn't think I stuttered, did I?"

She finally took his offered hand. "No. But I told you I didn't want to do this anymore."

He pulled her off the bed and onto her feet. "Woman, go home."

"D—"

"This ain't done."

"What are you saying?"

"We ain't done. Gonna figure it out. Just not here. Your place. Your bed. Me inside you."

"That doesn't sound like figuring it out."

"Right. It's a start."

"D..."

He shook his head; he didn't want to hear any argument. He was struggling with this as it was. "Go home, baby. Go home. Be there soon."

Diesel saw a look cross her face. She wanted to stick to her guns, she wanted to finish this, finish them. But she was wavering.

And when she finally whispered, "Okay," after one last look at him, she left.

He let the breath rush from his lungs and he muttered, "Thank fuck," to the empty room.

Chapter Ten

Jewel watched Diesel in the mirror above them. His ass flexed powerfully, his back muscles made his tattoos, the club's insignia and rockers, move as if they were alive, her legs wrapped around his bulky thighs as much as she could get them.

He was driving into her forcefully with each thrust of his hips. His mouth was to her ear, her hand wrapped around the side of his head holding him there, and with every grunt, her pussy clenched harder around him.

She was about to come. The sight and sound of him combined with his movement was driving her over the edge. She'd already come once when he had his mouth on her earlier. And a second time as soon as he'd taken her with his cock, because she had still been on a high from the first orgasm.

Where this man got his skill, she'd never know. It certainly wasn't in a bathroom with random females, which was his M.O.

Or, hopefully, his former Modus Operandi. Jewel didn't think she could stand to see him with another woman again. Not now, not ever, now that she'd had him.

Now that he'd had her.

"Feel you squeezin' me, baby."

The "baby" thing was new. Every time he called her that, it caught her off guard. She wondered if it had anything to do with her slipping up and telling him that she loved him.

She certainly hadn't gone to his room to admit that. It just happened. But it seemed to affect him, which shouldn't surprise her, but normally much didn't affect the man.

Though, she couldn't imagine that he'd had any other woman ever tell him that. He'd never let anyone close enough to even give them the chance to feel that way about him.

All the club sisters loved him, of course, but it was more like loving a big, bossy brother, not in the same way Jewel did.

"D," she breathed.

He grunted again in her ear.

"Going to come," she whispered.

"Yeah, baby, come," he urged, his voice gruff in her ear.

Then it hit her, her toes curled as the wave rushed over and through her. Her nails dug into the side of his head, the nails from her other hand raked over his shoulder and down his back as the currents swept through her for what seemed like forever.

He had stilled when it started. But he began to grind deep again when he growled, "You're fuckin' mine."

His statement sent a shiver down her spine. She didn't know what that meant to him, to them.

Where that would take them from this moment forward.

"Mine," he said again as he thrust deep one more time and spilled inside her with a low, long grunt. He shoved his face into her neck, his breath beating a tattoo against her throat.

"Yours," Jewel said softly as she cupped the back of his head. Her eyes flicked back up to the mirror. She looked so tiny under him.

He was such a beast.

And if what he had just said was true, he was her beast.

"Ain't gonna be like Z an' Sophie," his voice came muffled against her skin. He lifted his head and shifted until he was directly over top of her, catching and holding her gaze. "No ring, no weddin', no babies, no ol' lady status. Ain't doin' it now. Can't promise to do it later, either. Either accept it or don't, Jewelee. Can't give you more than that. Not now. Maybe not ever. Gonna take it as it comes, yeah?"

None of that sounded ideal to her. None of it.

But she loved him. Even if he didn't feel exactly the same way about her, she did recognize the fact that there was something there. He did feel something for her, she just wasn't sure what.

Whatever it was, she might be able to work with it and hope she didn't come out on the losing end later.

"We can take it as it comes," she agreed.

"No one else, woman. Serious. No one for me, no one for you. Can give you that. Comes a day we don't like that arrangement anymore, we can move on. No hard feelin's."

Now he was pushing it. No hard feelings? They get tired of each other and just move on? Simply brush each other off and go their separate ways? Even if that was easily done emotionally, the fact that they were both DAMC would make it more difficult. It would be hard to avoid him after something like that unless she totally separated herself from the club and gave up her job, her sisterhood, her family.

"Really, D? I get tired of being a booty call and decide to move on, you're not going to have any hard feelings? You'll be fine with that?"

He growled, "Ain't a booty call. Don't say that shit."

"But isn't that what I'll be unless you claim me as yours?"

He jerked his head back and stared at her for a moment before sliding his bulk to her side. He rolled onto his back and she stared at him through the mirror.

"Even if I claim you as my woman, not even my ol' lady, it can put a target on your back."

"You mean with the Warriors?"

"With anyone."

"Saying I was your ol' lady saved me with the Demons. Why would it be any different with anyone else, barring the Warriors. They're just assholes no matter what."

He didn't answer her. She didn't even get a grunt.

Club business was not a woman's business. His security business wasn't, either. He wasn't going to talk about it.

That was nothing new to any of the DAMC women. Though, Diesel had been known to say more than he should on past occasions because no one would challenge him on it. But today wasn't going to be one of those days.

She decided to go back to their previous subject. "So since, according to you, I'm not just a booty call, then are you still planning on rolling out of my bed in the middle of the night to go back to that disgusting shithole you sleep in?"

"Don't got a mirror over my bed. Got a mirror over yours."

"And that means..." she prodded, her heart thudding in her chest because she thought she knew what that meant but wanted to make sure.

"Want me in your bed?" he asked, turning his head on the pillow in her direction.

His dark brown eyes, his expression gave her nothing. He had a good poker face. Always had.

She rolled to her side up against him, placed a hand to his chest and stared down at him. "Yeah."

"Then I'm in your bed."

Just like that. From fighting her to not.

"Every night?"

His jaw shifted and his nostrils flared so slightly she almost missed it. "Can't promise that. Can't tell you what time I'll roll in. But I'll try to roll in every night. Got me?"

"Got you," she whispered. "So, no holding dinner for you."

The corners of his eyes crinkled. "No, but can cook me shit if you're good at it. Got a microwave. Know how to warm shit up."

She pictured the state of his room at church. "Got a rule, though."

"Nope. Diesel's number one rule: no naggin'."

"D, you can't be throwing your clothes all over the floor."

"Then pick 'em up."

Damn.

He continued, "Rule two: no bitchin'."

"Well, rules *were* meant to be broken," she muttered.

"Woman," he warned.

Jewel bit her lips together to keep from laughing.

"Rule three: No runnin' 'round partyin' with Kelsea. Wanna party, your ass is at church. Safe there. Not attractin' strange, either."

"D," Jewel started.

"No lip, woman. Make that rule four."

"Jesus, you're bossy."

"Yeah, you know it." He hooked her under her arms and pulled her across him from shoulder to hip, then smacked her ass. "You love it."

Jewel snorted. "Right, I can't say I love you being bossy."

"Love me?"

"Yeah," she breathed.

"Love bossy then."

She whacked his arm and rolled her eyes at him. "Yeah, right."

His eyes tipped up toward the ceiling and Jewel twisted her neck enough to see what he was looking at. Diesel laid naked on her bed, only covered by his tattoos and her. And his wide hand was planted firmly on her ass.

It looked good. It looked right.

"See that?" she asked softy.

"Yeah, baby. See it. Thankin' Jag for puttin' that up."

She lay her cheek on his chest and sighed. "About time you got some sense." His body shook beneath hers and she tipped her eyes up to him. "Are you laughing?"

"Yeah," he said and a smile cracked his face.

A fucking smile.

He was looking at her and smiling.

Holy crap! Her heart stilled, then started to thump wildly.

She melted into him more, wearing her own smile. "D..."

"Shut up, woman."

She stifled her laugh and closed her eyes to savor the warmth of his skin, the strong beat of his heart, and the security of his arms wrapped around her, holding her tight.

Gonna take it as it comes, yeah?

Yeah, she was going to take it as it comes. And see where it goes.

Chapter Eleven

Diesel's phone lit up. He put his whiskey down to pick up his cell. One of his crew was calling. He pushed away from the club's private bar and answered the call.

"Hold up. Headin' somewhere private," he grumbled without even greeting the caller.

Hellos and goodbyes were just a waste of needed oxygen.

He headed into the meeting room to the right of the bar and closed the door behind him.

"Go," he prompted Walker.

"Got some good news," Walker said, then stopped.

D waited.

"Got a bead on the prospect, Squirrel. Sent Ryder out to surveil the area. He was hittin' up some pussy in Homewood."

"Anybody else with him?"

"No. Like I said, just there for pussy. Low income housing."

"Get 'im?"

"Yeah."

"Before or after gettin' his dick wet?"

Walker chuckled low on the other end of the phone. "After. Came out with a smile. Then he saw Ryder, lost that lovin' feelin' real quick. Went from gettin' fucked to gettin' fucked in another way."

"Right. Where?"

"Got 'im at the warehouse."

The "warehouse" was were D kept his office, his equipment and everything else that was needed to run his business. "He cryin' yet?"

"Saw a couple tears. Did a little bit of blubberin', too."

"Gonna be doin' more before we're done."

"Yeah... Boss?"

"Yeah."

"Want in on this or gonna keep your hands clean?"

D thought about how he found Kiki and Jazz in that house that night. He not only wanted in, he knew Hawk would, too. Though he wasn't going to tell his brother. Not until afterward. He didn't need Hawk getting in a jam. Especially now that he'd settled down with Kiki.

D decided he would keep this on the D.L. Keep his brother out of it and on a need-to-know basis.

"Where's Mercy?" D asked Walker.

"At the warehouse."

Fuck. "He didn't start yet."

"Well, nothin' hardcore," Walker confirmed. "Waitin' for word from you."

"He got a plan?"

"Oh yeah," Walker said softly.

D just bet Mercy did. His name was Mercy for a reason. You get on his bad side, you're going to be screaming for mercy if it comes down to him exacting revenge.

No doubt about it, the man was a badass motherfucker. Sometimes he even scared D. And that wasn't easy to do.

"ETA?" Walker asked him.

"'Bout twenty."

"Got it."

D hit the End button and tapped his phone against his thigh. He then left the meeting room, crossed the common area and pushed through the side door to the courtyard. His gaze swept over the area, the only light coming from the bonfire in the fire pit and a few lights by the stage where Nash's band was jamming out, doing a tune D never heard before.

He spotted Jewel, eyes closed, drink in her hand, which was raised over her head, as she swayed to the music off to the side.

He needed to talk to her and get gone, but watching her made his feet freeze in place. She wore tight jeans, knee-high boots with a flat heel—*thank fuck*—and a hip-length black leather jacket that emphasized her narrow waist. As she rolled her head around, her long dark hair swept across her back and shoulders.

Jesus fuck. He wanted to fist that hair, bend her over and fuck her hard.

He forced his feet to move and when he approached her, her eyes opened and she held his gaze, her lips curved slightly. She turned away from him as he got close and backed into him, grinding her ass into his dick as she swayed to the beat.

"Jesus fuckin' Christ," he muttered. This was not the time to get a fucking hard-on.

"Gonna dance with me, D?" she asked. He detected a slight slur to her speech.

He never danced in his life and wasn't about to start tonight.

"How many?"

She bent over and shoved her ass harder against him. He grabbed her hair and forced her up. Wrapping an arm around her shoulders, he pulled her against him, his front to her back to keep her still.

"What?" she asked.

"How many drinks?"

She shook her head slightly, then took another sip of whatever she had in the red plastic cup. "Don't know."

"Jesus. Got business I gotta deal with. No drivin'. Got me? Get a ride home."

"I'll be fine."

He pressed his mouth to her ear. "Woman. Remember rule four? No lip."

"Just 'round your cock."

He snorted. "Yeah. That's acceptable."

She giggled and wiggled against him. "When're you gonna be home?"

Home.

Jesus.

"Don't know."

She turned in his arms and gave him a sexy pout. "Need you."

"Yeah," he breathed.

"Want you."

"Yeah," he breathed again. "Me, too, baby. Got shit to deal with first."

Shit she didn't want to know about. Shit she'd never know about. Things that would make her realize how much of a beast he actually was.

She slipped her hand between them and cupped his now hard dick. "Wake me up when you get home."

Again, with that *home* shit.

He hadn't even moved in. He showed up, fucked her, slept in her bed, then rolled out in the morning to go back to church to shower and find some less dirty clothes. He kept nothing at her apartment. He had never even eaten a meal there yet.

Though, he did get a spare key from his pop. Ace had handed it over to him with only a cocked brow and a shaking head. And once D had grabbed the key and turned to leave, he swore he heard Ace laughing.

That's because his father knew just how fucked D was.

Which was one hundred percent fucked.

"Might come back here after." As soon as that slipped out of his mouth, he regretted it.

She blinked up at him and frowned. "Then I'll stay here tonight."

Fuck.

"I sleep better with you next to me," she said softly.

Fuck him, so did he. He slept like the dead when she was tucked against him at night.

"Room's a shithole. Go home. Be there when I can."

She smiled and melted against him, pressing against his dick, which wasn't helping him to get moving. And he really needed to go.

"Woman, gotta go."

"Okay," she said, both her voice and eyes soft.

Jesus. What happened to the smart-ass biker bitch she was? She was getting all mushy and shit. Next, she'd be wanting babies.

"You still on the pill, right?"

"What? Yeah," she answered, confused.

He nodded. Thank fuck. He dropped a quick kiss on her lips and then set her away from him. "Behave," was his last warning before he headed out of the compound.

MERCY CIRCLED SQUIRREL, who sat tied to a chair. His face was hard, his body tight. And he'd only just gotten started.

When Diesel arrived, he hadn't expected quite what he saw... which was the metal chair Squirrel was tied to sitting in the middle of a bunch of plastic sheeting. Someone expected to make a mess.

And that someone was Mercy.

"Got any info?" D asked Walker, who was standing back, letting Mercy do his thing.

"Not really. Gave up Black Jack's name, which we already had, so that was fuckin' useless. Says he doesn't know where the fucker is."

"Need that info."

"No shit," Walker grumbled. "How far you gonna let Mercy take this?"

D met Walker's eyes, then let his gaze slide back to Squirrel who looked like he was going to shit his pants. In his mind's eye, he saw the prospect raping Jazz, carving "SWMC" into the skin of Jazz's belly, breaking her bones, and beating her beyond recognition.

And then what they did to Kiki, too...

He shook his head. He needed to keep his head clear. Otherwise, he might strangle Squirrel with his bare hands and they wouldn't get any info out of him at all.

"Diesel, c'mon, man. You can't do this," Squirrel cried out.

D ignored him. Mercy had already done some damage to the guy. But not nearly the damage Squirrel and Black Jack had done to Jazz and Kiki.

Not even close.

"Like beatin' up women? Rapin' 'em?" Mercy shouted in Squirrel's face, making the former DAMC's prospect flinch. Mercy grabbed his crotch and jerked it. "Make you feel like a fuckin' man?"

"Wasn't my idea," Squirrel croaked. "Swear, man. Wasn't me."

"The fuck it wasn't," Mercy growled. "Cops got the DNA you left in that poor girl. Got the proof. You're so fucked."

"Call 5-0. Hand me over to 'em," Squirrel pleaded.

Mercy laughed. "Too easy."

"She wanted it," Squirrel yelled in desperation.

Diesel sucked in a sharp breath and his whole body went solid. Before he knew it, he was next to Squirrel, his throat in his hand. "Say that again," he growled.

"She wanted it. Begged us."

D tightened his fingers and Squirrel coughed. D squeezed harder and Squirrel's mouth opened and closed like a fish out of water. His face turned a deep shade of purple, sort of like Jazz and Kiki's after they'd been beaten the fuck up.

Mercy murmured, "D."

Diesel blinked, took a breath, then released Squirrel's neck, who coughed as his coloring slowly went back to normal.

"Break any of his fingers yet? Jazz had broken fingers. Broken wrists. Broken arm. Only right to give him the same treatment. Both had broken ribs, too."

"C'mon, man," Squirrel whispered roughly. "Used to be a brother."

"The fuck you were. You were a prospect an' a fuckin' shitty one at that. Disrespectin' our women. No *brother* disrespects our women. Got me?" When Squirrel didn't respond, D bent over and screamed in his face, "*Got me*?"

"Yeah," he finally squeaked.

"Where's Black Jack?"

"Dunno. Already told 'im that."

"Too bad," D said, then turned and strode back to Walker, who was now leaning against the warehouse wall, one leg cocked, his foot flat against the wall, arms crossed over his chest, watching the whole thing without emotion.

Mercy might be a scary mofo, but Walker could be as cold as a glacier. Unreadable. He had a poker face like D had never seen before. And that was scary in its own way. It was always hard to get a read on him because he only showed you what he wanted you to see. And sometimes that wasn't even real.

"Steel and Ryder's on the NFL bitch since Mercy was needed here," Walker told him.

"Hunter an' Brick?" D asked, not taking his eyes off Mercy doing his thing with Squirrel.

Both of them ignored the prospect's screaming, crying and begging as Mercy played with him. And that's what the man was doing, playing. He wasn't even getting serious yet.

"En route so the second we get a bead on Black Jack, we can roll out."

D nodded. "Want that fucker in the worst way."

"Hear ya, brother. Gonna get 'im." Walker twisted his head D's direction. "Again, how far do you want Mercy to take this?"

D ignored Walker's question. He wasn't ready to answer that. He knew the answer; he just didn't want it set in concrete yet. He wanted to see how this played out first.

He approached Squirrel again and Mercy took a step back from what he was doing, which was carving the ex-prospect's name into his forehead with a knife.

"Didn't hear a location yet, Squirrel dick. Gonna hold out for someone who shows you no loyalty?" D asked.

"Got loyalty," Squirrel groaned, blinking quickly as blood ran down his face into his eyes. His head fell forward when Mercy released him.

"Fuckin' Warriors got zero loyalty." D made two fists and shoved them in front of Squirrel's face. "See that?"

The prospect didn't lift his head. Instead, he stared at the floor, his chest heaving from the pain he was in.

"Asshole, see what I got on my knuckles?" D asked again. His eyes flicked to Mercy and he gave the man a slight nod. Mercy stepped up behind Squirrel, grabbed the prospect's hair and ripped his head up.

"Look, motherfucker, the man's talkin' to you," Mercy demanded in a hard as steel voice.

Squirrel looked at D's fists.

"If you can fuckin' read, what's that say?" D asked.

"Dirty Angel," Squirrel croaked.

"Loyalty. Brotherhood. Family. That's what it says." D's nostrils flared as he looked at the piece of shit that destroyed Jazz and nearly destroyed Kiki. "Think you need to see it closer." And with that, D hauled off and slammed the fist that said "dirty" into Squirrel's face, not only knocking the chair over but knocking the rapist out. He stared at the Warriors' fallen prospect for a good minute before lifting his gaze to Mercy.

"When he comes 'round, do watcha gotta do to get info. Then you know what to do after. Got me?"

Mercy considered D for a moment, then nodded. "Got you."

"He gives up a location, I'll be in my office." D gave Mercy a chin lift before turning away.

As he walked out of the portion of the warehouse where Squirrel was being held, he gave Walker a chin lift, too. Then he went into his office, shut the door, and settled into his office chair to wait.

Jewel flipped over once again and punched the pillow attempting to reshape it to a more comfortable position. Like that was going to work.

It wasn't the pillow making her toss and turn, it was the fact that D wasn't home, wasn't in her bed yet and it was... She twisted her neck to read the digital numbers on her clock radio by her bed. Three in the morning.

She had no reason to worry about the man. He'd lived almost thirty-three years without her worrying. He was definitely able to take care of himself. But something made her gut churn. A feeling. Women's instinct. Something.

She should text him.

Fuck. That would break rule number one: *no naggin'*. He'd probably see her texting him at that ungodly hour as just that. Even though it wasn't. It was her caring about him.

She flipped again, this time onto her back with a sigh and suddenly she pictured him fucking some other woman in the women's bathroom at church. Her heart squeezed and her stomach did another churn.

He wouldn't.

He couldn't.

She didn't want to be that type of woman who couldn't trust her man not to fall into some other woman's pussy. Even though it really wasn't clear whether he was officially "her man."

Even so, he'd certainly had a long list of nameless pussy. A long, long, *long* list.

She reminded herself that he'd said he had business to take care of. Whether club business or In the Shadows Security business, she didn't know. And if she asked, he probably wouldn't tell her anyway.

Jesus, why did she have to go and fall in love with such a stubborn, domineering biker?

She heard the lock of her front door click, the door open and shut, his heavy footsteps, and then he was there, taking up a lot of space in her bedroom.

Looking at him, she answered her own question.

Because he was D that's why.

She'd known him forever. And wanted him for almost as long.

As she watched him move around the room in the dark, she heard him undressing. His heavy boots dropping to the floor, the whisper of leather as he slipped his cut off and threw it aside. And then the jingle of his keys in his pocket and the chain on his wallet, as his jeans fell to the floor.

She knew in the morning, wherever he shed his clothes, they would remain. Though, it was a small price to pay to have him come to her every night.

The side of the bed dipped low as he climbed in and rolled into her. "Baby," he murmured close to her ear.

She rolled onto her side to face him. "Yeah?"

"Home," he said simply.

"Yeah, kind of figured that out," she said with a smile that he probably couldn't see.

"Wanted me to wake you up," he reminded her.

"Yeah," she breathed.

"Still plastered?" he asked.

"No."

"Good."

"Why's that?"

"Want you to remember what I do to you."

"How about what I do to you?"

"That, too," he agreed.

Her smile widened. "Get your business taken care of?"

For a long moment, she only heard his breathing. Finally, he grunted, "No."

"Late night for nothing, then?"

"No. Got somethin', just not enough," he answered.

"Sorry," she whispered and reached out to touch his face. He had thick stubble along his jaw and cheeks. "Need a shave."

He grunted again. She wasn't sure if he agreed or disagreed.

He flattened his palm along her belly and moved it down until he cupped her mound. "New rule."

Oh shit. "Do I get a vote?"

"Nope." His finger slipped between her folds and he gently stroked her from one end to the other. "No shavin'."

"What?"

"No shavin'. My pussy now. Hate it lookin' like a little girl."

"You think I look like a little girl?"

He grunted. That was definitely a yes grunt.

"So, no shaving at all?" she asked, surprised.

"Do whatcha gotta do, but not everything."

"Ah, got it. Just do a little decorating."

He shifted against her and slipped two fingers inside her, curving them as he worked her. Her eyelids lowered as he hit *the spot*.

"Wet already," he grumbled.

"Always ready for you," she whispered.

His hand stopped moving for a few seconds and he said nothing, then he started moving his fingers in and out of her.

He pressed his mouth to her ear. "Gonna fuck your ass."

Her body jerked. "Now?" she squeaked.

"Not now. Soon."

"Do I get a vote on *that*?"

"Nope."

"D, you're not real... *small*."

"Yeah."

Yeah.

Jesus. "Can I at least campaign on that subject first?"

His body shook against hers. Did he think she was joking? "I'll consider your request for campaignin'."

"Well, aren't you generous for... *Ah... fuck*."

His fingers fucked her harder and faster, making her lose her thoughts, her breath, and her hips shot off the bed a few seconds later when her first orgasm of the early morning hit her.

"You were sayin'?" he asked, his voice deep and lower than normal.

"I... don't remember."

"Right." He moved over her. "Gettin' my dick now."

"Kind of figured that."

"Not gonna give me lip on that."

Hell no, she wasn't. She had been waiting for it all night. "About time," she breathed as he pressed the head of his cock to her entrance.

Before he took it any further, he took her mouth, sweeping his tongue through it once, twice, and once more while she squirmed beneath him. He had the control, though, and avoided her impaling herself on him.

He had barely lifted his mouth from hers when he asked, “Which?”

Anybody else wouldn’t understand what he was asking. But she knew. He wanted to know if he should bring his beast and fuck her hard, fast and furious. Or if she wanted him slow and gentle, letting them draw it out for as long as possible.

She knew exactly what she craved. “Beast.”

“Got it, baby.”

Then he brought his beast.

Chapter Twelve

HAWK LEANED over the bar and murmured to Zak, "We need to do this an' soon. Tired of that fucker."

"Hear ya." Z looked over at Diesel who sat to his right. "Didn't wanna do shit until after the weddin'. Weddin's over."

"Right," Diesel grunted.

"Ace on board?" Z asked Hawk.

"Yeah."

"Jag an' Dex are, too."

"Not up to just us, though," Hawk started. "By-laws state we gotta write up some writ of impeachment or some such shit. Can get Kiki to do that, but need to be brought up at a church meetin' before the whole club. Says we can't do it in an executive meetin'."

"She read the by-laws?" Z asked, surprised.

"Yeah. Asked her to. Wanna make sure when we do it, it sticks."

"Right," D grunted.

"Could do that or just wait an' vote Z back in when Pierce's term's up."

"Shit would be less messy that way," D suggested. "Also gotta decide if we're strippin' 'im of his colors."

All three of them looked at each other. No one wanted to do that if it wasn't completely necessary. But that's what they had to figure out.

Whether they needed Pierce out or just put in his place. His place being just a member and no longer the acting prez.

"Think the membership would want 'im kicked out?" Zak asked.

"Dunno," Hawk said. "Know Jag does. 'Specially after that shit went down with sendin' Ivy into Dirty Dick's for intel. Wasn't his place to decide that shit an' then keep it from us."

"Right," D grunted. He lifted his beer bottle to his lips and took a long pull.

Hawk continued, "Just need two-thirds of us to agree to oust him."

"No problem gettin' those numbers," D informed his brother.

"Also, gotta give 'im a heads up," Hawk added.

"What the fuck? Why?" D slammed his bottle down on the bar top.

Hawk shrugged. "Keeks said he needs the chance to defend himself. In the by-laws."

"Lemme just say, saw him eyeballin' Kelsea at Z's weddin'. Didn't like it. Wanna know what that shit's about. Could be more ammo against the fucker in gettin' 'im outta the head spot."

Hawk stared at his brother. "Didn't say anythin'."

No, D didn't. He wanted to do a little investigating first. He just hadn't had the chance.

Maybe he needed one of the women to take Kelsea aside and ask her if Pierce overstepped his boundaries as president with her. He tended to be one of the brothers who thought he had every right to any woman within the club.

"Want me or Kiki to talk to 'er?" Hawk asked.

D shook his head. "I'll get Jewelee since they're tight. Gonna talk to Annie, too."

Hawk nodded.

Between Annie being Kelsea's mother and also working part-time for Pierce at the gun shop, his aunt might have an idea if anything was going on between Pierce and Kelsea.

No matter what, Pierce had an ol' lady already—even though that didn't stop him from scoring snatch whenever he damn well pleased—and he was old enough to be Kelsea's father.

D couldn't imagine wanting such an immature piece of ass. But just because it wasn't his taste, didn't mean it wasn't for other men. Some liked to get them young. Kelsea might be in her mid-twenties but she acted so much younger.

"Jewelee gonna be on the back of your sled on the run Sunday?" Z asked, whacking D on the arm and smiling.

Fuck. He forgot about Sunday's ride that Jag, the club's Road Captain, set up. Only ol' ladies usually came along on the back of their man's bike. There were exceptions, but that wasn't the norm.

"Ain't my ol' lady," D grumbled.

"Livin' with her. Should make it official," Zak suggested.

"Ain't livin' with her an' ain't lookin' for a ball an' chain like you, Z."

"Ain't a bad thing," Z laughed. "Gettin' it on the regular, always good shit to eat at our place. Gettin' it on the regular," Z added again with a smirk.

"Like you ever had a problem gettin' it on the regular," Hawk said. "'Cept in prison. Don't want it on the regular in there."

"Fuck no. My ass went in a virgin an' made sure it came out one, too."

Hawk snorted.

Jag sidled up to them. "Came out with thick callouses on his palm, though."

"Take a fuckin' callous over a prison boyfriend any day," Z said, fake punching Jag.

"Hear you on that, brother," Jag answered, lifting his fists and tossing a couple fake punches back.

Jag then turned to D. "Bringin' Jewelee Sunday?"

Jesus. Not again. "Dunno."

"Ivy's comin', Kiki's comin', Soph's comin'." Jag leaned around D and shouted down to the other end of the bar. "Mama Bear's comin' too, right, Grizz?"

"What?" the older man yelled back.

"Mama Bear!" Jag shouted.

"What about the bitch?" Grizz bellowed.

D watched his brother's head drop. Hawk must have found something interesting on the floor behind the bar. Z snorted.

Jag released a groan before yelling again, "Mama comin' on the run Sunday?"

"For fuck's sake, Jag. Gonna ask the old fuck questions, walk the hell down there. Probably don't have his hearin' aid in," D muttered.

"Doesn't wear a hearin' aid," Jag returned.

"He fuckin' should, then," Hawk said, fighting back laughter. He then lifted his face to the ceiling and yelled, "Mama Bear comin' on the ride Sunday?"

Grizz had no problem hearing Hawk's booming voice. The old man swatted a gnarled hand in their direction. "Fuck no. Needs to stay in the kitchen where she belongs."

Jag eyeballed Hawk. "Mama in the kitchen?"

Hawk looked over his shoulder in that direction before saying, "Yeah."

"She comes out swingin' an iron skillet, I'm runnin'. Just sayin'," Jag warned.

"You an' me both, brother," Z said.

As a door opened, they all froze and looked at each other, wondering who to sacrifice first. Then, as one, they sighed in relief when they realized it was the back door to the private parking lot.

Slade walked in with Dex. Luckily, no one was carrying an iron skillet, instead Dex carried a black leather vest that clearly wasn't his since he was wearing his own colors.

"Man of the fuckin' hour," D grumbled.

Z shot a look his way. "Gonna be a good thing. 'Specially if we yank Pierce outta his seat."

"Get it. Not sure if I agree with the no prospectin' thing," D clarified.

"Right. Still waited 'til votin' on him. Maybe he didn't have to do grunt work, but he still had to wait."

"Didn't think he was in a rush to patch in anyway," Jag added.

"Yeah, was on the fence," Z said.

D cocked a brow at Zak. "An' now he's not?"

Z shrugged. "Kept on 'im."

Hawk shrugged, too. "Need some more solid members, brother. Know that."

D grunted his response and turned back to his beer when Slade and Dex joined them.

"Got 'im set up?" Z asked Dex.

D's cousin nodded. "Yeah. You gonna be inside?"

Z gave Dex a look. "Know I can't. Ain't on the board. Gonna wait out here. Chicken Hawk will catch me up after."

Dex leaned closer to the group and said in a low voice, "We doin' a coup?"

"A fuckin' what?" D asked.

"A coup. Watch the fuckin' news, D."

D scowled in Dex's direction.

"Hell, with your crew, you should know what that is, they all probably took part in that kinda shit," Z said. "Overthrowin' governments an' shit. You gotta good nose for sniffin' out badass motherfuckers to be on your *crew*."

D ignored him. "We gonna do this?" he asked no one in particular.

"Where's Ace?" Dex asked.

Hawk jerked his chin toward the meeting room. "In talkin' with Pierce."

D pushed away from the bar. "Then let's fuckin' get this done."

"D's gotta hurry up an' get home to Jewel. Big man went down hard," Dex said behind him.

D stopped his roll and spun on his boot. "Facin' you now, *Dexter*. Gonna repeat that?"

Dex lifted his palms up in surrender, laughing. "No harm, no foul, cuz. Just bustin'. Never thought I'd see the day my cousin got caught."

"Ain't caught," D grumbled.

Hawk pushed past Dex and whacked him on the back. "Good thing you're blood, dickhead. Otherwise, D would've had you flat on your ass before you knew what hit you."

Hawk moved into the meeting room. The rest of them followed, including Slade, their about-to-be newest patched member.

D wasn't sure if he was one hundred percent on board with that motion. The man hadn't been around long enough to get a good read on him. Since the *Dogs & Hogs* event, the guy came and went to club functions as he pleased. But Z and Hawk decided the man didn't have to prospect and do his time like any other recruit.

Why? Because he jumped in to save some of the women at the event when the Warriors tried to steal the donations Kiki earned for the charity. But any man who had a set of balls on him should've done the same. D didn't think that should give him a pass.

Most of the DAMC prospects were around at least a year before they'd even considered patching the guy in. During that time, they put the recruit through hell to make sure he wanted it bad enough.

Some of them washed out, some didn't. Like Abe aka Linc. And he figured Moose would go the distance, too.

Rooster he wasn't sure about and he'd been around the longest. He had gone from hang-around to prospect and that's where he got stuck. No one wanted him as a brother as of yet. The guy could be a bit of a whiny bitch sometimes.

Then there was Weasel. Another fuck up. Jesus. They needed better recruits.

D took his place at the table, ignoring Pierce's chin lift to him. He sat to the right of his pop, who sat to Pierce's right. Jag tended to pick a spot as far from Pierce as he could during the meetings, which was usually at the other end of the table. Ever since Jag had to drag Ivy out of Dirty Dick's and away from the Knights, he hadn't wanted to go near Pierce or he might be tempted to take the guy out.

They all agreed that Pierce never should've let Ivy go into their territory by herself. And that was the last straw with most of them. The president should've discussed it with the board first and brought it to a vote. He didn't. He and Ivy went behind all of their backs. And that created even more bad blood than there was previously.

Now, D needed to dig around to find out why the fuck the almost fifty-year-old man was staring down Kelsea at the wedding when she was dancing with a Dark Knight.

Shit was just not right with that and it bugged the hell out of D.

Maybe he needed to call Pierce out on it.

But the first order of business Pierce brought up was patching in Slade. The vote went as expected and no one, even Pierce, had a problem with making the guy a member. D's "aye" vote was done with reservation. If everyone else thought he'd be an asset then fine, he'd agree.

But D would keep an eye on him.

Plus, he could always dig around in the guy's past, if needed. As long as he didn't cause any shit, D would let him be. Once Dex handed Slade his cut with all his rockers and patches, he paid his dues to Ace, who was the treasurer, and then walked out the door to go have a drink with Zak.

After the door closed behind the newest brother, Pierce's gaze landed on him. "Got any news with the Warriors?"

D wondered if he should give the info he had or keep it to himself. He worried his brother might go ballistic when he found out D had Squirrel in his control and hadn't included him in the "questioning."

"Squirrel went to ground. Got a bead on him, then he just went ghost. Knows we're lookin' for 'im. Think he got scared when he knew we had his location. Doubt he's got the balls to show up 'round here again," D said and decided to leave it at that. He was only twisting the truth a little, because Squirrel definitely went *in* the ground and he had permanently disappeared. And it was certainly true he wouldn't be showing up again.

"Black Jack?" Hawk asked, his eyes steady on D, watching him closely.

D kept his face as blank as possible. "My crew heard a bit of chatter. Sniffin' his ass out."

"Want in, brother, if you get 'im. Squirrel, too," Hawk said.

Right. And that's why he wasn't sharing the truth with his brother. The less people involved in dealing with Squirrel and Black Jack, the better.

"It's possible Warriors took Squirrel out an' that's why he went ghost. Prospect's expendable. Hard to justify it with a patched member, but Squirrel dick? Don't need an asshole like that hangin' 'round when they know we're huntin' him down."

"We couldn't be so lucky that they'd take out one of their own," Ace grumbled next to him.

D shrugged and looked at his pop. "Could happen. Might be a bunch of stupid fucks, but sometimes they need to clean up their trash, too."

"Keep on it," Pierce ordered, which pissed D the fuck off since he did *not* need Pierce giving him orders. Not only on this issue but any issue. There was no way D was giving up the search for Black Jack and Pierce should know that. Hell, everyone else at the table knew better than that. That order was completely unnecessary. The fucker was just trying to get under D's skin. Which wasn't hard when it came to Pierce.

So D just grunted his response, letting Pierce take that answer as he wanted.

"Anybody else got anythin' on the Warriors?" Pierce asked.

Nobody else did.

"All right then, Jag. Sunday's run. Got that bitch all set up?"

Jag shot Pierce a look. "Yep. All set."

Pierce's gaze dropped back on D. "Wanna claim Jewel today before Sunday's ride?"

All eyes turned his direction.

"Nope."

"Just some fender fluff, then."

D's spine straightened and his eyes slid to Pierce's and held. "Yeah, fender fluff," he repeated in a mutter. Ace's hand dropped to D's arm below the table, which was the only thing stopping D from leaping across the table and throat punching the motherfucker until that smirk on his face disappeared.

"Which of your cum buckets is ridin' with you Sunday?"

Pierce was on his feet in a flash, his chair shoved back, his fists planted on the table as he leaned toward D.

Ace jumped to his feet as did Jag and Hawk.

"Boys," Ace warned in a low and quiet voice. "No reason to get in a tangle over pussy."

D cocked a brow at Pierce, making his challenge clear. "Wanna come at me?"

Pierce's gaze swept the table, then he said, "Feelin' a little outnumbered here. Will let it go this time, brother. Next time..." He let the last hang.

"Next time," D agreed. He glanced around the table. "We done here?"

"Motion to adjourn," Dex yelled.

"Second," Jag added.

Pierce sat down in his chair at the head of the table before asking, "All in favor?"

"Ayes," rose around the room.

"Gettin' the fuck outta here," D muttered to his father.

"Get gone. Go cool off. I'll keep Pierce here for a few," Ace said quietly.

"You do that," D muttered then caught Hawk's gaze and jerked his chin toward the door. D pushed to his feet and Hawk followed him out, Dex and Jag trailing just behind his brother.

"Bar," D grunted and headed through the double swinging doors of the commercial kitchen that sat between the clubhouse and The Iron Horse Roadhouse. When he pushed out into the bar, the dead quiet hit him since it was still early morning on a weekday.

The four of them gathered at The Iron Horse's long, lacquered wooden bar and within a few seconds, Zak came through the kitchen doors to join them.

"What the fuck happened in there?" Z asked, slipping behind the bar to grab a pop from the cooler.

"Just D bein' a little prickly over nothin'," Hawk answered, eyeballing Diesel.

"Ain't over nothin'," D grumbled.

"Fender fluff's nothin'," Hawk answered. "Ain't a bad term, D, you know that. Just hit you the wrong way. Any bitch on the back of a bike who ain't an ol' lady is considered that. Nothin' new."

"Never thought I'd see the day D was makin' a fuss over a b—" Jag's words stopped abruptly as he rethought them. "Woman," Jag corrected, wearing a smirk. "'Specially my fuckin' sister."

D ignored Jag.

Jewel's brother continued, "Believe me, if I thought that fucker was insultin' Jewel, I'd have been the first to introduce him to my fist. Gladly."

"Right," D grunted.

"So why we all in here for this impromptu meetin'?" Dex asked, ducking behind the bar and grabbing a can of Coke for himself.

"Gonna head out to the farm later, talk to Annie. Bringin' Jewelee to take Kelsea aside since they're close. See if we can get what's goin' on between Kels an' Pierce, if anything. If there is, more fuel for the fire to get his fuckin' ass out."

"We gonna do the writ? Or we gonna wait until his term's up? Let's decide that first," Hawk suggested.

"I'm up for gettin' his ass out ASAP," Jag said.

"Right. But again, might be a bit messy instead of just waitin' for the annual vote," Hawk answered.

"Gotta wait until January for that. Wanna wait that long?" Jag asked, looking a bit annoyed.

"Been president since Z went to prison. Had him at the head of the table for the last decade. What's another few fuckin' months? Might give us time to convince all of the brothers to vote Z back in an' Pierce out."

"Still wanna see what the fuck's goin' on with Kelsea an' him. I'll decide after that," D insisted.

"You do that, then we can go from there. If it's shit he shouldn't be doin' then we can kick his ass out an' turn our back on 'im," Hawk said.

"Strippin' his colors ain't just takin' his cut," Dex reminded them.

They were all well aware of what stripping his colors meant. It involved not only taking his cut and pulling his membership, it meant something would have to be done about all his DAMC tattoos. Because once they turned their backs on him, he was no longer DAMC and everything that once was had to be wiped clean. And those colors inked into his skin needed to be covered or removed in one way or another.

Plus, they needed to make decisions when it came to Shadow Valley Gun Shop and the gun range. Pierce managed it but didn't own it one hundred percent. Club funds had started the business, which was profitable and made the club a good amount of scratch.

What a fucking mess, D thought. He really didn't want to get into all of this now, not with the search for Black Jack still in full swing and trying to make sure everyone was safe from the Shadow Warriors. Because he predicted the next hit from them was coming soon.

In the last few months, things had been escalating with them. So he didn't expect the nomads to quietly ride off and never be heard from again.

D snorted. It would be way too easy. And when was shit ever easy?

"Want anyone to go with you?" Z asked.

"Nope. Takin' Jewelee. Good 'nough."

"When you goin'?" Hawk asked. "I'll give Pop a heads up."

"Later. Soon as Jewelee's done at the shop."

"Might wanna let her know first," Hawk said, amusement flashing in his eyes.

"Ain't whipped like you, brother."

Hawk threw his head back and laughed. "So you think."

Diesel grunted and headed out of the bar, striding through the kitchen before his blood pressure rose again.

Chapter Thirteen

DIESEL WATCHED his aunt pace across her small kitchen. She and Kelsea lived in one of the ten cabins that were situated behind his parents' farmhouse. The small farm had originally belonged to his grandfather, Doc. But since Doc was doing life at SCI Greene for murder, Ace and Janice had moved into the main house to take care of both the farm and D's cranky grandmother, Lonnie.

Ace's sisters, Annie and Allie, lived in two of the cabins so they could be close and help Janice take care of the crotchety old woman. D's grandmother certainly didn't make life easy on any of them.

Even though the older woman had lived the MC lifestyle being married to Doc, once D's grandfather got tossed into prison, the woman didn't want anything to do with the club or bikers. And since her son was a biker and so were her grandsons, it sort of made things uncomfortable when it came to holiday get-togethers since all she did was bitch about the MC. D and Hawk usually tried to find an excuse not to come to the farm at all. Unfortunately, Ace was stuck taking care of his mother, but because of that, he spent a lot of time at the pawn shop. More time than was necessary to run the business and D didn't blame him. He'd want to escape, too.

If it was up to Diesel, he'd stick his grandmother in a home and wash his hands of her. But D's mother, Janice, had the patience of a saint, so Lonnie still lived with them and probably would until the day she died.

If she didn't kill them all first.

Most of the cabins on the property were rented out long term since they were pretty decently sized. Ace had even offered one of them to Diesel so he could move out of church. He didn't accept since he wasn't sure if he wanted to be tied down to anything more than a room with a bathroom like he had now. Even if it *was* a shithole. And with his room at church, he could drink as much as he wanted and just head upstairs when he was done. He could raid the kitchen for grub when he was hungry and, even better, he could get one of the sweet butts to clean up his room, scrub his toilet, and do his laundry.

Out on the farm, he'd have to find someone else to do it. Someone would be needed to pick up his shit and make sure he had food. And that most likely meant having a woman around. Like a house mouse.

Or Jewel.

Even though the cabins were a good size, he didn't feel like sharing the space with a house mouse. Or anyone, period.

It was bad enough he was climbing in Jewel's bed every night. Even the thought of that little bit of commitment made his skin crawl. Though, once he was in bed with her, that uncomfortable feeling quickly disappeared.

And by morning, the opposite happened... He found himself not wanting to leave. But he did.

He wondered how the talk between Jewel and Kelsea was going. As soon as they arrived earlier, Jewelee locked her and his cousin in the bedroom so they could talk privately.

But now, D watched his aunt pace, which made him suspicious.

"So, no problems with workin' at the shop? Know Pierce can be handsy an' shit, Annie. Just wanna make sure he ain't doin' nothin' to you that you don't want done."

Annie paused in her pacing and turned her head his direction, her brown eyes bugged out. "Diesel, really... I'm not sure I want to talk about this with my nephew."

"Just tryin' to look out for you an' Kelsea."

"I get that, but still..." She stopped in front of the kitchen sink and stared out of the window. Since it was dark outside, there wasn't anything to see. But her face was clearly reflected in the glass.

That reflection showed that something was bothering his aunt and he needed to get to the bottom of it.

"Anythin' goin' on between him an' Kelsea that you know of?"

"What?" she whispered and turned to face him, her face paler than normal and showing a look of shock. "Why would you ask that?"

"Wanna make sure he ain't doin' shit to her, either."

"He wouldn't... he couldn't..."

Her insistence that Pierce wouldn't or couldn't didn't make any sense. The man thought he was God's gift to women and Kelsea was a woman. A young one, but still... "Why not?"

"Oh my God, D." Annie covered her mouth with a shaky hand, closed her eyes and then turned away again. This time he couldn't watch her face in the window since she stared down into the sink instead.

D scowled at his aunt's back. "What?"

When he didn't get an answer, his heart began to thump. What the fuck was going on?

"Annie, what?" he barked. Any patience he'd held onto was now gone.

"I... I always thought this would stay a secret..."

Diesel pushed off from where he'd been leaning against the wall and strode over to Annie. "What?"

When she still didn't answer him, he grabbed her arm and gave her a shake to snap her out of wherever she was stuck in her head.

"Annie."

She turned slowly and faced D, her face now as white as a sheet. "Pierce is..." She closed her eyes for a moment and when she opened them, she seemed even more uneasy. "Kelsea's father," she finished in a whisper.

His head jerked back and he dropped his hand, stepping quickly away from his aunt, as what she just revealed sunk in. Then it hit him. This complicated everything. Even more than it already was. "Jesus fuckin' Christ," he muttered. Suddenly, it hit him even harder. "Did Pierce force you?"

"Force me?"

Fuck. "To have sex."

"No."

Relief flooded through D because he knew the club president had an issue with being pushy with DAMC women in the past. And his aunt worked part-time for the asshole at the gun shop. He couldn't imagine that Annie would work for him if he'd forced himself on her. That wouldn't make sense.

But then, life could be fucking strange and things didn't always make sense.

"He got no idea?"

Again, Annie didn't answer him.

"Annie, fuckin' talk to me. Pierce know?"

"No."

"Sure?"

Eyes wide, Annie whispered, "You can't tell him."

Jesus Fuckin' Christ. D was definitely not telling him. But now that he knew that information, it made more sense why Pierce was watching Kelsea when she danced with a Knight. But that would be only if he knew.

Or suspected.

"Why'd you keep it from 'im?"

"For God's sake, Diesel, it's Pierce, that's why. I was young and stupid. I thought... *Shit.* I don't even want to admit to what I thought." She waved a hand. "We hooked up a few times, especially when we were partying heavily all those years ago. The club was a lot crazier back then."

"Nothin' happened since then." It wasn't a question. He wanted, no needed, for her to confirm that.

Once again, Annie stayed quiet.

D scrubbed his palm over his short hair. This was not good. Her silence revealed that Annie was still hooking up with Pierce on the side. And with Kelsea being Pierce's daughter...

"He ever ask you 'bout Kels?"

"Yes."

"An' you denied it." Again, not a question; in his gut, he already knew the answer.

"Yes."

"Anybody else know? Ace?"

"No. Nobody knows. Not even Kelsea. That's why when you asked if..." She shook her head. Her worried eyes hit Diesel. "Do you think..."

Holy fuck. He hoped not. Again, his take on it was Pierce might suspect something. But hopefully Jewelee was making sure that Kelsea wasn't doing anything stupid like hooking up with Pierce without anyone knowing.

Even if Kels wasn't Pierce's daughter, it would still be a whole fucked up situation if her mom and her were both having sex with the same man and neither knew the other was doing it.

Jesus fuckin' Christ.

D could even see Pierce thinking that was funny because he was getting one over on both women. The fucker. D had no idea why Randi, Pierce's ol' lady, didn't kick his ass to the curb. Or just fucking shank him.

But, that wasn't his problem. His problem was making sure Kelsea wasn't partaking in things that would turn most people's stomach. Like his. Because the thought of that possible snafu just made D want to fucking puke.

"Still don't get why you kept it from both of 'em," D finally said.

"Once I got pregnant, I stopped partying and backed away from the club. I didn't really want Pierce having a say in raising her. And you know what it's like with my mother. She hates the club now and all you bikers. It was bad enough when I was a single mother but to be knocked up by a biker..." She shook her head. "I didn't need to add any more to my grief. Didn't, and still don't, need her judging Kelsea, either."

"Think the woman would be more understandin' since she was married to a fuckin' biker..."

"One that committed murder and mayhem," Annie stated, lifting a hand, then shaking her head. "Not a proud moment for her. She totally switched gears after all that shit went down."

"Right," D grunted.

"Even so, Pierce's ol' lady at the time would've stabbed me in my sleep if she found out I was carrying his baby. He always preferred the crazy ones."

That was true. He still did. That's why he didn't understand why Annie was still chasing the man's dick. And when he thought back, he never remembered his aunt being with anyone. Not once. Never married, never dated. Nothing.

She was in love with Pierce. Had to be. D could figure out no other explanation why she'd deal with him all these years. And keep it a secret.

This made him reconsider how they would need to handle Pierce's removal from the president's spot. He wasn't sure whether they'd impeach him or wait for the next club election, and then have to decide even if they'd go so far as turning their back on him and kicking his ass out of the club.

Fuck.

He had ties now. Blood ties.

"Ain't gonna tell Pierce. Ain't gonna tell Kelsea. Gonna leave that shit up to you, Annie. If she finds out, she might never forgive you for keepin' that shit from 'er."

Annie nodded, walked over to the small kitchen table and pulled out a chair. She slid onto the seat and dropped her head into her hands, her dark blonde hair falling over her face. "You'll have to tell me what Jewel finds out," she said, her voice muffled.

"Yeah."

"Even if it's bad," she added, without looking up.

"Yeah."

She groaned. "Then I'll need to find a solution if it is."

Fuck. "Yeah." He glanced toward the kitchen doorway. He needed to talk to Jewelee, to hear what she found out.

The possibilities were churning his gut. He pulled his cell from his back pocket and texted her. *Got news. How long?*

His phone dinged not even thirty seconds later. *Now?*

He slowly typed a message back. *Yeah. Out front.*

Ok was her answer.

He lifted his head from his phone. "Gonna go out an' talk to Jewelee. Will let you know."

Annie took a deep breath, then nodded.

With a last look at his aunt, who sat there looking wrecked, D turned and left the kitchen, strode through the front room and out the door.

He approached his sled, then began to pace. He needed a fucking cigarette and he hadn't smoked in over five years. He actually dreaded to hear what Jewel may reveal.

He had to stop thinking the worst.

If he couldn't have a smoke, then he needed a whiskey. Not one shot, not even ten shots. The whole fucking bottle.

He kept his eyes peeled to the front door and he jerked when Jewel finally stepped out.

Thank fuck. He couldn't take any more waiting.

She had her eyes on him as she approached. She wore a serious expression and that scared the fuck out of him.

"Talk," he barked.

She frowned. "Jeez, D. Cool your jets."

"Woman. This is serious shit."

She looked up at him in surprise. "Why? What now?"

"Tell me first," he insisted.

"She's not doing Pierce, thankfully. Actually, the idea grossed her out. Hell, it grossed *me* out. Fucking perverted motherfucker."

Relief flooded D and he could breathe somewhat easier. "You sure?"

"Yeah, I mean Kelsea screws some questionable people, but I don't think she'd lie to me about that. Hell, she was doing that guy Slash from the Demons. I mean, if you want to talk about questionable..."

D's nostrils flared. "That his name? Slash?"

Jewel's mouth dropped open and her eyes rounded. She placed her palm flat on his stomach. "D, let that go. Don't cause enemies with the Demons because of Kels being stupid."

D blew out a breath. She was right. He had enough on his plate right now and so did the club. But if he ran into this Slash any time soon, he'd deal with it. Until then, he needed to deal with the Warriors and this whole Pierce thing.

It all made his fucking head hurt.

Then he had to deal with the woman who stood inches from him, looking good enough to eat.

But before he could do that, he needed to finish his business here and let Annie know that everything was okay. Or as okay as it was going to be with the secret she'd held for the past twenty-six years. D dreaded the day that secret ever broke. He had a feeling he and Hawk would have to hold Ace back from killing Pierce himself. And they would only do it for their pop's benefit, certainly not Pierce's.

"C'mere," he ordered Jewel.

She didn't even hesitate. When she stepped into him, he grabbed her and pulled her into his arms.

"Gotta tell you somethin'. Somethin' that's not for you or me to tell anyone else. But you gotta know 'cause you're close with Kels."

She blinked up at him. "What?"

He dropped his head down so he could lower his voice. "Pierce is Kelsea's pop."

Jewel jerked in his arms. "What?"

"Yeah."

"She doesn't know?"

"No."

"Pierce know?"

"Don't think so, but not sure. Annie never told 'im."

"That's fucked up."

"Yeah. See Kels gettin' too close with Pierce or him chasin' her, need to tell me right away."

"Holy fuck, D. The way Pierce is… he tries to get it from all of us."

D's spine snapped straight. "What're you sayin'?"

"He hits on all of us. Usually whenever no one else is watching." Her blue eyes blinked up at him in surprise. "You can't not know that."

"Know he's a fuckin' asshole. Know he'll be a dead man if he tries to touch you."

"How about Bella and Ivy? Diamond... Wouldn't doubt Sophie or Kiki, either. Hell, he hit on my mom, too. I saw it. So it wouldn't surprise me if he tries to get a piece of Kelsea if he hasn't tried already."

Blood rushed into D's ears and he thought his head was going to blow right off his shoulders. "None of you say shit 'bout it."

"Yeah, 'cause we're used to it, D. You gotta remember that he's been around us our whole lives. It's nothing new."

"How young were you when he first hit on you?" Jesus. He was about to burst a blood vessel and her answer may very well be the spark to cause it.

"D..."

He grabbed her chin and made her look at him. "How old?"

"You were right the first time. Question should be 'how young?'"

"Jesus fuck." He was going to beat the bastard to a bloody pulp. Then he was going to strip him of his cut and remove the club's colors off the man's back with an acetylene torch. Pittsburgh PD might find his toasted ass floating in the Allegheny River.

Jewel sighed. "Well, the good news is that Kels has resisted his so-called charms so far." She pressed her fingers into D's gut and he wrapped his hand around hers.

"Gotta tell Annie," he muttered.

"I'll wait here while you do that. Then you can take me home and fuck me."

"Right." He lowered his head until his lips were right above hers. "Fuckin' your ass tonight."

Her fingers curled against his stomach. "D..." she breathed.

He let her go and walked back into the cabin to deal with the shit. Then he was taking his woman home to fuck her until he could forget not only the Pierce business but the Warrior bullshit, too. At least for a little while.

Chapter Fourteen

JEWEL'S EYES popped open as soon as she awoke. Turning her head to glance at the clock radio on the nightstand, she was surprised to find it was only seven in the morning.

But D was wide awake. The reason, she knew, was because he was under the sheet, between her legs, sucking on her clit.

Well, *good morning* to her.

She wouldn't complain if she got woken up like that every day. Even if it was early on a Sunday morning.

She had planned on sleeping in since D was heading out on the club run later that morning. But if she had to suffer through being so rudely awakened, then she'd just catch some shut eye after he left.

When she lifted the sheet to peek at him, his eyes tipped to hers. She smiled and said, "Carry on," then dropped the sheet back in place.

Yeah, she'd have *no* problem waking up to that every morning. When the tip of his tongue circled her clit and the stubble on his cheeks scraped against her inner thighs, she dug her fingers into the sheet and threw her head back on the pillow while arching her back.

Oh yeah. Right there.

She wanted to tell him that, that he was hitting the perfect spot, and to not dare stop, but it was impossible. Instead, she hoped he could read her mind. Or at least her body's reaction to his wicked tongue movements.

When he rubbed his early morning beard growth over her delicate skin as well as her sensitive nub, she almost screamed *"Gooooal!"* like one of those soccer announcers on TV as she came.

This man could eat pussy. No doubt about it. And the intense orgasm she just had proved it.

She relaxed and gave herself a lazy smile in the mirror that hung above her. She loved that mirror now, but when she first moved in, she almost had her brother, Jag, rip it down since he was the one who put it up.

Because Ace certainly hadn't installed it.

Plus, she didn't want to think of her brother having sex with Ivy. Or think about him having sex at all.

That aside, she wasn't sure she wanted to wake up every morning and see herself with bed head, sleepy eyes and creases from her pillow on her face. But now...

Fuck yes, it needed to stay.

There was nothing more of a turn-on than watching Diesel fuck her in that mirror. Watching his muscular ass—which Sophie rightfully called the Eighth Wonder of the World—flex as he pumped in and out of her, whether fast or slow, always drove her over the edge.

It was her own personal porn that she couldn't get enough of.

She had seen it pumping plenty of other times when he was fucking some bitch in the church bathroom, but now that he was using those hips and ass to drive into her? It was even better. It was great. Spectacular. And...

"Woman," D murmured, the sheet now thrown off of his head, though he still remained on his stomach between her spread legs.

"Yeah," she breathed.

"Sore?"

Her relaxed state quickly disappeared. "If that's your way of asking if I want a second round back there after last night, then fuck no. You're going to have to give me time to recover," she huffed.

He pulled himself up and over her so they were face to face. His dark brown eyes stared into hers as he frowned. "Wasn't askin' to stick my dick in your ass, woman. Was worried you were sore an' hurtin'."

Oh.

Well, that was sort of sweet.

"I'm not sure we're going to do that again anytime soon," she added.

"Why?"

"Well, that thick, hard thing that's pressing into my thigh right now?"

His cock flexed against her leg.

"Yeah, that. If you haven't realized it yet, it's not *real* small."

"Got a monster cock."

Jewel snorted. "No, don't take it that far. It's not a python hanging between your legs but it isn't a garter snake, either. And I'm a delicate little flower back there," she added.

He dropped his head and pressed his face into her neck as his body shook.

She arched a brow. "You think that's funny?"

"Baby," he said against her skin, making her shiver. "Had no problem takin' my snake last night. You loved it. Wanted more. Begged. Pleaded. Came all over me."

"Yeah, okay. Well... Today I'm kind of regretting my decisions from last night."

His body shook some more.

Jesus, she loved it when he actually laughed. That *she* made him laugh. Even if it was only a slight chuckle that he hid against her throat.

"You'll get used to it," he finally grumbled.

"Not so sure about that," she told him.

"You will."

"Mmm," was her non-committal answer.

He lifted his head and shifted until the head of his cock pressed against her slick folds. "Ain't sore there," he declared.

"Nope. You've got a green light for that location." She smirked up at him. "Have at it." She reached under the sheet and grabbed a handful of his ass, encouraging him to take her.

"Need your mouth," he said, his low, gruff voice washing over her, making her tingle all over and her nipples bead hard.

"Then take it," she encouraged.

"Didn't ask your permission, woman," he reminded her. "Take what's mine."

Take what's mine.

She bit her bottom lip to hide the smile that wanted to break out across her face. "Then shut up and take it," she said again.

He crushed his mouth down on hers and he kissed her like he was starving. It wasn't gentle or loving. It was hot, wet, and forceful. Just how she liked it from him.

His tongue found hers and they tangled together. Playing, teasing and sparring.

A groan worked up from her chest and he swallowed it before it could escape. One hand gripped her throat, the other dug into her hair. Again, not even close to being gentle.

He was unleashing his beast. Her pussy throbbed violently for him, and he still barely pressed the head of his cock against her slit. He hadn't taken it any deeper, hadn't driven himself home yet.

And she so needed that. Needed him inside her. Completing her. Claiming her... at least in this bed, if nowhere else.

Time and patience, she told herself. That's what she needed to hold onto. Time and patience was also what she needed to give him.

She knew he'd be worth the wait.

With a tilt of his hips, he finally drove into her with a grunt.

Oh, yes, he was going to be worth the wait.

She whimpered into his mouth at his pounding, but he wouldn't let it go. His breath became hers and hers his.

His grip on her neck tightened for a moment before his fingers relaxed and moved down to twist a tightly beaded nipple. He rolled it hard and thumbed the tip until she squirmed beneath him, begging for more without needing to use words.

She dug her nails into his ass and he grunted into her mouth, fucking her even harder, faster. Her whole body jerked with each pound, but he still held her mouth. He wasn't letting go. His tongue moved lazily, so opposite to the rest of him. He tasted of her, something she was getting used to since he loved to go down on her. Which made her one lucky woman.

She'd be even luckier when she finally had him. All of him. His heart, his loyalty, his...

Bucking against him, she came as hard as he fucked her. The orgasm rushed through her like a tidal wave, her inner walls clenching around him tight.

And that's when he finally released her mouth with a hiss. He curled his body over her, trying to avoid crushing her as he relentlessly pounded her, sliding in and out of her wetness.

He pressed his forehead to hers. "Baby, gonna come again?" His voice was ragged as if he was having a hard time catching his breath.

He wasn't the only one.

"Wanna come, D," she whispered, trying to meet his gaze, but his eyes were squeezed shut as if he fought for control.

"Come, then," he growled. Slipping his hand between them, he circled her clit with his fingertips. And that wasn't gentle, either.

He could be gentle, but she rarely saw it from him. She only caught glimpses, brief moments before it was gone again. It was like he purposefully hid it away, buried it deep.

Like he was afraid to expose that side of himself.

"Coming," she cried out as she jerked against him.

He grunted and thrusted a few more times until he felt her fall and then joined her, spilling himself deep, giving her the only thing he was willing to give.

Which wasn't enough. Not for her.

Time and patience, she reminded herself once again.

What she was looking for was there. She just needed to draw it out.

THAT PATIENCE she kept telling herself she needed was being sorely tested at the moment. She'd made him coffee and now she leaned back against the counter, her arms crossed over her chest, watching him eyeball her.

They were at an impasse.

Jewel hadn't bothered to get dressed because her plan was to slide back into bed after he left and catch some more winks.

But now he stood there glaring at her like she was the one in the wrong.

"Comin' with me," he growled.

"That's the third time you've said that, but it doesn't change the fact that I'm not," she returned matter-of-factly.

His eyes narrowed even more, his expression hard. "No lip."

"I'm not giving you lip, D. And even if I was, tough shit."

"Jesus fuckin' Christ," he muttered. "All the ol' ladies are goin' on this run."

Jewel lifted a satin covered shoulder in a half shrug. "Yeah? And? Did my status change and someone forget to tell me?"

His mouth became an angry slash as he took a step closer, his eyes trying to burn a hole in her. "Don't push me, woman. Don't gotta be an ol' lady if you're invited."

She kept her face blank. "I didn't hear an invitation. I heard a demand," she stated. "And I'm not going as fender fluff." She tugged the sash on her robe tighter. "Sorry, not doing it."

"Ain't a bad thing."

Her eyebrows shot up her forehead. "Right. So you say."

"It ain't," he insisted.

"Are you trying to convince yourself or me?"

He moved another step closer until she could feel his heat through her satin robe. She put up a hand to keep him from coming any closer, as if that could stop him.

"I'm heading back to bed to catch up on some sleep, then I'll meet you later at church."

She knew why he wanted her to go. Because all the brothers who had an ol' lady or someone regular were bringing them along on this ride. She suspected he was going to get a bunch of shit if Jewel didn't come along since they were practically living together.

Or so everyone thought. Technically, he showed up every night. In reality, he had never left one personal thing behind at her place. Which was telling.

She was actually starting to wonder if her apartment had been turned into a state park, where everything you carried in with you, you carried back out, leaving no indication afterward that you were ever there.

And that was not what she wanted.

Sophie, Ivy and Kiki had also been on her about coming along on the run. Being D's regular piece earned her the right to ride on the back of his sled. *If* he wanted her there.

Surprisingly, for some reason he did.

But she wasn't going to agree to it unless she was officially his ol' lady. She'd already made that decision and she was sticking to her guns.

Too bad if Diesel didn't like it.

And there was no doubt that he didn't. He was making that quite clear.

If she had actually asked to go and he didn't want her on the run, there would be no discussion about it at all. He wouldn't *allow* it. And that stuck in her craw.

So, she was determined to be just as stubborn as him and hold out.

"Get dressed."

She sighed. "I'm going back to sleep, D." Then for good measure, she rubbed her eyes as if she was sleepy.

"Ain't sayin' it again," he muttered.

Dropping her arms, she plugged her hands on her hips. "Good."

"Wanna wait until you're my ol' lady to be on the back of my sled durin' a run, gonna be waitin' a long time."

She jerked her shoulders up. "Fine."

His head jerked back and his face got dark and stormy.

She'd had enough of this. She pushed away from the counter, but he blocked her. "Woman," he grumbled.

She looked up and squarely met his eyes. "D, unless you plan on dressing me yourself, then dragging me by my hair down the steps and physically putting me on your bike… I'm… not… going." She patted his stomach. "Now, go. Have a great time. See you later at church."

After verbally dismissing him, he simply blinked at her and she fought back a smile. Though, now would not be a good time for her to laugh at his frustration. Too many people were afraid of Diesel, not only due to his size, but his *don't-fuck-with-me* attitude, so he was rarely challenged.

Because of that, he had no idea what to do with her defiance.

She pinned her lips together, pushed past him, went to her room, slipped out of her robe and back into bed.

Then she waited for his next move.

She sighed in relief when a few minutes later, she heard her front door open and close, his bike roar to life, and him hit the throttle hard as he sped away.

Jewel smiled to herself and snuggled deeper into her bed.

"What the fuck's up your ass?" Hawk asked as they approached the lineup of bikes in the back parking lot at church.

Diesel's eyes slid to his brother, then away. They landed on Kiki as she waited near his brother's sled.

The club's attorney had integrated herself quickly and seamlessly into their biker lifestyle. She already had all the gear needed to be on this run since it was a cool, early fall day. And she even had her own custom brain bucket.

Hawk was definitely a lucky fucker since his woman looked not only hot in jeans and a leather jacket, but even more so when she wore her business wear, which usually included a tight blouse, a short skirt and high heels to show off her legs. And she was smart as fuck. Brains, looks, and loyalty, Hawk's woman had it all.

Diesel was taking the tail on this run and Hawk decided to ride toward the back along with him. Jag, as Road Captain, was taking lead.

And D's cousin Ivy, Jag's ol' lady, was standing near Sophie and Zak as the women talked. They were all looking his way. And so was his mother who stood by Ace toward the front of the line.

Fuck him.

They were all probably wondering why Jewel wasn't coming along. They all probably thought D didn't want her on the run. Probably thought he was being a complete asshole and excluding her. Which was far from the truth. But he wasn't going to explain himself.

"Think you're gettin' the evil eye from most of the women."

"Yeah," D grunted.

"Shoulda asked her," Hawk suggested.

Maybe that was his mistake, he didn't ask, he *told* her she was coming.

Even so, she needed to listen to him. Ol' lady or not.

She needed to understand she'd never become an ol' lady if she didn't obey her man.

D looked up the line of bikes. Almost everyone was here this morning. Even the prospects. The lineup included almost twenty bikes. Because of that, they'd need to keep a tight formation and run double.

Jag was good at organizing the runs and that's why he'd been unanimously voted in as Road Captain for the past few years. Grizz used to do it, but with his arthritis, bursitis and every other itis that ailed him, he and Mama Bear didn't always participate anymore.

But as much as the old man griped about Mama the other day, she was there, ready to ride. And so was Pierce's ol' lady, Randi.

The executive committee still needed to find the time to sit down and talk about ousting his ass. They needed a solid plan.

Without warning, his mother was standing next to him, giving him a look. D groaned silently. His gaze caught Hawk's, who was turning away to hide his laughter. Kiki just gave him a big smile, then turned away, too.

What the fuck.

"D..."

"Ma," he warned.

"Heard you're getting serious with Jewel..."

Jesus fuck.

"Heard wrong."

She lifted her brows like she didn't believe him. "Your father says your bike's in the pawn shop's lot every morning and has been for a while. Sounds serious to me."

"Ma," he warned again. He wasn't going to discuss his sex life with his mother. Over his mother's shoulder he spotted Ace lifting his arms and shrugging in his direction. A lot of help he was.

Jesus fuckin' Christ. Did the women sic his own mother on him?

"Jewel's a gem," she said then laughed at her own joke. "She'd be great for you to settle down with."

"Ma!" he barked.

But that did no good because she kept going, "You find the right woman and look what happens..." Janice waved an arm toward Hawk. "Look how happy your brother is."

"Pussy whipped," D said under his breath.

"What was that?"

"Nothin'. Ma, seriously, not havin' this conversation with you."

"I was just telling Ace now that Z's married and Sophie's pregnant, the next generation of Dirty Angels has begun. The seal has been broken."

He gave his mother a frown. Jesus. His mother thought the "seal" being broken meant everyone was going to start popping out kids.

"Not in the cards for me, Ma," D assured her.

"Bullshit, D. Jewel would make a great mother. And wife," she added. "Plus, she grew up in this lifestyle so she understands it. She's your perfect mate," she stated, then turned and walked away.

What the fuck. He didn't need a "mate." Perfect or otherwise. His mother had gone off the fucking deep end.

He'd never given her any indication that he would ever "settle down." Just the thought made his chest tight and his stomach churn.

Live free. Die free.

Women were clingers and nags. And he did not need that in his life.

Fuck no, he didn't.

Jesus fuck, they needed to get the hell out of there. He needed to feel the wind on his face and hear the roar of the sleds in his ears. He needed to think about nothing but the road ahead of him.

Keep it simple.

Fuck.

"Jag! Let's hit the fuckin' road," Diesel bellowed toward the head of the formation. What should be an enjoyable ride was already turning into a shit show and they hadn't even left the lot yet.

Just then, a vehicle came rounding the building into the lot. D twisted his head and noticed it was Jewel's. She must have come to her fucking senses.

Thank fuck.

She pulled her Jeep close to the lineup and as soon as it rolled to a stop, Diamond climbed out of the passenger side.

What the hell? Why was Diamond here?

As Slade broke away from a few of the other brothers, Jewel's sister rushed up to him and he snagged her waist, pulling her tight against him. She gave him a huge smile and giggled.

Diamond *giggled.*

What. The. Fuck.

His head spun toward Hawk. "Know 'bout this?"

Hawk shook his head. "No fuckin' clue."

"Not likin' this," D grumbled.

"Not sure you got a say," Hawk answered and mounted his sled, Kiki quickly climbing on behind him.

Jag yelled out, "Okay, now everyone's here, mount up, we're headin' out."

D turned his attention back to Jewel's four-by-four and waited for her to get out to join him.

She didn't. She sat in her Jeep with her head turned to watch her sister get on the back of Slade's sled.

The rumble of the engines and straight pipes filled the chilly air. D hadn't moved toward his yet.

"Comin', brother?" Hawk yelled over the noise.

He nodded but didn't move, nor did he look at his brother. His gaze was pinned on Jewel sitting in her jeep. He could only see the back of her head.

And still, he waited.

She was going to get out of her vehicle and join him any minute now. Especially since she had rousted herself from bed and saw all the women who were going on the run.

She'd want to join them. Join him.

For some fucking reason, she wasn't getting out of her Wrangler.

So, he waited longer.

Out of the corner of his eye, he saw Jag look his way in confusion. Then after a quick glance at Hawk, Jag lifted his hand and circled it. Giving his bike gas, he circled the lot and headed out, the line of bikes and their riders following him.

"Comin', D?" Hawk shouted again.

His gaze slid to his brother. "Yeah, I'll catch up," he shouted back. Hawk pulled his skull bandana up over his lower face, pulled down his goggles, gave him a chin lift, twisted his throttle, and then he, with his woman hugging his back, rolled out.

The parking lot now was deserted, the rumble of the Harleys fading more and more every second he didn't move.

He finally unfroze his feet and stalked to the driver's side of her Jeep, which was still running.

Jewel rolled her window down, her stomach churning as Diesel stared down at her, looking a bit grumpy.

"Ain't gettin' out," he grumbled.

"Nope. I'm not coming. Di called me last minute since her car had a flat. She told Slade she'd meet him here, so she asked if I could do her a favor and drop her off."

She knew it was going to be a bad idea for her to show up at church to drop off her sister, but Diamond had begged. Slade had asked her if she wanted to come along and she was excited about riding on the back of his bike.

And Slade was hot, so Jewel didn't blame her sister for being thrilled about the invitation. Plus, Diamond seriously needed to get laid, so Jewel hoped that would work out. If sleeping with Slade would take some of the sting out of Diamond, then he would become the club hero.

"Got outta bed an' came here for Diamond."

"Yes, because she's my sister and she needed my help." And the bitch needed to get laid so the world would be a better place again.

"Couldn't get outta fuckin' bed to come on the run with me."

Shit. Did she actually hurt his feelings? No. Couldn't be. That meant he actually had some. "I *was* out of bed, D. I went back to bed because I told you I'm not coming on the run with you. I made that clear."

"Woman," he growled.

"We already had this conversation. Now I'm heading back home."

"The fuck you are, woman. Dressed. Here. No reason not to go."

"Yes, I'm going to go as in *go home*."

Diesel closed his eyes for a moment, and if she leaned out of the window she was pretty sure she'd see his hands balled into fists.

She was pushing his buttons, she knew. But she was trying to make a point.

Most of the DAMC women fought against becoming ol' ladies and here she was, fighting to become one. Of course, she had to pick the most stubborn shit out of all of them to do that with.

But, now, there was no one else but Diesel for her and she doubted there would be again. The heart wanted what the heart wanted.

What a stupid fucking saying that was. But unfortunately it was true.

Only, she wished her heart had picked someone more easygoing. Less pigheaded. More loving. But then D wouldn't be D. He'd be totally different and she'd probably want nothing to do with him.

Diesel ripped open her car door and for a moment when he leaned into the Jeep, she thought he was going to physically pick her up and haul her over to his bike.

And she was certainly not dressed warm enough for a long bike run in this weather.

But instead, he turned the ignition key to off and yanked it out, tossing it onto her lap. With a hand gripping her upper arm firmly, he said, "Get on my sled."

If she had been smart, she should have just dropped Diamond off in the front lot of The Iron Horse and made her walk around back. D never would've known she was there. And then they wouldn't be in their second standoff of the day.

But it was too late for that. Even so, she was determined not to give in to his demands.

"No," Jewel said softly. She needed to stay strong.

Stick to your guns.

But, if she was honest with herself, there was really nothing more that she wanted but to cling to D's back as they went on a club run. She wanted to be on the back of his bike with her arms wrapped around him. But not in the capacity that he wanted her there...

As his regular piece, and not his ol' lady.

And to her there was a big difference. Maybe other women didn't care, Jewel did.

She wasn't asking for a ring; she wasn't asking for a wedding. She wasn't asking for a white picket fence. She only wanted Diesel to claim her as his. And not just when he was fucking her. She wanted to be claimed at the table.

And, for fuck's sake, she had no idea why this was so important to her.

It shouldn't be. In the real world, being an ol' lady meant nothing. Here, in her world—hell, *their* world—it meant everything. At least, to her.

It meant more to her than anyone would ever know or could understand.

And he needed to understand that, too.

"Woman," his chest heaved suddenly as if he was struggling to breath, "get on the back of my bike."

Jewel closed her eyes slowly, let the burn in her stomach subside and tried to control the quiver of her lower lip when she said, "I'm not your ol' lady, D."

She couldn't see it on his face but she could hear the anger mixed with what sounded like desperation in his voice. "Jesus fuckin' Christ, Jewel, get the fuck on my bike."

"Diesel, no. I'm not your ol' lady." This time she said it loudly, more firmly. She wasn't going to bend to his will, to be broken.

She sucked in air, trying to fight the instinct to just do what he said, to make it easy on herself. Make it easy on him. But she couldn't.

Because if she did, she lost. She would never get what she wanted from him.

No. *Needed.*

His words came rough, low, gravelly. "Last time, woman. Get—"

She snapped. "No, Diesel!" Her eyes popped open. "I'm not your *ol' lady*!"

His face turned hard, his eyes like coal, his jaw tight. He reached into the Jeep and grabbed her other arm.

When he started to drag her out of her seat, she shouted the first word that exploded through her head. "Beast!"

D froze, his nostrils flared, his eyes blinked slowly.

He released her so quickly it was like he had touched lava. He jerked himself two steps back, his chest rising and falling rapidly as he practically panted. A look Jewel didn't recognize crossed his face and he shook his head, as if to clear it.

Without another word, he stiffly spun on his heel and stalked to his bike. After swinging a leg over, he kicked it to a start and heeled the stand up. He never looked her direction again.

She watched him tear out of the lot, his Harley's engine roaring. The longer Jewel sat there, the more the sound drifted off until she could no longer hear him.

She needed to move. She needed to leave in case he came back angrier than ever.

She'd return later, when the run was over and everyone came back to party. He'd be cooled off by then.

Hopefully.

If not, she may very well be sleeping by herself tonight. And that was the last thing she wanted.

As much as she wanted Diesel, as much as she loved him, she really needed him to feel the same way.

Chapter Fifteen

JEWEL WAS HALFWAY up the steps to her apartment when her cell phone dinged.

She paused and read the text.

Yo! Diesel wiped out his sled. All fucked up. Askin 4 ya.

What the fuck!

Her heart raced as she reread the text. The only problem was she had no idea who sent it to her.

This Slade? she quickly texted back. She didn't have his number programmed into her phone yet. So, it would make sense that his would come up "unknown." And Diamond had been with him, so maybe she made him text her.

Her phone dinged again. *Yeah.*

Holy fuck. Her mind spun and she felt panic seep into her bones. She wondered how hurt he was.

Where, she texted back. Running down the steps, she rushed back to her car, fumbling with the key fob as she tried to unlock her door. Finally, the locks beeped and she jerked the door open and climbed in.

She still needed an address. Her phone dinged again.

Church was the one-word answer.

Fuck. If he was hurt, why didn't they take him to the hospital?

She turned the key in the ignition and her Jeep roared to life. After shoving the shifter into reverse, she texted, *how bad?* Because she needed to know.

Hurry was the only answer she got. With a shaking hand, she shoved the gearshift into first gear and popped the clutch, spinning the tires as she raced out of the pawn shop lot and headed back to church.

Within ten minutes, she was hauling ass through the front lot of The Iron Horse, around the side of the building and through the open gate to the back lot of the clubhouse. She slammed on the brakes and her Wrangler skidded to a stop.

What the hell? The lot was empty.

Not one bike, and a few empty vehicles still sat where they had been left earlier before the run. She shoved her Jeep into neutral and jammed her foot on the emergency brake.

Maybe they left and took him to the hospital. Which was something they probably should've done in the first place.

A chill ran through her. Something wasn't right.

She couldn't place what it was. Maybe someone had been left behind to give her an update and were waiting for her inside.

Though, they should have called or texted first. She picked up her phone and saw she didn't miss any calls or texts on the ride over.

When she glanced back up, she screamed. A head appeared in her window. One she didn't recognize.

Before she could hit the automatic door locks, her door flung open. "Diesel's ol' lady?"

What?

"You Diesel's ol' lady?"

Who the fuck was that? He wore no colors. Maybe he was a new hang-around? "Is he okay?"

"No. Needs you."

"How bad is he? Where's he at?"

"Lemme drive," the guy demanded.

What? "Uh, no." This guy was creeping her out. He looked like a biker, he talked like a biker, but he didn't wear a cut. He definitely wasn't DAMC. And hang-arounds weren't allowed at the club without a club member.

"Yeah, get out an' lemme drive."

What the hell was going on? "Who the fuck *are* you?"

"Get out!" the guy screamed, leaning into her vehicle.

Jewel smashed the clutch to the floor and before she could shove the Jeep into first gear, she was dragged out of the Jeep and thrown to the ground. She landed on her hands and knees on the pavement.

Holy fuck! This is what happened to Kiki!

When she tried to push to her feet, she flinched as something flew toward her head.

A boot, was her last thought, then everything went black.

DIESEL FOLLOWED the line of bikes back into the parking lot. One by one they parked and everyone dismounted. He shut his bike down then crab-walked it backward into an open spot between Hawk's and Zak's sleds and kicked the stand down.

After ripping the goggles off his head, he tugged his bandana down as he watched Kiki stand in front of his brother's bike stretching her legs and arching her back.

"Sore?" Hawk asked her.

Kiki rubbed her ass. "Ass hurts," she answered with a smile. Hawk let out a low chuckle.

D had a flashback from this morning. He and Jewel practically had the same conversation, though for quite a different reason.

His temper had cooled off twenty minutes into the run. And after an hour, his thoughts had cleared.

The second hour into the long ride through the back roads of southwestern Pennsylvania, reality had fucking hit him. By the third hour, he knew what he needed to do about Jewel.

And, fuck him, he had expected to clear his head on that ride, not complicate his life.

But that's exactly what happened.

The fourth hour made him anxious to return and find her ass, tell her what he decided and judge her reaction to what he had to say.

Things had to change, that was for sure.

Being at the back of the pack, he was subjected to watching his brothers riding with their women. Everyone seemed content and happy for the most part. Even Grizz and Mama Bear.

Hell, even Diamond and she was just fender fluff for the day. But D swore she was the one wearing the biggest smile out of everyone.

And the one time they stopped by the river, she and Slade had disappeared for a little while. The brother had probably gotten a quick head job in the woods.

Not that he blamed the man. Especially, if Di sucked cock half as good as her sister...

Diesel flipped up the flap on his saddle bag and pulled out his phone. He'd text Jewelee and let her know they were back since her Jeep wasn't in the lot yet.

When he turned on his phone, multiple messages dinged at him.

Jesus fuckin' Christ.

Someone was trying to get a hold of him. Hopefully, shit wasn't going down with his crew or that NFL douchebag that they babysat. He hit the message app and pulled up a long string of texts from Jewel.

Call me.

Call me soon. Important.

Call me right away.

Where r u?

Why arent u callin?

U need 2 fuckn call me.

Fuck! What the fuck was that about? He jabbed the Call button with his finger and put the phone to his ear.

The phone was answered on the first ring. But the voice on the other end of the line wasn't hers and the deep voice made him go solid and ice rush through his veins.

"Got your ol' lady."

Every vertebra snapped straight in his spine as his fingers tightened on his phone.

Jesus fuck. He sure hoped Jewelee was messing with him. But if she was, she was getting her ass beat because this was not fucking funny at all.

"Jewel ain't my ol' lady." At least, not yet.

"Sure she is. Heard a rumor, then Demons confirmed it."

Fucking Demons. Fucking Warriors.

D's mind spun. What the fuck was going on?

"Don't believe everythin' you hear," he growled.

"Right. So here's the deal. Got your ol' lady. Thinkin' 'bout fuckin' her up or fuckin' her... Or both." The man on the other end of the line laughed. "But I'd rather deal."

"Who the fuck is this?" D snarled into the phone. When he felt a presence next to him, he glanced up to see Hawk watching him carefully, his face a blank mask.

His brother cocked an eyebrow at him. D shook his head and lifted a *hold-on* finger.

"Tired of you lookin' for me, cocksucker. Tired of havin' to hide out. Tired of your bitch ass all together. Shit's gonna stop. Willin' to deal. An' now I got the wildcard to win this game."

"This fuckin' Black Jack?" he barked into the phone. D noticed the expression change on his brother's face and Hawk's head twisted quickly toward Kiki.

Kiki's eyes were wide and pinned on them, her face pale.

"Get inside church," Hawk ordered her. When she didn't move, he yelled, "Now!"

D turned his back on them; he needed to concentrate on what this fuckstick who had Jewel's phone was saying.

"See? That's the fuckin' problem. You know my name. You an' those spooks of yours have been tryin' to snag my ass like you did Squirrel's. Ain't likin' any of it. An' now you got the Knights on my ass, too."

"You're fuckin' dead," D muttered before he could stop himself.

"Yeah. Ain't gonna happen. Got your bitch. She's a sweet number, too. She as tight as that young one?"

D's jaw locked and he saw nothing but red. And it was Shadow Warrior blood that tinted his vision red, not to mention his fury.

If that fucker touched one hair on her head...

If he violated her in any way...

D tried to swallow but his Adam's apple jammed in his throat. His vision narrowed and he was back in that fucking house all over again.

Kiki. Jazz.

And now Jewel. Spread out naked over the floor, blood, bruises... broken. Both mind and body.

History couldn't be repeating itself.

It just couldn't.

If he found Jewel the way he found those women, he'd be destroyed. Shattered into a million fucking pieces, never to be put back together again.

He couldn't lose her. Not when he'd just decided to claim her not even an hour ago.

She was his. And only his.

And that sadistic fucker had her.

He needed to keep his shit together and not completely lose his mind or he wouldn't be able to function and find Jewel. He needed to find his woman and he needed to do it fast.

"So you wanna win this game. What game are we playin', asshole? What do you want?" It killed him to have to try to negotiate with this fuckwit.

Suddenly, he was surrounded by a bunch of brothers, all listening, all watching him carefully. No one saying a word. Dex, Jag, Zak, Hawk, Linc, Slade, Crow, Rig, Crash, Ace, Dawg, Nash, and even Pierce.

He glanced around and couldn't find any of the women. Not even Diamond. Thank fuck. Someone must have had sense enough to send them all inside to keep the drama at a minimum.

Last thing he needed was a bunch of women freaking the fuck out.

It was bad enough that he was freaking the fuck out. And he had to keep a lid on that.

"What do you want, asshole?" D shouted into the phone.

"Want the slate wiped clean. Want you to forget I ever existed. Want your spooks or shadows or whatever the fuck they are, off my fuckin' tail."

Diesel pushed through the crowd and walked away from them, hoping no one would follow. He headed to the other side of the lot.

"You gimme my woman an' you just want me to forget everythin' you did to the other two?"

"Bingo."

"Gotta get 'er back untouched." The hesitation on the other end of the phone made him suck in a breath. "You touch 'er, the deal ain't even on the table. Got me?"

No answer.

He repeated himself much louder and slower this time, "Touch 'er, you're dead. No deal. You fuckin' got me?"

Still no response. The ice that ran through his blood had turned to molten lava. "One hair. One bruise. Anythin'. You're done."

"She fuckin' didn't come with me willin', you asshole," Black Jack yelled into the phone. "Got a little banged up in the process."

Got a little banged up in the process.

His heart was thumping so hard, he thought the veins in his neck were going to bust out of his skin.

"Ain't bad, though."

Ain't bad, though.

Jesus fuckin' Christ.

He was going to kill the fucker. He was going to jam his hand into the man's chest and rip out his fucking heart. Then he was going shove it up the Warrior's ass.

"I agree to this, when do I get 'er back?" he growled into the phone.

"Once I get my guarantee, you get her back... soon as you can find 'er. Need a head start, motherfucker. Don't trust your ass not to take me out. Know all 'bout your so-called crew. I give you the location before I'm outta Dodge, then I'm toast. I ain't stupid."

Oh, yes, he was. Not only had he touched and damaged DAMC property, he had the balls to take D's woman. And that was fucking the stupidest move he could ever make.

The Warrior had every right not to trust D or his Shadows. Because there was no way Black Jack was going to walk the Earth after today.

He had already signed his fate with what he did to Kiki and Jazz. But now...

Now his fate was going to be so long and drawn out, he was going to beg for it to be over.

And D wasn't going to leave the room when Mercy did it. He was going to help.

"This the game? I gotta find her?" D cursed silently. He had nothing to go on except Jewel's cell phone, which he doubted Black Jack would leave behind. If the fucker had even a few working brain cells, he'd realized that's how D and his crew found him last time... by pinging Kiki's cell phone.

"Yeah. Like I said, need a head start. But didn't hear you agree to the terms."

D looked over his shoulder back toward the clubhouse. Night was moving in, so the day was starting to lose light. Everyone stood in a group, staring in his direction, waiting for word.

Hawk had a hand on Jag's arm, holding him back. He seemed the most agitated and for good reason.

"She need a doctor?" D needed to know. Because he figured as soon as he agreed to Black Jack's terms, the man would hang up and he'd have no further info.

"Maybe. Maybe not."

Asshole.

Black Jack continued, "Ain't playin' twenty questions. Agree or not? Don't agree, I'm takin' 'er with me."

"Gonna gimme a clue where to find 'er?"

"Yeah, only get one, though. Gonna text it to you once I'm far 'nough away. Then I'm gonna dump her phone. Ain't gonna find me with that. Ain't gonna find her with that, either."

"Gonna gimme a time when to 'spect the text?"

"Now you're askin' too much. Agree or not?"

Fuck him.

The fucker had his balls in a jam. He hated being this helpless. Jewel could be anywhere. They had been on the club run for over four hours. He had time to take her at least a state away.

"Agree. But if it takes me more than an hour to find her, deal's off."

"That's not the terms."

D closed his eyes and let the evening air fill his lungs, then he pushed it all back out in a rush. "Whatever, asshole. Make sure you text a decent fuckin' clue ASAP."

Black Jack laughed. "Fuckin' pussy makin' you weak, Diesel. Little bit of snatch makin' you agree to shit you'd never agree to before. She must be good. Now wishin' you didn't agree. Temptin' me. She'd prolly fight me as hard as that other one. Made it even better. Like 'em when they're a challenge. Makes it even sweeter when I stick my dick in 'em."

The line went dead.

D's nostrils flared. He wanted to whip his phone across the lot. But he couldn't. He couldn't. He needed it. He needed to get that text. He needed to call his crew.

He was going to lose his fucking mind.

DIESEL PACED the common area of church like a tiger stuck in a cage. He'd called his crew, had them standing by for more information. But now they just waited. He had Rooster and Weasel go to Jewel's apartment to look for clues.

But Zak got a text from them saying they hadn't found anything. No struggle, no blood, nothing. D had no idea where she was snatched from. He just knew her Jeep wasn't at the Body Shop, her apartment, or at church.

She had completely disappeared.

Brick was getting their connection at the phone company to ping her cell phone. But they hadn't heard back from the guy yet.

Time and his patience were running out.

He looked at the time on his cell. It had been fifty-eight minutes since Black Jack called him.

Fifty-eight fucking minutes and no text.

Jesus fuckin' Christ! He couldn't take much more of the waiting. And if that fucker was lying and didn't ever send a text?

He stepped up to the nearest pool table, grabbed the cue-ball and whipped it across the room. The wall exploded where it hit, showering plaster and drywall onto everything around it. He stared at the gaping hole it left but he didn't feel any better.

"Brother," came the low murmur behind him and a hand landed on his shoulder.

He would've shrugged it off but he remembered how Hawk felt while kneeling next to Kiki on the floor in that house. D had tried to comfort him at the time, too, and Hawk hadn't welcomed it. He'd been hurting too badly.

Now, D got it.

His gut was a hollow pit, his chest and shoulders painfully tight, his nerves shot.

This was the longest hour in his life.

His phone dinged. Hawk made a noise next to him. Then Zak and Jag were there, too. Hovering.

D turned away and hit the power button on his phone to light it up.

Fuck you, motherfucker read the text.

D's heart dropped into his stomach and he closed his eyes, his fingers holding his phone in a death grip. Now he had no idea how to find Jewel, where to even begin looking.

Like a needle in a haystack.

When his phone sounded again, D opened his eyes and glanced at the next text.

It was a photo of Jewel bound in ropes. Wrists behind her back. Ankles tied together and then tied to the binding on her wrists. Gagged and blindfolded, she was trussed up on her side, her hair covering her face so he couldn't tell if she was conscious. He couldn't tell how hurt she was. But he knew that body well, so he definitely recognized her. And she was still dressed in what she had worn this morning. Thank fuck for that. That gave him hope that the asshole hadn't raped her before leaving her wherever she was.

Which he still had no clue. He needed more than a photo of her to start looking. Black Jack hadn't held up his end of the deal. But then D wasn't planning on holding up his end, either.

"Info?" Hawk asked.

"Photo," D grunted, then scrolled through his contacts and found Hunter's number. He hit send.

"Boss," his man answered.

D stared at his boots, a hand on his hip, trying to keep the panic out of his voice. "Only got a photo. Ain't gonna do us any good."

"That's all we need," Hunter said softly. "Even better than some random clue."

D glanced up and his gaze hit Hawk's. "What the fuck you talkin' 'bout?"

"Unless your woman disabled the GPS on her phone, or that motherfucker did, the coordinates should be embedded in the photo's metadata."

"That fuckwit is too fuckin' stupid to do that."

"Hope so," Hunter muttered.

"Done this before?"

"Fuck yeah," Hunter said on a breath.

Relief flooded through Diesel. "An' that's why your nickname's Hunter."

The man chuckled, but it wasn't done warmly, it was fucking frigid. "Not the only reason, but yeah."

"Got you, brother. Meet you at the warehouse ASAP. Gotta get the location an' head out."

"Ten-four, boss. ETA fifteen."

"Make it ten," D muttered into the phone.

"Hear ya." The call dropped.

"Got a location?" Hawk asked.

Ace rushed up to them. "Want 5-0 searchin', too? Can call Mitch."

"No. We're handlin' it. Gonna find Jewel. Gonna find Black Jack."

Ace frowned. "Son, don't do shit that's gonna land you in a concrete box."

He looked at his father. He couldn't miss the concern on his pop's face. "Gonna do what I gotta, Pop."

"Right," his father murmured.

"Gonna call the Knights' president," Pierce yelled across the room. "Need all boots on the ground searchin'."

"Just tell 'em to stand by," D yelled back. "If what I got don't pan out, we'll get 'em on it. Already owe 'em a marker. Don't need two."

"They'll do it without a marker," Z murmured. "Want 'im as bad as us."

"Not as bad," Hawk answered.

His brother was right. No one wanted Black Jack more than Hawk or D.

"Gotta head to the warehouse an' meet Hunter. Knows how to get Jewel's location from the photo." He looked at Hawk. "You, Z, an' Jag with me." His gaze landed on Ace. "Everybody else needs to hang here an' wait for word. We need 'em we'll call. Gotta watch the women. Keep 'em here. Got me, Pop?"

"Hear ya, boy. Got it covered."

"Slade, too," Z suggested.

D still didn't know if he could trust Slade, so he wasn't thrilled with that idea.

"Former Marine, brother," Z reminded him. "Might be good to have 'im with."

"Yeah," D grunted. "Wastin' time here."

"Let's roll," Z said, jerking his chin to the small group of brothers.

Almost as one, they moved out the back door and into the lot, heading toward their bikes.

Before they could mount up, the back door flung open and Diamond ran out. "I'm coming, too."

"No," Hawk barked.

"Yes, Hawk. It's my sister," she screeched. "Jag! Tell them I'm coming."

Jag just shook his head. "Ain't gonna have to worry 'bout you gettin' snatched up or in the way. Stay here."

"No!" Her eyes wild, she turned to Slade. "Going with you."

Slade scowled at her. "No you ain't. Stayin' here like you're told."

Surprise hit her face at his answer. She probably thought she had the newest member wrapped around her finger already. D was glad to see he wasn't.

"The fuck I am! She's my sister."

"Diamond, you're wastin' time," Hawk growled.

"Then stop arguing with me!" she insisted.

"Woman, you're stayin' here," Slade stated firmly. "Get inside an' don't leave church 'til I get back. Got me?"

"You can't tell me shit," she screamed at Slade.

"No, but I can," Diesel bellowed at her. "Get inside an' shut the fuck up."

"D..."

"Get the fuck inside. Don't need your shit on top of everythin' else."

"Di, do it!" Jag yelled at his sister.

She opened her mouth then snapped it shut. With a huff, she turned and went inside.

"Jesus fuckin' Christ," D muttered and looked toward Slade who was getting on his sled. "More power to ya, brother."

"Ain't a thing," Slade grumbled, avoiding his gaze.

There wasn't time to debate that. And, honestly, D could give a fuck who Diamond was sinking her claws into, as long as it wasn't him.

One by one, bikes came to life and they rolled out.

Chapter Sixteen

HEADING into the warehouse with his brothers on his heels, D's phone rang.

"Go," Diesel barked into it.

"Gotta bead on his last known location," Brick answered. "Probably where he ditched her phone. Signal went dead after that last text went through."

"Where?" D grunted.

"Past the Ohio line, heading west."

"Gotta get 'im before he gets too far," D stated.

"Hear ya, boss. Gonna do our best."

"Know it. Owe you big time."

"Not doin' it for you. Doin' it for them."

Them.

Kiki, Jazz and now Jewel.

"Yeah," D answered. "You an' Walker head that direction. Meetin' Hunter now at the warehouse to get the location of Jewelee."

As long as Black Jack hadn't moved her after taking the photo, he had all the faith in the world Hunter would get an exact bead on her.

"Keep me updated, got me?" D said.

"Copy that," were Brick's last words before he hung up.

D yanked the door open to the warehouse and they all filed in. He headed directly to the surveillance room and found Hunter in there waiting for them, sitting behind one of the computers.

Hunter held out his hand. "Phone."

D dropped it in the man's palm. He wanted to pace but the room wasn't big as it was and it was now full of his brothers.

Jesus, if he was a religious man, he'd be feeling fucking blessed about now. He had good men at his back. Couldn't ask for more.

Well, he could. He needed to find Jewelee safe.

Hunter did his thing with D's phone and the picture and after a minute, plugged the latitude and longitude into Google Maps on the computer.

"Got 'er," Hunter said in a low voice, staring at the screen. He looked up and met D's eyes. "Long as he didn't move 'er."

For fuck's sake, if he moved her, they were screwed.

"Where's Mercy?" D asked him.

"En route. Got Steel an' Ryder in the city babysittin' McDouchebag."

"Right. So you're with us to find Jewelee," he told Hunter. "Brick and Walker are lookin' for Black Jack. Gonna need Mercy to meet up with them. Gonna need him on scene when he's found."

Hunter met his eyes, then a knowing look crossed his face and he jerked his chin up. "Pluggin' these coordinates into my phone an' yours, too, boss."

"Yeah," D grunted. "ETA to get to that locale?"

"Maybe forty-five."

"Gotta do it quicker than that."

"Hear ya," Hunter said, his gaze circling the room. "Takin' lead. Everyone keep up." He pushed his big body from the chair. "Make a hole," he grumbled and headed out of the room toward the lot behind the warehouse.

JEWEL HADN'T CRIED ONCE. Not once since she woke up from being knocked out by that asshole motherfucker.

She did a mental scan of her body. Her head ached, the skin on her wrists and ankles burned from the rough rope, her muscles were stiff from her limbs being bound and her laying in that position for who knows how long.

At least she was dressed and alive.

A gag was shoved in her mouth and a blindfold covered her eyes. She had no idea where Black Jack had taken her. Even worse, she had no idea what he planned. However, she couldn't hear a thing. Wherever she was, the silence was deafening.

She couldn't hear traffic, voices, or even birds. There weren't even any identifying smells other than a slight musty odor. Otherwise, nothing to identify her location.

She just knew the floor was concrete because the cold seeped into her bones and the surface was rough beneath her cheek. A shiver skittered down her back. She could be in a bunker somewhere never to be found. She could lay here until she eventually starved or froze to death.

Kiki and Jazz had been found by someone pinging Kiki's cell phone. She could only hope that Black Jack had kept hers with them. However, she had no idea where he was, either.

She closed her eyes behind the bandana that blindfolded her, and in her mind's eye she saw D racing to her rescue. She only hoped that was true. His Shadows were good at finding people, as well as making people disappear. But she didn't know much more about them.

She couldn't blame Diesel if he was still angry about her not going with him on the club run. If she hadn't been so obstinate and did as he demanded, she never would have given Black Jack the opportunity to take her.

But, no, she had decided to be as stubborn as D in an attempt to bend him to her will. And anyone who knew D knew he didn't bend. Not ever. Not for anybody.

She had been stupid to believe she would be the one who could do it... and look where she ended up...

Royally fucked.

No, she was not going to cry. She wouldn't show any weakness.

Fuck that asshole Warrior. She was DAMC through and through and tough biker bitches didn't cry. They didn't beg. They fought.

Though, it was hard to fight when you were trussed up like a pig about to go to slaughter.

Fuck!

She didn't know how long she laid there while her thoughts raced and played tricks on her mind. Every time she thought she heard something, she was wrong, she'd imagined it. She didn't know if it was an hour or two since she came around. But still no Black Jack. No Diesel.

No one.

She'd never been afraid of being by herself before, but the fear was clawing down her spine and up her throat. She might not survive this.

If she didn't, D would probably be really pissed. And then she would have to haunt his ass.

She snorted. Then sobered quickly when she realized she was losing her mind.

This waiting. This unknowing. Her mind was going to snap, break like a dropped mirror, shatter into countless shards of glass, unable to be put back together.

She needed to keep her shit together.

Then she heard the roar of a motorcycle and her stomach dropped. Black Jack was back.

DIESEL NEEDED to keep his shit together. He was falling apart inside, but he had to hide it. From his men, from his brothers, from Jewel once he found her.

This wasn't him. Shit didn't tear him up like this.

But it was.

Black Jack was right. Pussy was making him weak, vulnerable. He never thought that day would come where a woman meant enough to him that she could be used as a weapon against him.

That day was today.

He was so fucking fucked.

But it was Jewel. And, goddamn it, she was worth it.

Hunter was just ahead of him in his blacked-out Range Rover. His hand came out of the driver's side window and gave D a signal. They were turning right.

D gave the same signal to the group behind him and he followed the four-wheel-drive vehicle off the main road onto a stone lane. His back wheel kicked out in the loose gravel and he righted it quickly.

He didn't need to dump his bike. He needed to find Jewelee.

Hunter was driving slowly down through a thick of trees and D followed carefully. Then suddenly the patch of woods opened up to a clearing and D spotted a small concrete block building next to what remained of an old baseball field. One that hadn't been used in quite a long time.

He raced past the Range Rover, tempted to lay his sled over and use the momentum to launch himself into that building... because she was in there. He knew it in his gut.

Instead, he parked it calmly but quickly and he went to the wood door to see there was a latch on it with a padlock.

"Jewel!" he bellowed through the thick door. "You in there?" When he got no answer, dread washed over him. "Jewelee! Answer me!"

He listened carefully for a moment. Nothing.

Fuck.

He cocked his leg back and then forcefully kicked the door. It didn't budge.

"Jesus fuckin' Christ!" he yelled to no one in particular.

"Boss," Hunter said. "Step back."

D looked behind him. Hunter stood with his .45 in his hand. His brothers, all anxious and tense, gathered behind his man.

Moving away from the door, he waved everyone back behind the vehicle. He didn't need anyone getting hit from a ricochet or shrapnel.

"Ears!" D yelled and covered his own.

Hunter moved to the side of the door jamb and shot at the lock. Then he was moving forward and kicking the door open.

D jogged forward and followed on his heels into the dark interior of the windowless building.

"Fuck. Need a light," D grumbled. "Jewelee!"

Something moved in the corner.

"Jewel," he yelled again.

Suddenly, the headlights of two bikes were pointed through the open doorway and D spotted her. She was in the exact same position as in the picture.

He fell to his knees next to her, ripping off the blindfold and then the gag. "Jesus fuckin' Christ." He moved the hair out of her face carefully in case she was injured. She turned her head toward him, blinked, then gave him a crooked smile. "Jesus fuckin' Christ," he whispered.

She was okay.

"Knife!" he yelled over his shoulder and one appeared. "Gonna cut these ropes off, baby. Gotta stay still, got me?"

"Yeah," she croaked. "Water."

"In a sec," he reassured her. In the limited light, he could see a bruise on her temple and a little bit of dried blood, but she was in nowhere near the shape Kiki or Jazz was in when he found them.

Black Jack had hardly touched her. Thank fuck.

"Stay still," he told her again and he sawed at the ropes until her hands were free. She moved them in front of her and began to rub her wrists. "Still," he said again as he sawed at the bindings at her ankles.

When the final thread of the ropes cut free, relief rushed through him.

His woman was safe. She had a knot on her head and a cut, but she was whole.

She tried to sit up but whimpered. "Legs are asleep," she said.

He fell to his ass onto the concrete floor and yanked her into his lap. With his arms wrapped around her, he held her as close as he could. Which wasn't nearly close enough. "Thank fuck," he whispered in her ear. "Thank fuck."

He pinned his forehead to hers and just breathed. She was alive. She was whole. She was his.

"D..." she whispered.

"Yeah," he breathed.

"Sorry I didn't go on the run."

Jesus fuck.

Diesel closed his eyes, not willing to let her go but knew they had to move. They needed to get her out of there. Someone needed to get her to the emergency room to get checked out. And he still needed to find Black Jack.

Shit wasn't done yet.

"Woman, gotta listen to your ol' man," was all he could say so he wouldn't lose it.

"If I had an ol' man, maybe I would," she murmured, looking up at him with a small grin.

"Got one," he grunted.

She jerked in his arms at his words, then said softly, "Love you, D."

"Know it, baby" he answered into her hair.

Jesus fuckin' Christ. It felt as if the world was crushing his chest.

He couldn't keep sitting there. And everyone else agreed.

"Gotta go, D," came from Hawk.

"Need to find that fucker," came from Jag.

He got a better grip on Jewel and pushed to his feet while she was still in his arms. He looked to his brother.

"Need you to get 'er to the hospital. Make sure everythin's okay."

Hawk shook his head. "Goin' with you."

He could argue with his brother, but that would just waste time and he didn't think he'd win that argument. He looked to Jewel's brother. "Jag, take her, got me?"

"Yeah."

"You an' Slade. Take Hunter's cage. Give 'im your bike."

Jag's eyes widened. Diesel knew he was asking a lot of him but, luckily, the sled Jag was riding wasn't one of his fancy customs. That had been trashed not long ago by the Warriors. Even though he'd been working on a new custom for the past few months, it would take another year or so to complete. So in the meantime, he was riding a temporary bike. One he'd eventually customize and sell once he completed his own.

"Lucky I ain't that attached to my sled," Jag grumbled.

"Will take care of it," Hunter said. "Promise, brother."

"Ain't a keeper. The only one I have right now, though."

"Hear ya," Hunter said. "Take care of my ride, too. I *am* attached to it."

Jag nodded and followed D as he carried Jewel out to the Range Rover.

"What are you going to do?" she asked him.

"What needs done," D muttered.

"D..."

"No lip, woman," he told her as Hawk opened the passenger side of the vehicle for him. He set her carefully on the seat. "Belt on. Don't give Jag any shit, got me?"

Jewel rolled her eyes at him as she pulled the seatbelt into place.

"Get checked out, go back to church, wait there."

"I'll be fine."

"Yeah you will. 'Cause you're gonna listen to me an' listen to Jag."

"That's not what I meant."

"Know it, but you're gonna do it anyway."

He leaned into the vehicle and kissed her hard. "Gonna see you in a bit."

He went to close the door and she stopped him. "D..."

"Yeah."

"Don't do anything crazy."

He shut the door and gave a chin lift to Jag, who moved around the front of the Range Rover. Before getting in, Jag slipped off his cut and leaned in to hand it to Jewel. Then he climbed into the driver's seat and, a few seconds later, took off with Slade following on his bike.

As D watched them head down the lane, his phone rang and so did Hunter's. He looked at his screen.

"Mercy," D said to Hunter.

Hunter looked at his phone. "Brick," he announced.

D turned one way and Hunter the other to grab their calls.

"Yeah," D grunted into the phone.

"Gonna let me play with him?" Mercy asked.

"The longer the better," D answered and he heard Mercy make a pleased sound on the other end of the phone.

"Hoped so. Otherwise, would've just took care of business and called you when it was over."

D didn't doubt it. "Got a bead?" D asked.

"Better than that. Got him cornered. Holed up at a house in Ohio. 'Bout ten klicks past the state line. Jeep's out front."

"He know you're there?"

"Fuck no. We're in the shadows. Gonna wait for the boss man to get here."

"Brick with you?"

"Yeah. Talking to Hunter now."

"Hunter's with me. So's Hawk an' Z."

"Sure you want them involved?"

No, he didn't. Except he didn't think he would get either of them to stand down and head back to Shadow Valley. But then if he was in their shoes, he wouldn't, either.

Tonight they were going to start with Black Jack. Then they'd take all the Warriors down. One by one, if need be.

"Don't got a choice, brother," D finally said.

Mercy grunted before saying, "Gonna text Hunter coordinates."

D's phone went dark and he glanced toward Hunter, who was glancing his way. The other man gave him a chin lift and D returned it.

It was time to ride.

Chapter Seventeen

SHIT WAS GOING SIDEWAYS. Once they arrived at the location Mercy gave Hunter, they couldn't find him or Brick at first. D's men were truly in the shadows.

Diesel stared at Jewel's Jeep which was parked next to the little cabin in the woods. Smoke billowed from the stove pipe coming out of the roof, and lights were now off inside so he couldn't see any movement.

Didn't matter, though. Black Jack was in there and they were going to go in and get him if they had to. They weren't going to wait for the Warrior to make the first move, they had planned to go in hard and fast.

Problem was, the fuckstick now knew they were out there. It was hard to get anywhere near the cabin without him hearing their bikes. Which was the reason why the lights had gone out. Better night vision for Black Jack, plus kept him under the cover of darkness.

Fucker might not be as dumb as D thought.

Even so, they weren't leaving until this was all settled.

And by settled, D meant *game over* for the Shadow Warrior.

He'd let Mercy play for a while, then D would come in for the final hand.

"Didn't think you'd keep your end of the bargain, motherfucker," came from the cabin.

"Touched my woman. Touched my brother's woman. One of your brothers tried to grab Z's woman."

"Made a deal," Black Jack shouted his direction.

D yelled back, "Deals were made to be broken." And so were bones.

They'd start by breaking every bone on the bastard that he and Squirrel broke on Jazz. Then go from there.

"Figured you'd break your word," the Warrior yelled.

"Figured right, asshole."

Mercy appeared from nowhere and murmured to D, "Fucker's armed. Couple handguns an' long guns from what I could see. Got close enough to take him out, but that wouldn't be any fun."

"Brick?" D whispered to Mercy.

"Behind you," Brick answered.

D looked over his shoulder and could make out his brother, Z, and his crew. "Should leave 'im to the experts," D muttered.

"But you won't," Mercy answered. "Not sure what kinda shot he is."

"Right," D grunted.

"Can't flush him out an' can't wait him out, so gotta make the first move," Hunter said.

"We can spread out an' approach. Can't have eyes on all of us at once," Z suggested.

"He's gonna be watchin' D," Hawk said.

"Maybe," Brick answered. "Maybe not. Knows about our crew, so might be more worried about us than boss man."

"D's a big target," Walker said, approaching from the rear. "Could be a good distraction to let the rest of us make a move."

"Not much cover close to the cabin," Mercy said.

"Gonna stand here an' chit chat or we gonna get that fucker?" D finally asked, impatiently.

"Thought we were having a meaningful conversation, boss," Brick joked.

"Need to get this done so I can check on my woman," D grumbled.

"Don't gotta be here, boss. We can handle this one little flea," Mercy said.

"Know it. But it's personal."

"Wanna piece of him, too. Been waitin' too long for it," Hawk added, stepping closer.

D studied his older brother. Even in the light of the moon, he could see Hawk's face was as hard as granite.

"Gonna distract him. Don't let the fucker escape. Take 'im down but not out, got me?" D got a response from everyone but his brother. "Got me, Hawk?"

"Yeah," he finally grunted.

"This ends here," D told him.

"Just this piece. Lots more pieces to the puzzle, brother," Hawk muttered. "Don't get fuckin' shot."

"Not plannin' on it," he answered. But as soon as he did, a shot rang out, and he stepped back from the impact. A burn hit his chest and he lost his breath as he dropped to his knees, a hand automatically going to where he was hit.

"Fuck," D groaned.

"D," Hawk called out, but ducked as another shot pinged off a nearby tree.

"Boss, you hit?" Walker asked, moving in closer.

"Fuck yeah."

Another shot rang out and everyone dropped to the ground flattening themselves in the dirt.

"Stay down," Mercy yelled. "Brick."

"Yeah," Brick answered. "Got it."

Brick crawled on elbows and knees deeper into the woods and disappeared.

D sucked in a breath as he tried to remain calm. The spot where the bullet entered was throbbing with each beat of his heart. What made it worse was his heart was pumping a million beats a minute.

"Where you hit?" Walker asked next to him.

"Chest. Right. Upper."

"Just a scratch then," Walker said. "Long as nothing's nicked—lung, artery, heart—then you're good."

Right, D thought. Hurt like fuck, though.

"Don't look like I'm gonna get to play, boss." Mercy said, sounding disappointed as he crawled up next to D.

Jesus fuckin' Christ.

A few more shots rang out and everyone ducked their heads. "Anybody else hit?" D asked, then winced when the pain shot through him.

"Nope, just you. Your mama knew how to grow 'em big," Hunter said. "Makes for an easy target. Even a bad shot like that asshole in there can't miss you."

D ignored Hunter and called out, "Z?"

"Good," Zak answered from behind him.

Yep, he was the only stupid ass to get shot.

Hawk handed him his bandana. "Pressure to the wound."

D grunted and took it, doing exactly what his brother said. He sucked in a breath at the burning pain.

"Text Rig, Z. Get 'im rollin' this direction ASAP. Need to get the Jeep outta here after this is done. Tell him no delays. Got me?"

"Yeah."

Black Jack took a few more shots, kicking the dirt up around them. One hit a tree and the bark exploding overhead before landing on them.

"Fucker. Shit shot. Wasting ammo," Walker grumbled.

"Be glad he's a shit shot," Hawk said. "We just gonna sit here an' wait 'til he's out?"

"Fuck no," Mercy said. Then said nothing else.

"What the fuck we doin' then?" Hawk asked. D could hear the impatience in his brother's voice. "Brother's shot, need to get 'im to a hospital."

"Needs a fucking Band Aid and a beer," Walker said. "He'll be good."

Suddenly a bunch of shots headed their direction.

"Asshole got one of his rifles," Hunter growled. "What the fuck's takin' Brick so long?"

"Patience," Mercy said.

"Hard to be patient when it's rainin' bullets," Hawk growled.

"You ain't hit, so quit bitching," Walker told him.

Just when Hawk started crawling in Walker's direction acting like a man on a mission, a final shot echoed through the clearing. This one didn't come from the direction of the cabin. It came from their left.

Then the cabin was eerily quiet. Dead quiet.

"Holy fuck," Z whispered in awe. "Head shot?"

"Former Navy SEAL sniper," Hunter muttered, climbing to his feet and dusting himself off. "'That city is well fortified which has a wall of men instead of brick.' That's a quote by Lycurgus of Sparta. Only with Brick, the saying is, 'That city is well fortified which has a Brick instead of a wall of men.'"

"He that good?" Z asked, surprise clear in his voice.

"Yeah, fucking the best."

"Damn," Z whispered.

"Rig en route?" D asked Zak.

"Yeah."

Hawk pushed himself up to a stand. "Gotta get you to a hospital."

"Not here. Home."

"D, there's one closer to here than home."

"Gotta get to Jewel."

He heard his brother make a noise, but Hawk said, "Let's hit the road, then," finally. "Don't need you bleedin' out before we get there."

"Just a scratch," Walker said again.

"Shut the fuck up," Hawk shot in Walker's direction, making the man laugh.

"We'll stay and clean up this mess," Mercy said to D as he helped him to his feet. "Get your brother to drive you back in the Jeep. We'll stay until this Rig gets here with the rollback. I'll get him to take your bikes instead. Yeah?"

"Yeah," D answered him. "Thanks, brother."

"Wish the night ended differently, but whatever. Next time. Plenty of more pieces to the puzzle to play with, yeah?"

"Yeah," D said on a pained breath. Hawk came from behind him and braced an arm at his back. It was good timing, too, since he was starting to feel a bit light-headed.

"Let's go," Hawk said and helped him toward the Jeep. "Z, ridin' with us or followin'?" his brother asked over his shoulder.

"Stayin'," Z answered. "Gotta check out this head shot an' will ride back with Rig."

"Jesus," D muttered.

"Don't be surprised if suddenly he's hangin' at the range with Brick," Hawk said low as he helped him into the passenger seat of the four-by-four.

"Fuck me," D muttered.

"Gotta a bit of a ride home, lots of time to tell me what you're gonna do 'bout Jewel."

"Fuck me," D muttered again.

"STOP FUSSIN', woman!" D barked as Jewel fluffed a pillow and tried to tuck it behind his head.

"I have to take care of my ol' man," she stated with a smirk.

"Ain't your ol' man," he grumbled.

"Swore I heard you say it."

That he did, but he wasn't going to admit it. At least not when she was being cocky. "By accident."

She rolled her eyes at him. "Right."

"Ain't true unless it's official."

"I'm sure Pierce will have no problem setting up a special meeting for that."

Fucking Pierce. They still needed to deal with his ass. And here he was sitting in the hospital. With everyone being more worried about his flesh wound, they wouldn't want to discuss that issue.

As soon as Hawk got him to the hospital, he was rushed into surgery and they dug out the bullet, cleaned out the wound, and sewed him shut. They said he was lucky he had a lot of heavy muscle to take the impact.

Nothing major was damaged besides flesh due to the caliber used and the distance he was shot from. But he would have a badass scar for the rest of his life. Though, it did fuck up one of his tattoos.

That wasn't what pissed him off. No. He never got to see Jewelee when he'd arrived. No matter how much he demanded he see her before he went into the OR, they all ignored him.

Hawk found that amusing since that wasn't something Diesel was used to.

But he did assure D that he'd check on Jewel and be waiting for him once he got out of surgery.

His brother kept to his word, of course. He certainly wasn't the only one waiting when he finally woke up from the anesthesia.

Ace and his mom were there, and just about everyone else. Z and Rig arrived not long after he came out of surgery and Z assured him that things were "cleaned up." He told him Mercy would give him a full report once he was out of the hospital.

That was good enough for him since he trusted his crew one hundred percent.

The nurses had insisted everyone leave since he was still groggy from the surgery and they reluctantly all filed out. All except Jewelee. Even against the nurse's orders. And D backed her up by telling the nurse that he'd rip out his IV and leave the hospital if she couldn't stay with him.

Because that's how pussy whipped he'd become in a fucking day.

Jesus fuckin' Christ.

However, now he was starting to regret having her stay since she wouldn't stop fussing over him. He needed to do something to get her to stop.

He grabbed her wrist above the ligature marks and pulled her close. "Woman, lemme see your head."

She swatted a hand in his direction. "I'm fine. Just a bump, a bruise and a couple stitches."

"Lemme see." He cupped the side of her face and brought her even closer so he could press his lips to her forehead. He pulled back a little and murmured, "Fuckin' woman had me scared."

"Nothing scares you," she scoffed, perching herself on the hospital bed by his side.

"Thought of losin' you did."

She frowned as she reminded him, "Almost lost you, too."

"Been shot at before." Which was true.

She sighed. "Yeah, but never hit."

That was true, too.

"Can we not make that a habit?" she asked, her brows low, her blue eyes worried.

"Gettin' shot?" he asked.

"Yeah."

"Yeah, baby. Promise not to make it a habit."

"My fault. I should've listened to you," she whispered to D.

"Ain't your fault, woman," he said, his voice gruff.

"If I had been on the ride, he wouldn't have got me."

"Could've snagged you anywhere."

As she curled her legs up and leaned into his good side, his arm snaked out and wrapped around her, holding her close.

Jesus, she felt good against him.

"If I'm hurting you, I'll get off the bed."

"Ain't movin', woman, stayin' right there."

She smiled at him. "So, it took me getting snatched to get you to make me your ol' lady?"

"Nope."

She raised her brows at him. "Changing your mind?"

"Nope."

"Then what?"

"Decided before that asshole got you."

"You did?"

"Yeah. On the run this morning. Had time to think."

"And you thought it would be a good idea?"

"No. Ain't a good idea."

Jewel snorted. "D..."

"Never a good idea to have some woman hangin' 'round your neck like a fuckin' noose, squeezin' your balls in a vise, naggin' an' bitchin', rollin' her eyes at you. All that shit sucks."

Jewel pinned her lips together for a moment, then said with a smirk, "Yeah, I can see that being a bit of a deterrent."

"More than a bit," he grumbled. He lifted her hand and brushed his thumb lightly over the broken, brush-burned skin at her wrist from the rope. His heart seized when he thought of how badly it all could've gone.

Instead of him lying in a hospital bed, it could have been her. Instead of her teasing him, she could have had her mind and spirit broken like Jazz had. His woman would've been changed forever.

And that would have fucking killed him.

"Sure you wanna be my ol' lady?" he asked.

JEWEL MET HIS GAZE. There was nothing she wanted more.

When she'd gotten the news he'd been shot, she just about collapsed. She had just gotten to church with Jag after a short stint in the emergency room. She had only been there long enough for the doctors to make sure she didn't have a concussion and to get a couple stitches. Then not even an hour afterward, she found herself back in some fancy black Range Rover heading back to the hospital, Jag driving like a crazy man with Janice and Ace in the back seat. She could tell D's parents were trying not to freak out, and she was trying to put on a brave face, also.

When they arrived at the hospital in record time, they were relieved to find D's gunshot wound wasn't life threatening. She went from almost collapsing in panic at church to doing it in relief at the hospital instead.

She loved him too much to bear losing him. Not this soon.

Hell, not ever.

"Never a good idea to have a man hanging around your neck like a fucking noose, being bossy and demanding, expecting you to obey all commands like he's your master."

"Yeah," he breathed. And she could tell he was fighting a smile.

"It sucks. Can't get dick anywhere else now, either," she added.

The crinkles at the corners of his eyes disappeared and he shot her a scowl. "Woman, ain't even goin' there."

She laughed. It was too easy to push his buttons.

He looked up at the ceiling and blew out a breath. "Jesus, woman, what'd you do to me?"

"Nothing you didn't want done," she said matter-of-factly.

She waited for him to argue that point, but, surprisingly, he didn't.

"I don't give a shit," a loud female voice could be heard from outside the room. "I need to see my cousin."

"Ma'am!"

"Don't *ma'am* me. For fuck's sake, I'm not that old." Bella came barreling into the room and turned in time to shut the door in the nurse's face. "Ol' biddy," she huffed. Her eyes turned to Diesel and Jewel over on the bed and she smiled. "Thank fuck," she whispered and rushed over to them.

"Ain't no lock on the door," D warned. "Probably will get security to come in an' drag your ass out."

Bella lifted a shoulder. "Just wanted to make sure you're okay."

"Alive," he grunted.

"I can see that." Bella glanced across the bed at Jewel. "He really okay?"

"Fuckin' woman! Said I'm okay," he barked impatiently.

Jewel turned her head to hide her laughter.

"Well, don't be a fucking grump," Bella barked back at him.

"Just got shot. Allowed to be a grump."

"And him being a grump is different from when?" Jewel asked Bella.

Bella smiled at her. "True."

"Jesus fuckin' Christ," D muttered, raising his eyes to the ceiling again.

The door suddenly swung open and all eyes turned in that direction. Jewel was sure it was the nurse or security coming in to escort Bella out.

It was someone in a uniform but not who they expected.

"Fuck," Diesel said under his breath, but loud enough for Jewel to hear.

Bella frowned in the new arrival's direction. "What're you doing here?"

Axel stepped into the room, then firmly closed the door behind him. He pinned his gaze on Bella. "You supposed to be in here?"

"Are *you* hospital security now?" she asked smartly. "Get a demotion?"

Axel's lips flattened and he stepped closer.

"Whataya want, pig?" D barked.

"Jesus, Diesel," Axel grumbled. "Can't you ever be civil?"

"Not to you."

Jewel could see Axel take a deep breath. Probably so he wouldn't shoot Diesel in the other side of his chest.

"Axel, he doesn't want you here," Bella stated.

"Well, he doesn't have a fucking choice. I'm here to question him."

"On what?" Jewel asked her cousin.

"All GSW's have to be investigated."

She frowned. "GSW's?"

"Gunshot wounds," Axel clarified.

"Slipped, fell, shot myself. Fucked up," D grumbled. "Now get gone."

"We've got the bullet, D. We can do ballistics and see if it matches any of your weapons."

"SVPD isn't doing ballistics," Bella said, swatting a dismissing hand toward Axel.

"Someone was shot, Bella."

"Yeah, an' it was an accident an' I'm just peachy," D said, frowning. "Now get gone."

Axel shook his head. "You can tell me that a thousand times, but I'm not leaving until I get the info I came for."

"Ain't sayin' shit."

Axel looked at Jewel, who gave him a shrug. "I wasn't there."

Axel stepped closer to her, seeing the injury to her head. "What happened to you?" His eyes slid to D. "He hit you?"

"No!" Jewel exclaimed. "Holy shit, Axel. Don't even say stuff like that. I clocked my head on one of the shop's lifts."

Axel gave her an *I-don't-believe-you* face. "Just making sure he isn't taking out his miserable temper on you." Before he could question her further, D got his attention. Luckily.

"Fuckin', pig. Steppin' on thin ice. Can still get outta this bed," D warned.

"Smart, threatening a cop," Axel proclaimed.

"D would never hurt Jewel," Bella stated.

Axel's gaze slid to her. "You know what happened?"

Bella shut her mouth and averted her eyes.

Did she know what happened? All Jewel was told was that after D got shot, Black Jack got away.

Now she wondered if something else went down.

"I don't know shit. Just what D told you."

"Bullshit," Axel growled. He stepped closer to Bella and grabbed her arm. "If you know the truth, you need to tell me."

Bella yanked at her arm. "Don't know shit, Axel."

"Get your hand off 'er," D growled, sitting up.

Jewel put a hand on him. "Don't get out of this bed, D."

"Woman," D growled.

"It's not going to do you any good to get out of bed. You just had surgery," she insisted.

"Gonna kick your ass, pig, as soon as I'm outta this bed an' you ain't in uniform."

"Again, with the threats." Axel shook his head. "I'll take that as you aren't going to cooperate."

"Fuck no."

"There's still going to be an open investigation," Axel warned. "We're going to question a bunch of people. Including your *crew*. Someone will slip." His gaze slid back to Bella. "One way or another, someone's going to say something."

Bella locked her gaze with him and shrugged. "It's not gonna be me."

"I could arrest you for obstruction of justice."

Bella pinned her wrists together and held them out to him. "Go ahead. Kiki will have me out in under an hour. You can't prove I know anything."

"Bella," he said, his voice low.

"Axel, get gone," Bella said softly.

"We'll talk later."

"Doubt it," she answered.

His lips flattened out as he stared at her. "Don't be so sure."

"Don't be threatenin' my cousin."

His gaze turned to D before landing on Jewel. "And make sure you don't hurt mine."

"Since when do you care about family?" Bella asked softly.

"Jesus, Bella," Axel said just as softly, something passed through his eyes that Jewel swore was pain. Or hurt. Or maybe even regret.

"Axel, get gone," Bella repeated, her face mournful, her eyes reflecting the same emotions as Axel.

With a frown, he nodded. "You know how to get a hold of me if any of you want to make a statement," he said to the room in general, then he gave Bella one last look. "Or whatever." With that, he spun on his heel and left.

Chapter Eighteen

Diesel eyeballed his brother first, then Jag as their executive committee meeting broke up.

Shit was done. At least one important thing was. But there was more business to take care of. Just not in this room.

"Congrats, son." Ace whacked D on the back making him wince.

"Pop, he just got fuckin' shot a week ago!" Hawk barked.

"He's a tough fucker. Or at least I thought so. Now he got an ol' lady maybe he's softenin' up." His father laughed.

"Right," D grunted.

D, Jag, Ace, Dex, and Hawk held back and let Pierce leave the meeting room first with them following closely behind.

As the man stepped out into the common area, he stopped short. "What the fuck is this?"

D pushed past him to see all the brothers and prospects gathered like they had planned. It was time for a surprise church meeting.

Hawk shoved the writ of impeachment into Pierce's chest, which had been signed by three of them: D, Hawk and Jag. "Know you're supposed to have time to read this, but ain't givin' it to you. Read it now."

Pierce glanced down at the paper he had taken reluctantly. After a moment, he glanced up, his face showing a mixture of shock and anger. "What the fuck? You impeachin' me as prez?"

"Yeah," Hawk answered, squaring off.

Diesel did, too. Though he doubted Pierce would get into a brawl right there in front of the whole club.

"Why?"

Hawk shrugged. "Need this club to remain progressive, you ain't on board with that, but that's not the major issue. Shit you pulled with Ivy—"

"Ivy!" Pierce spat out. "That bitch came to me; I didn't go to her."

Jag bumped into Diesel as he tried to push past. D grabbed Jag's arm, stopping him from taking Pierce out right there in front of everyone. Jag shot him an annoyed look, but D ignored him.

"Don't matter, sent her into Dirty Dick's without us knowin'. Shit coulda went sideways."

"It didn't," Pierce stated.

"Right. 'Cause Jag stepped in," Hawk answered. "Got her ass outta there, where it didn't belong."

Pierce shook his head, then his eyes widened and his face paled. "You strippin' my colors?"

Hawk hesitated, his nostrils flaring. Diesel could see the internal battle his brother fought. Hawk wanted to tell him to hand over his cut and get the fuck out, but they all had decided Pierce's actions weren't bad enough to kick him totally out of the club, just out of the head spot. Besides, the man was good at running the club's gun shop and range. No matter all his other problems, he had a good head on his shoulders for business.

And though D didn't tell anyone but Jewel, the fact remained that Pierce *was* Kelsea's father. If they turned his back on him, he didn't want that causing issues down the road if either of them found out the truth. This club was still about family and loyalty, no matter how much of an ass Pierce acted like sometimes.

But D was going to let the women know that they needed to come to him ASAP if Pierce made any unwanted moves on them. That shit was going to stop. No fucking doubt about it.

"No. But be on notice, this vote goes through an' you're impeached, keep your shit clean, stay loyal, an' you'll be able to stay. If not..." Hawk let the last hang out there.

"This is bullshit," Pierce growled.

"Want out?" Diesel asked him. "Got no problem turnin' my back on your ass."

Pierce shot him a look then glanced out over the common area. Everyone's eyes were turned their way.

"For fuck's sake," Pierce muttered. "Don't gotta have a vote, can see you guys planned this shit. I'll step down." Then he added, "For now." He crumpled up the writ and threw it on the floor.

"Be for the best," Hawk murmured.

"Ain't givin' up my fuckin' colors willingly, though," Pierce muttered as he strode away from them, his body tight, his head shaking.

Hawk stepped behind the bar, grabbed a crate, then set it up in front of the bar before climbing on it.

"Yo! Listen up," he shouted. The room got quiet. "Called you all here for a special meetin'. Pierce decided bein' president ain't for him, so he's steppin' down."

A grumble moved through the large room.

"Anyone interested in bein' prez needs to step forward. Hafta be patched in least a year to be eligible. Gonna have a vote. Majority rules. Gonna just be temporary 'til the vote in December. Got me?"

"Yeahs" and "Got yous" were shouted out.

Hawk surveyed the room. "Anybody?"

"Know who it should be," came from Dex.

"Right. Still gotta ask," Ace said from beside D.

Zak stepped up to the bar.

D's gaze met Hawk's. Both were relieved since they wanted Z back at the head of the table. But they also knew that Z had mixed feelings about it. It was not only a lot of responsibility, but he had a kid on the way. And Z had been a target before for the Warriors, being club president again might make that target a little bigger.

That problem with the remaining nomads needed handled, too.

And would be, if D had anything to do with it. The only way the ongoing beef between the two clubs would ever come to an end was if one of the clubs came to an end.

And he needed to make sure it wasn't the Dirty Angels.

Their club motto was *Down & Dirty 'til Dead*. But it wasn't up to the Shadow Warriors to determine DAMC's time of death.

"Well, it looks like Z's the only taker. We need a vote?"

"Fuck no," came from Grizz, who sat on his regular stool at the end of the bar.

"How 'bout this..." Hawk started. "Anybody got a problem with it? Speak now or forever hold your fuckin' peace. Or at least 'til December's elections."

"Nobody got a problem with it," came from the group.

"'Kay then." Hawk glanced down at Zak, who stood to the side. "Guess you're it, brother."

A chorus of hoots and hollers, along with boot stomping rose up.

"Meetin' adjourned. Down an' dirty..." Hawk yelled.

"'Til dead," came the answering roar.

As Hawk climbed off the crate, D stepped up to Zak. "Glad to have you back as prez," D murmured.

"Doin' it 'til December an' then see."

"Understood. Got that you're gonna be raisin' a family. Just know we've always got your back. Forever family, brother."

"Brother," Z said, his voice gruff. They clasped hands, bumped shoulders, and D smacked him on the back. "Gotta keep this club on the up an' up, D. 'Specially since my kids are gonna be the next generation. Gotta set a solid foundation. Gonna need your crew to do what they do best."

"Know it. It's covered. Findin' Black Jack was personal for them, too. But I'll get 'em on huntin' the rest down. Might take a while since the nomads tend to scatter when shit gets hot, but my guys are good."

"Yeah, they are. Witnessed that shit out at that cabin."

"Right. Don't like that Rig was out there. Brother gotta keep his mouth shut."

"Already had a long talk with him on the ride back."

"Think he's gonna keep it quiet?" D asked.

"Yeah," Z said quietly. "He better."

That didn't mean he would. D didn't like any of the brothers seeing what his crew could do. He tried to keep the brothers' hands clean as much as possible. It was important to Z and almost everyone else to keep the club legit. Pierce had been their biggest obstacle when it came to that. He had always preferred the old ways of murder and mayhem, but then he was old school DAMC.

D glanced around but couldn't spot Pierce anywhere. Probably went off to lick his fucking wounds. Not that D blamed him. The former president had an oversized ego and what they did to him would be a serious blow to it.

He'd get over it. Eventually.

Or eventually be outside looking in with a few tattoos removed.

"Gonna give Jewelee the good news?"

"Should make her sweat it out," D grumbled.

Z laughed. "Fuckin' woman's a trip as it is. Gonna drive her fuckin' bat shit crazy."

"Ain't as bad as Diamond, thank fuck."

"That's fuckin' true. Not sure if Slade's tryin' to tackle that mess or if she's tryin' to do the tacklin'."

"Think it's her, brother. Don't think he'd have any problem gettin' pussy anytime he wants it."

"Yeah. Hear ya," Zak murmured, then he laughed. "Maybe he'll take your place in the bathroom fuckin' random snatch against the wall."

"Jesus. I gotta give that up now?" D asked.

Z's head jerked back as he stared at Diesel. "You wanna keep your fuckin' balls?"

D cupped his crotch. "Yeah, kinda like 'em. They're useful."

"Right, word of advice then..."

D cut him off with a snort. "Just fuckin' with you, brother. Don't want to get shanked while I'm sleepin'."

Z grinned. "Could see Jewelee doin' that, too. You givin' up your room here?"

D's chest tightened. "Didn't give it thought."

"Her apartment's better."

Right. No doubt about that.

"Take one of the smaller rooms like I keep for backup. For when your ass in the fuckin' dog house."

"Ain't gonna be whipped like you," D told him.

"Whatever you say, brother." Z grinned. "Gonna go home an' get a piece of ass." He headed toward the back door flicking two fingers above his shoulder.

Home.

Now that he'd claimed Jewelee at the table earlier, he needed to make some decisions for him and his ol' lady.

His ol' lady.

Jesus. He fell down that fucking slippery slope. The same one Z, Jag and Hawk tumbled down.

He was fucking fucked.

Then it hit him. No, he wasn't. He was a lucky fucker instead.

He got a good woman who loved giving him head and was good at it, one who came all over his dick, and best of all...

She loved him.

She. Fucking. Loved. Him.

That punched him right in the gut. And it wasn't a bad feeling. Nope. He had someone who belonged to him. Someone he needed to take care of, protect. Someone to come *home* to. A warm, soft, sexy woman to climb into bed with at the end of the night. One who wanted to be with him because of who he was, what he stood for, where his loyalties lie. Not for only what hung between his legs. Or for his status in the club.

And for once he was interested in a woman for what wasn't between hers, either. Jewel was much more than a hole to bust a nut into. She'd willingly stand by him, or ride behind him on his sled. She'd take care of him, too.

The best part was, she understood how he lived, what made him tick. And she accepted it all. She accepted him as he was. Like him, she was DAMC through and through.

She was not the kind of woman to try to change him.

She loved him, loved what she called his beast. She took everything he gave her and asked for more.

Jesus fuckin' Christ. He loved his ol' lady.

He loved Jewel.

He realized his pop had been standing there watching him for who knew how long.

Ace wore a knowing smirk on his face. "Just hit you, didn't it, son?"

He blinked at his father.

"Gonna have grandbabies. Lots an' lots of fuckin' grandbabies between you an' Hawk. Your ma's gonna be happy."

Before D could unhinge his jaw to set his father straight, Ace laughed and walked away.

His gaze bounced over the brothers and prospects who remained behind to hang out after the church meeting. It landed on Crash and Rig, who were playing pool with Moose and Dawg.

His feet started moving and then he was there, catching the rolling cue ball to stop the play.

"Hey!" Crash yelled.

"Need you to pay attention," D told him.

Crash leaned on his cue stick. "What?"

D looked over at Rig. "You payin' attention?"

"Yeah," Rig answered.

"Jewelee's quittin'."

Both of their mouths dropped open and their eyebrows rose. "What?

"Quittin'. She's done."

"Why?" Rig asked.

"But she's good at running the fuckin' shop," Crash whined.

"Know it. Woman got mad skills when it comes to runnin' a business. That's why she's comin' to work for me."

"Who's gonna run the office?"

"Get Di or Kelsea. Jewelee can train 'em."

"But—" Crash started.

D raised a palm. "Brother, ain't havin' a discussion. Decision's been made."

"She know?" Rig asked.

"Nope. Gonna go tell her now."

Rig laughed. "Good luck with that, brother."

He didn't need luck. He had Jewel. She was all he needed.

DIESEL RODE his sled up to the body shop's office and shut it down. He stared in through the window and saw Jewel staring back at him, a sly smile on her face.

Before he could dismount from his bike, she was out the door, standing on the stoop, her hands on her hips. "Got news for me?'

He pulled his bandana down and his goggles off. "Got two things to tell you, woman."

Her smile got wider. "Yeah?"

"Yeah. You just quit."

Her smile disappeared and her eyes widened. "What?"

He took it that his announcement wasn't the news she was expecting. "You heard me, woman. You're comin' to work for me."

She took two steps forward and stopped. "D..."

"No lip, remember?"

"But—"

"Woman, can't give your ol' man no lip," he said more firmly.

"I can't?" She arched a brow at him. "Who's my ol' man?"

"Lookin' at 'im."

She crossed her arms over her chest and tilted her head. "I'm looking at a beast. Why would I want someone like that?"

"Ain't gotta choice now. Too late. Wanted it. Got it. Now stuck with it."

"Stuck with it, huh?" She smirked.

D shook his head and snorted. "Woman, get on my sled."

"Damn, you're fucking bossy. What was I thinking?"

"That you love big dick, an' you love bossy."

"Well, you have the bossy part covered. Wondering when I'm getting the big dick."

"Gonna get that in a few if you get on my fuckin' sled."

"D, I have my car."

"Jeep's fine here. Want you on my sled," he repeated. "Ain't got an excuse this time."

"What excuse is that?"

"That you ain't my ol' lady."

She smiled. "That is true."

She stepped closer to his bike and he snagged her, bringing her close. "Kiss me, woman."

He cupped the back of her head and pulled her to him, then he took his ol' lady's mouth hard. And she tasted fucking great. When her tongue tangled with his and she moaned into his mouth, it hit him right in the dick.

He needed to get her home.

Yeah, that's right. *Home.*

Epilogue

Jewel's head dropped forward as she rode Diesel's cock. Her gaze fell on the still red reminder of his gunshot wound at the top of his chest, just below his collarbone.

He'd been lucky.

And she was even luckier to still have him.

In her life. In her bed. In her heart.

She couldn't believe how much she loved the man beneath her. And she knew he loved her back. Though, he showed it—in his own way—he hadn't actually told her yet.

She wasn't sure if he ever would.

He wasn't a man who showed or talked about his emotions and she was okay with that. Sometimes she could coax it out of him and when she did, it made it so worthwhile.

A smile. A laugh. A look.

The rarity of them made those moments extra special to her.

Right now, he was watching her in the mirror as she rode his cock. She looked up, too, and cursed silently when she spotted all his clothes strewn about the bedroom floor.

"Jesus," she groaned.

"Like that, baby?" rumbled deep from his chest.

"No."

"No?"

"Fucking you, yes. Your pigsty habits, no."

He dropped his gaze from the mirror to her. "What the fuck, woman?"

She stopped riding him and waved an arm around the room. "And before you start reciting your *rules—*"

"Shut up, woman, tryin' to fuck you."

"You're not trying; you're just lying there."

"Yeah."

"Yeah," Jewel huffed.

"So get movin'," he said, smacking her ass.

She fell forward onto his chest with a laugh, then gave him a quick kiss. "Hey," she whispered, unable to hide her smile of happiness.

He grunted.

"Gotta tell you something," she continued.

He grunted again.

"I love you, beast."

No grunt this time, instead he sucked in a breath, spun his big body, and flipped her onto her back.

Now face to face, she cupped his cheek. "You're a beast, baby, but you're my beast."

Diesel smiled...

Actually smiled.

Then grunted in satisfaction.

Sign up for Jeanne's newsletter to learn about her upcoming releases, sales and more! http://www.jeannestjames.com/newslettersignup

Welcome to Shadow Valley where the Dirty Angels MC rules. Get ready to get Down & Dirty because this is Axel's story...

When you're a cop, life can be complicated when the woman you love is MC born and raised...

Though the club blood runs thick in Axel's veins, he's despised by them for being a cop. They also hate him because his family turned their back years ago not only on the club but his brother, the president of the Dirty Angels MC. However, he's loved Bella forever, watched her marry the wrong man, one who broke her in almost every imaginable way, and yet she's still the strongest person he knows. Despite their rivaling families, he won't let anything stand in the way of making her his this time.

Bella hasn't known anything other than alpha bikers her whole life. Her marriage to one turned into a tragedy, one that changed the rest of her life. She was never the same after that one fateful night that Axel came to save her. Though he remains on the outskirts of her life, he's always there: watching, waiting, worrying about her. Especially when a rival MC continues to wreak havoc on all of their lives.

Like Romeo and Juliet, his family may never accept her, and hers him, but they're both determined to tear down the wall that divides them.

Turn the page to read the prologue of Down & Dirty: Axel (Dirty Angels, Book 5)

Down & Dirty: Axel

Prologue

Axel couldn't remember the last time he'd been with a woman.

It'd been way too long, and it was all her damn fault.

Bella climbed into her purple Dodge Challenger and within minutes, pulled away from the bakery's back parking lot.

Just like he did almost every night, Axel hit the starter on his custom Harley and headed the other direction, so she wouldn't spot him following her. Because if she did, she'd have a shit-fit and punch him in the fucking nuts if given half the chance. And he happened to like his balls the way they were. Though, right now, they could be considered blue since he hadn't done anything with them in a while except found relief with his own palm.

He rounded the corner and hit a side street, riding parallel to the one she was traveling. He knew where she was going. He knew exactly how she'd get there.

He only wanted to make sure she arrived safely, then he'd head home.

Like normal.

Because he had no fucking life.

Nope. He'd go home, crack open an Iron City Beer and kick his feet up to watch some TV.

And she'd go home, double lock her front door, check to make sure all her windows were secure, set her security alarm, then make something to eat and climb into bed.

Without him.

She never dated. Never brought a man home. She always went to bed alone.

Although, that should make him happy, it didn't.

Not that he wanted her to be with another man, he didn't. But it also didn't give him much hope for his own chances.

Not at all.

It wasn't like he hadn't been trying. He had. Every chance he got. But she resisted, and she was downright stubborn.

Which was to be expected.

Tenacity ran deep when it came to the women of the Dirty Angels MC and Bella was a biker chick through and through. Born and raised within the club, she was third generation Dirty Angels MC.

Years ago, she had even married into it, became an ol' lady, a biker's claimed property. That day had been one of the darkest days of Axel's life.

Although not the darkest. No, that day came later.

After the worst day of both of their lives, she became "Property of No One." No longer claimed by anyone. And she shouted that to the rooftops. She made that statement loud and clear, even wearing it on her tank tops and sweatshirts. He was surprised she didn't have Crow tattoo it across her forehead.

But he didn't want her to become his property, no.

Yes, he was a biker, but he didn't want her to be his ol' lady.

Yes, he rode a Harley and wore a cut, but he wasn't DAMC.

No, he wasn't that type of biker, even though the club's blood ran thick through his own veins, as well.

No.

Instead, he belonged to the Blue Avengers MC.

Because he was a cop.

BELLA PEEKED out of the window pretending to check the latch, but in all reality, she already knew it was secure.

Axel didn't think she knew what he did way too often, which was follow her home after she finished working her shift at Sophie's Sweet Treats. She noticed him doing it after the trouble with the Shadow Warriors, a rival MC, had become more frequent.

Sometimes he was in his patrol car, sometimes on his sled, sometimes in his truck.

But she knew he was there.

He was always there.

He'd always been there.

She wished he'd give up.

She *needed* him to give up.

But no matter what she said to him, no matter how shitty she treated him, no matter how many times she'd told him to "get gone," he never did.

Yes, he'd back off but only to give her space. He'd always be there waiting on the outskirts of her anger.

It wasn't him. It was her.

She didn't want any man.

Not a biker. Not a doctor. Not an accountant.

Not even Axel.

Or at least, that's what she tried to tell herself.

With a sigh, she leaned her forehead against the window pane and could see him sitting on his Harley, the custom one Jag built for him, in the shadows just outside the circle of the street light.

He probably thought since he didn't have illegal straight exhaust pipes that she wouldn't hear his sled outside her house. But, hell, being raised in an MC meant she could easily recognize the deep rumble of his Harley, legal pipes or not.

So many times she'd pushed him away. But he never gave up. The man was tenacious and determined.

And as much as she wanted him, she couldn't have him. For more reasons than one.

Sucking in a ragged breath, her nipples tightened at the thought of having her way with him just for one single night.

Only one night.

Maybe then she'd get him out of her system. And her out of his.

She needed to prove to him and to herself that this wasn't meant to be, no matter what their bodies said.

No, she couldn't crack that shell to let him in, even for a split second.

Her feet moved without her permission and suddenly she was at her front door punching in the security code, turning the deadbolt, and removing the security chain. Everything her cousin Diesel, the club Sergeant at Arms, had installed for her safety. Before she could stop herself, she ripped open the door.

Barefoot, she stepped out onto her front stoop, put her hands on her hips and stared directly at him.

What was she doing? Why couldn't she fight his pull?

Within seconds, his sled roared to life and he rolled into her driveway, heeled the kickstand down, quieted the engine and stared back at her.

Without saying anything, Axel dismounted, took long strides in her direction and bumped her backwards with his chest against hers until he pushed them beyond the threshold enough so that he could slam the door shut.

Then her back was pinned against the wooden door, his chest to hers, effectively trapping her as he took her mouth.

Her lips parted on a whimper and he took advantage of this by shoving his tongue deep to explore the recesses of her mouth, to tangle his tongue with hers. She moaned as his fingers dug deep into her long, loose hair, pulling hard, imprisoning her head against the door so he could take the kiss even deeper.

A moan bubbled up from the back of her throat but he held her still, his cock hard and long as it pushed against her belly.

It had been a long time for her and she so wanted to accept what he offered but she couldn't.

She shouldn't.

He finally released her mouth, his breath beating rapidly against her parted lips. "Bella," he whispered raggedly.

Then his face was buried against her neck, his tongue tracing along her throat, along the artery that pounded so violently that it might escape. She stared at his dark head, his tightly trimmed hair, as he moved farther down, brushing his lips along her skin, over the large shoulder cap tattoo that ran from the bottom of her neck and down her left arm. He kissed each colorful rose, each lily, each daisy that Crow had inked permanently into her skin in an attempt to make her feel beautiful again.

His thumbs swept lightly over her beaded nipples that pushed against her snug camisole. The one she wore to remind herself and others that she belonged to no one but herself.

As he kneaded her breasts, he pushed a knee between her thighs, separating her legs just enough to cause a rush of wetness that she hadn't experienced in ages.

Tentatively, she brushed her fingers over the shaved sides of his head then over the slightly longer hair at the top as he murmured her name against her skin, working his way back to her lips.

After another long, deep kiss, his forehead pressed against hers and they both panted as their gazes met and held, his blue eyes darker than normal.

His fingers slipped down over her waist to her hips, then snagged the bottom of her cami, beginning to tug the stretchy fabric up her belly. As soon as she felt the air against her bare skin, she froze, turned her head to break their connection and moaned for him to stop.

He didn't. Instead his warm fingers traced along her bare waist and up her ribs, pushing the fabric higher.

She pressed her palms against his chest and screamed, "Stop!"

He went solid, his breathing harsh, and she couldn't bear to look at him, so she closed her eyes and let the darkness behind her eyelids calm her racing heart.

"Bella..."

His voice was gentle, not angry, which made her heart squeeze and her chest tighten.

She shook her head slightly, still unable to look at him.

"Let me in, Bella," he said softly.

"I can't," she whispered back, her voice breaking, her eyes stinging even behind her lowered eyelids. She sucked in a breath to gather her strength since she needed to be strong to turn him away, to say no to this man.

A man who knew her secrets, her past. A man who knew her better than anyone. And he shouldn't.

Knowing what he did, he certainly shouldn't want her.

Not only did Axel know things about her no one else did, they were complete opposites, with families that didn't accept each other. Like the Montagues and the Capulets in *Romeo and Juliet.*

She was DAMC. He was a cop.

She was not accepted in his family, and he wasn't in hers.

Her lips trembled as she repeated, "I can't. You need to let me go. Let this go."

He slowly smoothed her camisole back down until it covered her completely, then stepped back.

Bella mourned the loss of his solid frame, of his burning heat against her. Something that brought her both solace and anguish.

"Look at me," he urged softly.

Reluctantly, she opened her eyes and studied the man she'd known all her life, the one who looked so much like his older brother, Zak, the former president of the DAMC. Like his father, Mitch, a veteran cop.

Sadness softened his strong features as he traced a thumb over her bottom lip, admitting, "Like you, I can't."

A long moment later, he stepped back as his gaze raked over her, then reached for the knob. Bella quickly moved away from the door to let him leave.

Because that was the smartest thing for her to do.

Let him go.

After she heard his sled roar to life and race away, she finally took a complete breath.

Get *Down & Dirty: Axel* here:
mybook.to/DAMC-Axel

If You Enjoyed This Book

Thank you for reading Down & Dirty: Diesel. If you enjoyed Diesel and Jewel's story, please consider leaving a review at your favorite retailer and/or Goodreads to let other readers know. Reviews are always appreciated and just a few words can help an independent author like me tremendously!

Bear's Family Tree

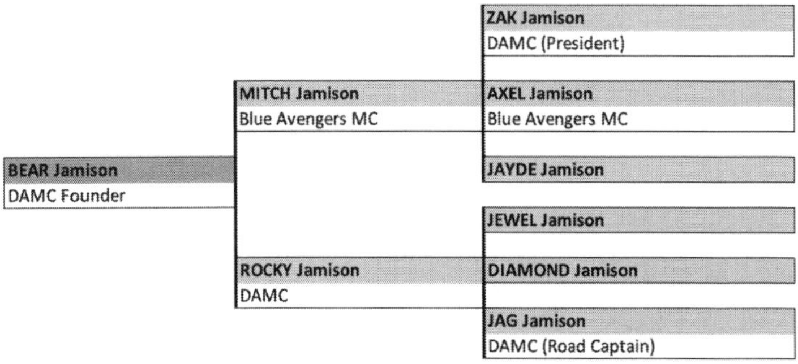

BEAR Jamison
DAMC Founder
MITCH Jamison
Blue Avengers MC
ROCKY Jamison
DAMC
ZAK Jamison
DAMC (President)
AXEL Jamison
Blue Avengers MC
JAYDE Jamison
JEWEL Jamison
DIAMOND Jamison
JAG Jamison
DAMC (Road Captain)

Doc's Family Tree

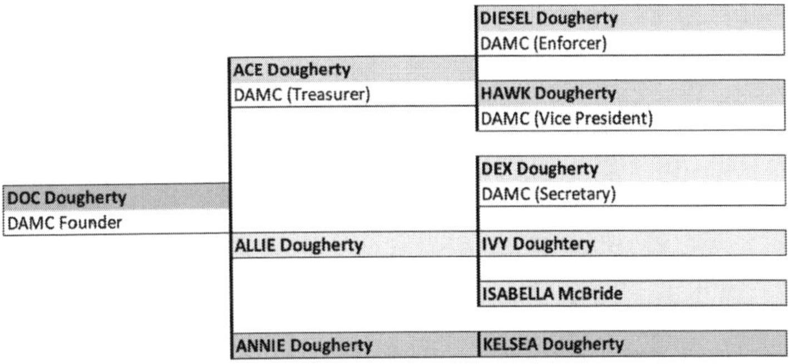
DIESEL Dougherty
DAMC (Enforcer)
ACE Dougherty
DAMC (Treasurer)
HAWK Dougherty
DAMC (Vice President)
DEX Dougherty
DAMC (Secretary)
DOC Dougherty
DAMC Founder
ALLIE Dougherty
IVY Doughtery
ISABELLA McBride
ANNIE Dougherty
KELSEA Dougherty

Also by Jeanne St. James

Find my complete reading order here:

https://www.jeannestjames.com/reading-order

Standalone Books:

Made Maleen: A Modern Twist on a Fairy Tale

Damaged

Rip Cord: The Complete Trilogy

Everything About You (A Second Chance Gay Romance)

Reigniting Chase (An M/M Standalone)

Brothers in Blue Series

A four-book series based around three brothers who are small-town cops and former Marines

The Dare Ménage Series

A six-book MMF, interracial ménage series

The Obsessed Novellas

A collection of five standalone BDSM novellas

Down & Dirty: Dirty Angels MC®

A ten-book motorcycle club series

Guts & Glory: In the Shadows Security

A six-book former special forces series

(A spin-off of the Dirty Angels MC)

Blood & Bones: Blood Fury MC®

A twelve-book motorcycle club series

Motorcycle Club Crossovers:

Crossing the Line: A DAMC/Blue Avengers MC Crossover

Magnum: A Dark Knights MC/Dirty Angels MC Crossover

Crash: A Dirty Angels MC/Blood Fury MC Crossover

Beyond the Badge: Blue Avengers MC™

A six-book law enforcement/motorcycle club series

COMING SOON!

Double D Ranch (An MMF Ménage Series)

Dirty Angels MC®: The Next Generation

WRITING AS J.J. MASTERS:

The Royal Alpha Series

A five-book gay mpreg shifter series

About the Author

JEANNE ST. JAMES is a USA Today and international bestselling romance author who loves an alpha male (or two). She writes steamy contemporary M/F and M/M romance, as well as M/M/F ménages, and has published over 63 books (so far) in five languages. She also writes M/M paranormal romance under the name: J.J. Masters.

Want to read a sample of her work? Download a sampler book here: BookHip.com/MTQQKK

To keep up with her busy release schedule check her website at www.-jeannestjames.com or sign up for her newsletter: http://www.jeannest james.com/newslettersignup

www.jeannestjames.com
jeanne@jeannestjames.com

Newsletter: http://www.jeannestjames.com/newslettersignup
Jeanne's Down & Dirty Book Crew: https://www.facebook.com/groups/JeannesReviewCrew/
TikTok: https://www.tiktok.com/@jeannestjames

facebook.com/JeanneStJamesAuthor
amazon.com/author/jeannestjames
instagram.com/JeanneStJames
bookbub.com/authors/jeanne-st-james
goodreads.com/JeanneStJames
pinterest.com/JeanneStJames

Get a FREE Sampler Book

This book contains the first chapter of a variety of my books. This will give you a taste of the type of books I write and if you enjoy the first chapter, I hope you'll be interested in reading the rest of the book.

Each book I list in the sampler will include the description of the book, the genre, and the first chapter, along with links to find out more. I hope you find a book you will enjoy curling up with!

Get it here: BookHip.com/MTQQKK